MAGIC BORN

THE ELUSTRIA CHRONICLES: MAGIC BORN - BOOK 1

CAETHES FARON

THE MAGIC BORN SERIES

Magic Born

Magic Unknown

Magic Betrayed

Magic Hunted

Get sneak peeks and stay up to date on new releases by signing up for the author's Insider Newsletter. You'll also get a free copy of the Insider exclusive story *Magic Tracked*, a prequel to *Magic Born*:

http://CaethesFaron.com/magic-tracked

CHAPTER 1

A web of green vines exploded from the hand of the imp facing me. Maniacal laughter erupted from her purple lips as I activated my concealment spell, dodging her attack. She jumped from foot to foot, her long green limbs flailing as she goaded me. I was in no mood to fight, but I needed to get by her to retrieve the scroll the Circle of Sorcerers had sent me to fetch. It contained the instructions for the next part of my quest, and I'd tracked it for days. If I had to, I'd kill the imp for it, and it looked like I had to.

The decision made, I unleashed a rain of hellfire on her head. The spell drained me of all my magic, but I didn't anticipate needing more any time soon, and I didn't want to mess around with lesser spells. The imp fell to the ground, her three-foot frame consumed in flames. I ran past her to the tree that held the scroll and stabbed the unveil charm into the trunk. Directly below the charm, the bark melted away to reveal a compartment. Inside sat the scroll I'd spent all day searching for. As I pulled the scroll out, a giant black cloud descended. The dark mist swirled and took the form of a demon.

"Shit."

I didn't even have time to see which spell of his killed me before the load screen of *Wizards and Fae*, my massively multiplayer online game of choice, mocked me with its familiar art of giants, elves, and wizards that looked way more impressive than the actual in-game graphics. The graveyard appeared, and I claimed my body. There wouldn't be time to make another attempt at the scroll. There was only a five percent chance of the demon spawning when a player removed the scroll, and he had to appear the one time I wasted all of my magic on the stupid imp.

No time to wallow. I wasn't just Kat Thomas, college senior. I was, more importantly, Serafina, Dark Sorceress, and if I didn't get a move on, my guild would boot me. I teleported Serafina to my guild's meeting place and joined our voice-chat line.

"Hey, guys, Serafina here. Sorry I'm late."

"No problem. We're still waiting on Hector." The voice of Jabber-wocky, the guild leader, sounded in my headset.

No surprise. Hector got away with everything, including showing up late. The fact that he gave his avatar such a mundane, human name was a turnoff, like giving a human name to a dog, especially since it was a female elf—talk about squicky. But he was the best tank in the game, so we all put up with his foibles. It was his job to take the hits from all the bad guys we fought while the rest of the group and I tried to take them down. And, of course, he did all this while wearing armor that amounted to a metal bikini. Gotta love those authentic details in a game created by a guy. I cast some long-lasting enhancement spells on the rest of the group then got up for snacks.

My gaming rig was set up in the living room of my one-bedroom apartment. It was the most expensive thing I owned. In the kitchen, the fridge revealed some cans of grape soda and leftover mac and cheese. I nuked the leftovers for a minute and grabbed a couple of sodas. It should be enough.

With soda within easy reach for a quick swig between fights, I folded my legs up under me and settled in for a long night of gaming. While waiting on Hector, I took the opportunity to scarf down the mac and cheese. The dry, congealed mess wasn't appetizing, but all I needed was something to keep the hunger at bay for the next few hours. A private message appeared in the lower right-hand corner of my screen.

GreyMist: Did you hear back about the master's program yet?

GreyMist was the healer of our group and my best friend in the guild. We bonded over being around the same age and in college. The rest of the guild was made up of professionals, adults who had careers and mortgages and their shit together. The only guild-member younger than us was Rintin, a high schooler whom we tolerated because his DPS—damage per second—was through the roof.

Serafina: No.

I didn't provide more. This was game time, time for me to hack away at some baddies, not think about my life. That wouldn't be the last I heard from GreyMist on the matter. Nicole—GreyMist's real name—always looked out for my interests, but right before a raid wasn't the time to get into my dysfunctional relationship with the future. Two minutes later, Hector made his grand entrance, and our raid on the light fae castle commenced.

The game lulled me in as it always did. My mind calmed as I went through the familiar battles. The fights were challenging, but I was up for it. Our guild had been together for years, and we could anticipate each other's moves even without the assistance of voice chat. The satisfaction of doing a difficult task well filled me. The guild was my world. I had no family anymore, and people in my real life didn't get me the way these guys did.

During a fight with a coven of cursed elves who controlled dozens of miniature demons, a series of knocks on the door startled me enough to make me miss the elf I aimed for.

"Damn, sorry," I told the guild. I regrouped as I focused on the elf. During encounters at this high level, distractions could cause our whole group to wipe. I had to be on top of my damage and magic management, careful not to burn through my magic too quickly or too slowly, maximizing each spell while also making sure I didn't pull the attention of the baddies off of our tank. It would only take two blasts from one of the demons to kill me. The knocker at my door would go away. I couldn't remember when I'd last had someone over. I took the elf down and searched for my next target.

The knocking continued. When would this guy get a clue? After a few more knocks, the rhythm intensified. I muted my microphone and turned my head to the door as much as I could without taking my eyes off the screen. "Go away!"

We almost had the elf leader down, only ten percent health left. His armor got a boost when he was that low. He sent shockwaves of damage through the group. I had to keep my eye on my health and step back should I get too low. It would take concentration to make sure I did enough damage without running out of magic or dying.

The knocking got louder. "Hello?" A male voice sounded from the other side of the door, but I didn't let it bother me. We'd been working on this castle for weeks, and I couldn't let my team down. My most powerful spell finally finished charging and I cast it, holding my breath to see if our combined effort would be enough to bring the leader down. I didn't have enough magic left to cast another if it didn't work.

The elf wobbled, let out a few curses, then fell over. The entire group cheered as we healed up and readied to fight the next boss.

Bang, bang, bang.

"I'll be right back. Someone's at the door." I removed my headset and opened the door to find a delivery guy with a package in his hands about the size of a shoebox. Yay for persistence. This had to be the new wireless headset I'd ordered.

"Oh thanks, I wasn't expecting this so soon." I snatched the package and shut the door. Too bad we were already in the middle of a raid or I'd set it up. It'd be nice to not be tethered to my computer by a cord anymore. I grabbed a knife from the kitchen on my way back to the computer. Everyone would be taking a short break now, and I at least wanted to take a look at this beauty that had arrived early.

The knocking on the door resumed. With a few minutes of break left, I decided to go ahead and get rid of this guy now rather than risk him disturbing the next fight.

"What is it?" I glared as hard as I could at the dark-haired delivery guy when I answered the door, hoping he would get the message and leave, only to be taken aback by a pair of strange dark yellow eyes.

"I need to talk to you. It's important." His voice had a smooth accent I couldn't place. Definitely not local or any other American accent. Even though he looked Latino with his thick black hair and warm tan skin, his voice didn't have the lilt of a Spanish accent.

"I don't know you. Go away and leave me alone." I almost had the door closed when he stuck out his hand to stop it. Before I could give in to my instinct to pull the door back and slam it on his hand, he spoke.

"You don't know me, but I know you, sort of. I have information about your mother."

Ah. This had happened a few times, but I thought it would have stopped by now. A lot of victims' families from the plane crash that had killed my parents sought each other out. I didn't understand it, but people in general tended to baffle me.

His dark yellow eyes peered so earnestly at me that I decided I could give him a second of my time. I saw a hint of grief in them that was familiar. He appeared older, not a student, maybe late twenties or early thirties. The black jeans and T-shirt fit the tall frame of a guy who hung around the gym more than the guys I knew.

"Look, I'm kind of busy, and I've already made peace with my parents' death. Maybe you should check out the support group. If you need the information, I can get it for you." He should have it already, but I didn't mind giving it to him if it would get him to leave.

His eyes shifted from side to side and he lowered his voice. "No, I don't mean her. I mean your real mother."

Ice slithered down my spine. I'd given up looking for my birth mother years ago. It seemed disrespectful to my parents. A couple months after they died, I picked up the search again, but quickly abandoned it. Nothing good could come of it. I already had parents, and they were dead. Nothing I might find would change that.

"My mom's dead. Leave. I don't want to see you again. Don't make me call the cops." I put the full weight of my body, all one hundred thirty pounds of it, behind the door and secured the deadbolt before he could stop me. I rested against the door, the cool metal penetrating my shirt, and took a deep breath to stop the slight shaking that overcame me. I played the game to forget, and the stark reminder of my parents' death brought a wave of grief crashing against my body. I rode it out until my hands steadied. Game night with the guild had no place for grief.

Settling back in my chair and putting my headset on, I tried to push the entire thing from my mind. "I'm back. It was just some guy at the door."

"You okay?" GreyMist asked.

Trust my best friend to question my effort at nonchalance. "Yeah, I think he finally got the message to leave. So are we ready to move on?"

The next fight did a great job of driving the strange incident from my mind, but during the next break, I opened the package, knowing now that it wouldn't have my headset in it. What I saw confounded me.

"What the fuck?"

CHAPTER 2

*T*he package distracted me for the rest of the raid. I decided long ago to not let the fact that I was adopted bother me. Whenever I thought about my birth mother abandoning me, I remembered how damn lucky I was to have my parents. So why did I care so much that she'd sent me a package?

"What's up with you?" Nicole asked in a private voice chat after the raid.

"Nothing." I didn't like lying to my best friend, but I didn't have the energy to talk about the encounter with the stranger. Nicole was always encouraging me to go to therapy to talk through my feelings about my parents' death. She also thought I had buried issues about being adopted to unpack. If I told her about the guy, she'd start back in on her quest to get me to therapy. My parents were dead and I was adopted. No amount of talking would change that. A therapist wouldn't bring my parents back to life. A therapist could only help me continue with my life, and I wasn't ready to be happy. The only time I really felt anything was when I played *Wizards and Fae*. That's why I latched onto the game. I didn't feel any other time, because if I did, it would be too much. The pain would be too much. My parents had died on their way to see me. I could drive myself insane with the guilt and grief. Not happening. I may not be living the life my parents and I had planned, but at least I wasn't miserable, and that deserved some points in my mind.

Even though Nicole's persistence annoyed me, I secretly loved her for it. There were worse things in the world than knowing someone cared.

"Really? Nothing? So you just started to suck all by yourself?" she asked.

"What are you talking about?" There wasn't much for me to be proud of in my life right now, but my gaming skills gave me what little pride I had.

"I had to take like three potions just to keep myself in enough magic to heal you tonight. You kept pulling aggro but then slacking off on the DPS. Rintin had twice as much DPS as you tonight and didn't pull aggro once."

Pulling aggro meant I pulled the monster's attention away from Hector, our tank, who had enough armor and health to absorb the blows. The trick to my role in our guild's raids was to do a lot of damage per second without pulling aggro. The fact that Rintin the high schooler outdid me on damage added to my embarrassment. "I just had an off night."

"You don't have off nights. What's going on?"

I wanted to tell her, I just didn't want to delve into my psyche with her. "If I tell you, do you promise to not get all psychoanalytical on me?" Nicole was a computer science major at MIT, but she had a strange fascination with pop psychology.

"Of course. Just two friends talking. What's up?" She tried to sound uninterested, but she couldn't hide the bubbly sound her voice got when she anticipated hearing something juicy.

"The guy who kept knocking on the door, he said he had information about my mother."

"Some conspiracy theorist about the crash?"

"No." That was about the only thing that could have been worse. After the plane crash, conspiracy theories started popping up all over the Internet. Those nutcases didn't care that there were real grieving families who only wanted some privacy. They made life hell. Escaping into the game helped me avoid them. "He wasn't talking about my mom. He was talking about my birth mother."

"Oh. Wow. That's"—she trailed off then seemed to remember her promise to me—"not at all big or emotionally impactful or anything."

"Stop," I said through a slight laugh. "I told him I had one mom and she was dead and to go away and leave me alone."

"Good for you." She paused for a beat, and I knew what was coming. She couldn't resist. "Were you curious at all about her?"

Wanting to move away from any talk of feelings, I focused on the package. "No, not after I saw what she sent me."

"Wait, she sent you something?"

"Oh, yeah, I thought he was a delivery guy at first bringing my headset, you know, the wireless one I ordered that you told me was the best."

She didn't take the bait. Normally, Nicole loved talking hardware, especially gaming hardware. I didn't know what half the specs actually meant, but she took pride in her recommendations. "So what was it?"

I grabbed the package from my desk and looked inside one more time, as if it might make more sense now. "It's a necklace."

"A necklace?"

"Yeah, just shows how much she doesn't know me. I don't know how I could be related to a woman who chooses a piece of jewelry as her first overture to the daughter she abandoned."

"What kind of necklace is it?"

I pulled it out to get a better look. "Nothing special. An amber stone fixed to a gold chain."

"I'm impressed you could identify the stone."

"Amber is what trapped the mosquito they used to bring back dinosaurs in Jurassic Park. Duh."

I could practically hear Nicole's eyeroll through my headset. "Of course. Do you think it's some kind of family heirloom?"

"I don't know. What do heirlooms look like?" My parents, the ones who adopted and raised me, hadn't left me anything I'd consider an heirloom. We were a tight unit but didn't have much of an extended family. "It seems too simple to be something worth passing down."

"Well, there has to be some reason she sent it to you. Maybe if you'd let the guy who brought it talk to you, you'd know."

"I thought you supported me telling him to go away."

"I support you standing up for yourself, but you have got to get over this fear of talking. When did talking ever hurt anyone?"

"Now. Right now. I'm in physical pain." It was a joke, but it didn't stray far from the truth. There were times when the grief hit me harder than a physical blow could. Just the thought of talking about my birth mother as if I could simply replace my mom and move on from my grief threatened to crush me. "I don't need to know why she sent it or anything else. I'm fine."

"If you say so. Hey, you should wear the necklace with your skirt to the hearing tomorrow. It doesn't hurt to look nice when pleading your case."

Shit, between the game and the visitor, I'd forgotten about the hearing. It was to determine if my scholarship would continue through next semester despite my subpar grades. I only had to get through one more semester to graduate, but there were days when it felt like a taller mountain to climb than when I started as a freshman. Without my scholarship, I wouldn't be able to do it. There was a lawsuit underway against the airline responsible for the crash that killed my parents, but it could be years before I saw anything from that. My dad's life insurance policy had barely covered their debts and funeral expenses. "You're probably right. At least it'll be good for something."

I only had one skirt in my wardrobe, and it would need all the help it could get. However, I couldn't help thinking that Nicole would somehow use me wearing the necklace as an excuse to try to get me to explore my feelings about my birth mother. The only thing the necklace did was illustrate the difference between my mom and my birth mother. One knew me and one didn't.

"Are you nervous?" Nicole asked.

"No." That should be a good thing, but I knew it wasn't. People who cared got nervous. Indifferent people didn't get nervous. Depressed people didn't get nervous. "Thanks for helping me prepare what I'm going to say. I've got it all memorized. It'll be fine."

"Good." Nicole was the closest thing I had to a sister. I didn't deserve her and I knew it. The fact that she cared so much even when I didn't gave me hope that maybe one day I'd get out of the funk I was in. She was strong for me when I wasn't.

Time to stop this train of thought before misty eyes turned into tears. "Oh, I have something for you. You'll never guess what it is." I navigated to my in-game inventory to locate the item and send it to her. "The key to unlock the quest line for the Circlet of Eternal Youth!"

"No! Really? You're awesome. I can't believe you did that."

I'd worked for weeks to get the key for her, and the excitement in her voice made it all worth it. The circlet was a legendary item that I knew Nicole wanted but was too busy to get by herself. I met up with her in-game to do the quest line. The game sucked me in, and hours passed with my best friend. If only life could stay this simple and fun.

CHAPTER 3

I sat on a bench in the quad in shock. I knew I'd let my life get a little out of control since my parents' death, but I hadn't realized it was this bad. The chairman of the scholarship committee's voice echoed in my head. The old white-mustached man had sounded like a grandfather scolding a wayward child.

"Your scholarship is revoked. Normally we'd place you on academic probation with the opportunity to regain your scholarship, but since next semester is your last, that's a moot point."

When the committee asked what my plans for the future were, I didn't know what to tell them. Given my status as a full-ride scholar at the school, they expected me to regale them with exciting opportunities I was pursuing. That used to be me: dedicated, driven, looking to take the world by storm. That would still be me if Mom and Dad hadn't died. But they had, and I coped the best way I knew how. Despite what they had thought, perhaps I wasn't meant to be extraordinary. Earth was filled with ordinary people leading ordinary lives and being ordinarily happy. I was fine with that.

But I had shattered the one dream my parents had for me. I'd chosen Stapleton University because it had been their alma mater. I worked my ass off every day in high school to get a full-ride scholarship. I'd known from a young age that I'd been adopted, and I never wanted my parents to regret that choice, so I'd dedicated my life to making them proud. It seemed smart at the time. But now without them, I was lost. I hadn't just lost my parents, I'd lost the cornerstone of my life. It was time to figure out who I was without them, but I wasn't prepared. Now it may be too late.

This wasn't who they raised me to be. I wiped away the tears that had silently fallen and gathered myself. I could fix this. One more semester, that's all I had to go. Maybe Nicole was right. Maybe it was time to accept some help. If therapy could get me on track, then it was worth looking into. I had Nicole and I had the work ethic I'd spent a lifetime building. I headed to the parking lot with a new sense of optimism. All I had to do was figure out how to pay for one more semester.

When I got to my car, a bright orange flier fluttered in the wind underneath one of my wiper blades.

Attention: A rare panther has been spotted near campus. Do not venture into the woods alone. If you see the panther, call Animal Control at 555-347-0908. Illegal hunting of the panther will not be tolerated.

Going into the woods alone or otherwise was never a possibility for me. No Wi-Fi, no Kat. I crumpled the flier and tossed it on the passenger seat.

My little red, two-door clunker stalled twice on the way home. The hills in the area were too much for her. My baby needed a long, flat stretch of asphalt to be at her best—somewhere I could let loose and push her to the fifty-five-mile-per-hour limit at which she started to shake so hard she could double as a carnival ride. At least I didn't have to worry about being without a car. No one would give me any real amount of money for her, so she wasn't worth selling to raise funds for tuition.

As I stepped onto the sidewalk that led to my apartment building, I pulled off my heels. Blisters had formed where the straps lay.

Bringing a pair of comfy shoes to change into would have been wise. When I got to my door, a folded piece of paper stuck out of the side. Probably some stupid flier or takeout menu. Turned out, it was neither. After I let myself in, I read the handwritten note.

I have something very important to speak to you about concerning your mother. Please call me.

Alex

His phone number appeared underneath the signature.

"Give up already." I crumpled the note and tossed it in the kitchen trash along with the junk mail. My keys landed on a little table inside the entryway to my apartment. I walked past the kitchen on my right and into the bedroom, throwing my overflowing messenger bag onto the unmade bed. The state of my room should have been the first clue that I didn't have my life together. Tomorrow, I'd start taking better care of myself and find some way to get through my last semester, but I couldn't think about that now. I had a date with Nicole.

I slipped into a pair of comfy, green plaid pajama pants, threw my auburn hair up into a messy bun, and grabbed a toaster pastry from the pantry, no time to heat it. Nicole would be wondering where I was.

"So you are coming. I thought you might have gone to that party instead," Nicole said when I joined a private voice chat with her.

I let Nicole's jovial tone pull me away from my depressing thoughts just as it always did. I'd tell her about the hearing later, and we'd come up with a plan to fix it. I just wanted to enjoy one last night with her in-game, and then we'd tackle my scholarship problem.

"Ha ha, very funny. The only reason to go would be for the free food to avoid cooking." Some guys in my complex were throwing a party centered around some sporting event. Football? Baseball? I had no idea. If I hadn't been so shocked at the committee's decision, I probably would have popped in for some free pizza.

"You know, it wouldn't kill you to actually make an effort, have some real friends outside the game."

"Yeah, yeah." I never understood the appeal of other friends. Bonding with other people invited disappointment and heartache.

"And cook?" Thick disbelief coated Nicole's voice. "I didn't realize toaster pastries qualified as cooking now."

I couldn't allow her to demean my skills. "Hey, you can burn a toaster pastry. If you can burn it, it qualifies as cooking."

"You clearly missed your true calling as a home economics major."

"Do they even have such a thing?" It sounded slightly horrifying in a Stepford wife kind of way. "Hey, do you mind if I do my daily first? I don't want to forget."

"No, go ahead. I'll be here killing forest pixies until I'm fifty at this rate."

"Thanks. I'll be quick." Each day, players got a random daily quest to complete. They were usually simple, if annoying, and the rewards definitely exceeded the effort put forth. The game awarded bonuses for maintaining a streak, and I was up to a one-hundred-sixty-two-day streak. I didn't want to blow it by losing track of time as Nicole and I talked.

I retrieved the quest from my in-game mail and read through the instructions.

Elemental magic has run amok!

These elemental magic quests were getting boring. I'd already had this one a few times.

Call the ice to you as you harness the power of elemental water. Feel the power of the ice coursing through you. Now take this ice spell and show the

flame monsters of the Western Ridge who really controls the elements!
Collect ten of their cores for your reward.

A wave of shivers went through my body and goosebumps emerged on my arms. The power of suggestion had me realizing I needed to turn up the heat in the apartment when I finished the quest. I equipped the ice spell in my spell bar and teleported to Western Ridge.

"Which one'd you get?" Nicole asked.

"Fighting off some flame monsters at Western Ridge."

"It should just take a minute then. In chat, people are saying the drop rate is pretty good today."

I hoped so. When I arrived in the area of the flame monsters, a scroll popped up to let me know that I'd reached the zone for my quest. One of the more annoying features of these daily quests was that players couldn't start blasting right away like normal. The spell didn't unlock for a few seconds, probably to force players to read the scroll.

Feel the elemental power of the ice coursing through you. Cast your frost
storm on one of the monsters and see whose power is strongest.

As I read, cold enveloped me. Nausea churned in my stomach and my head ached. Had that chicken at lunch been bad? If so, did salmonella really hit this fast?

The instructions were repeated in the strange fictional, universal language of the game. Some fans went so far as to learn the language, but my interest lay more in killing and collecting loot. As my eyes scanned over the foreign print, my teeth chattered with the chill. What was happening? I looked down to my chest where the cold concentrated around the amber stone of the necklace I'd worn for my hearing. The skin around the amber stone had turned purple from cold. What the hell? The heater must have broken again, and the cold stone only felt like the source.

I read the last line of the scroll while waiting for the spell to unlock. Little bits of frost formed where my hands sat on the mouse and keyboard—actual little ice crystals. This wasn't an issue with the heater. "Shit."

"What is it?" I jumped at the sound of Nicole's voice. "Some rare spawn giving you trouble? Do you really need my help with a daily?"

Crap, I'd forgotten I was on an open chat line with her.

"No, sorry. I just forgot about something. I'll be right back." I muted my mic. Be right back? What on earth made me say that? What could I possibly do that would make this better in a few minutes?

CHAPTER 4

I took a hard look at the stone resting on my chest since it
seemed to be the epicenter of the cold that had taken over
my body. It didn't appear to be anything special or out of the ordinary, just an amber stone connected by a little setting to a gold
chain. Either this necklace somehow caused my body to form ice or
I was hallucinating it. I honestly didn't know which would be worse.
Typical that I'd have a mental breakdown when I finally decided to
get my life together.

I felt my way around the chain, searching for the clasp.
Removing it would test my hypothesis that the necklace caused the
cold. My fingers didn't find a hook, and the chain was too short to
draw over my head. Pulling with all my strength against the thin
metal only resulted in little chain-link imprints on my palms. I'd
never been a jewelry person, but this was ridiculous. It shouldn't
take this much work to get a necklace off.

Maybe pliers would work. Destroying the necklace to get it off
would actually give me a little satisfaction, as if I were throwing
away all this nonsense with my birth mother. It had probably served
as a bad-luck charm with the scholarship committee anyway.

I got the toolbox Dad gifted me freshman year out of the corner of my closet where it had gathered dust and spider webs. Rummaging through it on the bed, I found a pair of needle-nose pliers that might do the trick. Standing in front of my bathroom mirror so I could get a better view of the chain, I located the clasp, which appeared impossibly small. I didn't know how I had gotten the necklace on in the first place. After trying to open the clasp with no luck, I positioned the pliers in one of the links. It barely fit, but it should be enough. I squeezed the handle together as hard as I could and twisted. My hands turned white with the effort, but nothing happened to the chain. Wasn't gold supposed to be a soft metal? Sweat lined my palms from the exertion. I wiped them off and took another go. The link should be weakened from my first effort. This time it would bend and open up.

I closed my eyes with the effort, putting all of my strength into bending the delicate link. The chain warmed, the amber stone growing hot against my chest until I couldn't take it anymore. I opened my eyes and released the link. It hadn't so much as bent.

"Grrr." I threw the pliers into the sink and they burst into flames. "What the fuck?" The water from the faucet wasn't enough to douse the flames. I ran to the kitchen and grabbed the fire extinguisher from under the sink. White powder swooshed out of the nozzle and coated my bathroom vanity, extinguishing the fire and my will to continue on. The mess would take forever to clean.

The only option I could think of was to go to a jeweler. But what if ice randomly came from my hands or things spontaneously combusted around me? Retracing recent events in my mind, I couldn't figure out how or what had caused the ice or fire. It was completely out of my control. The last thing I wanted was for it to happen in public. Even if the embarrassment wasn't enough of a deterrent, I couldn't risk hurting someone. Ice wasn't likely to hurt anyone, but fire was too dangerous and painful to mess with.

A text notification sounded on my phone.

Where'd you go?

Nicole. I'd completely forgotten that I left her hanging. I didn't have any other ideas or options. Nicole would think I was crazy, but this was what best friends were for. Instead of replying to the text, I went back to my computer.

"Sorry about that," I said as I put on my headset.

"No problem. What happened?"

Moment of truth. I didn't know how to tell her, so I blurted it out. "That necklace the guy delivered yesterday…it's doing some weird stuff."

"It's a necklace. What could it possibly be doing? Define weird stuff."

I took a breath. This was my last chance to back out, but I didn't know what else to do. "It made ice come out of my hands."

"What? Ice did not come out of your hands." Nicole's tone said this was a joke.

"Yes, it did. And then I couldn't get the damn thing off, so I took pliers to it to try to pry it open, and instead the chain just got hot and the pliers burst into flames."

All I could hear for several seconds was Nicole's breathing and the game soundtrack in the background. "This is the necklace you wore to the hearing?"

"Yes." My skin crawled with the dread of where this was headed.

"How'd the hearing go?"

"I just told you that ice came out of my hands and my pliers spontaneously combusted and you want to know about my scholarship?" Defensiveness wouldn't help my case with her, but this line of questioning infuriated me. Not everything could be solved with psychology. This was an actual physical problem. "It's not relevant."

"I think it is."

"I lost it for next semester. But this has nothing to do with that. I was going to tell you later tonight. I'm not worried. We'll think of something. I can even get student loans if I have to."

"Kat, you're spread too thin. You're not sleeping well. Your depression and avoidance aren't getting any better. And now the stress is causing hallucinations."

"You think I'm hallucinating this?" This was exactly why I'd resisted therapy. It would just be someone trying to talk me out of the way I feel, trying to change what I know.

"Of course. What other explanation is there?"

"This is not a hallucination." I turned on my webcam. "Allow video chat and I'll show you."

Nicole's face appeared in the corner of my screen. Her black hair was done up in her trademark pigtail buns with purple streaks running through them that contrasted with her pink bangs. Her dad immigrated from South Korea when he was a kid and grew up to marry a WASP who was rebelling against her family by living as a hippie in northern California. Nicole had inherited her dad's flawless fawn skin, wide brown eyes, and black hair, but she got her mom's wavy locks, delicate jawline, and kiss of freckles on her nose and cheeks. The result was a woman who seriously didn't realize how pretty she was. She quirked her eyebrows, the right one featuring a piercing on the outer edge with a little barbell through it, and said, "Okay. Show me."

I didn't know how to get the ice to form on command. Thinking about it didn't do the trick.

"I don't see anything."

"Hang on. These things take time," I said, as if I were some kind of expert. I went back to my in-game quest log and read through the elemental quest that I was doing when it first happened. Just as before, the amber stone turned into a chunk of ice on my chest. My palms frosted. "This good enough for you?" My voice quivered as my teeth chattered and I held up my hands for Nicole to see.

"Holy shit." Nicole's eyes went wider than I'd ever seen them, her eyebrows disappearing under hot pink bangs. "Does it hurt?"

"No, it's just really cold." I closed out the quest and thought warm thoughts. Nicole sat in silence as if she expected me to speak. "So what do I do?"

"How should I know?"

"You're my more beautiful, more talented, and more intelligent friend. You have your shit together, and I think we can both agree that I'm a hot mess. Tell me what to do."

"Umm, there is no class covering this at MIT. It also isn't in the adulting manual. This is crazy."

"Thanks. I'm so glad I came to you with this problem." If Nicole didn't have any ideas, it meant I'd exposed this insanity to her for no reason.

"Why don't you go to a jeweler?"

"Did you hear the whole 'pliers spontaneously combusting' part? I can't risk something like that happening in public. Not only would it mortify me, but there's a chance I'd hurt someone. I can't do that."

"Well, if you can't get it off, I think the best option is to try to get a hold of the guy who gave it to you. Did he leave a card or anything?"

I glanced at the trash can in the kitchen. "He left a note on my door today with his phone number. It said he had important infor-mation about my birth mother or something."

"Since he's the one who gave it to you, he probably knows how to get it off, if nothing else. Give him a call and have him come take the thing back."

That sounded reasonable, except I didn't like the idea of inviting him back over. "I'd really rather do this without him."

Nicole glanced to the side, thinking, then focused back on me. "Did he give off any creepy vibes or do you just not want to talk about your birth mom?"

I thought back to the previous evening. His yellow eyes should have unsettled me with their strange color, but they hadn't. When I remembered them, warmth spread through my body, like seeing an old friend. My dislike of him came from his delivery—both the necklace and his desire to talk about my birth mother. "No. The opposite actually. He looked like a nice, clean-cut guy."

"You're a pretty good judge of character. Trust your gut. But just in case, you have that panic app on your phone. Just push the button and I'll have the police there so quick it'll make your head spin. And if you don't check in with me, I'll call the police anyway."

My options were to invite a stranger over or live in solitude with random ice and fire coming from my body. "Fine."

I turned off my webcam and fished his number out of the trash. The phone rang and rang and rang. He must not have set up his voicemail. That was his problem, because I was getting answers even if I had to let the phone ring all night. With each ring, my irritation grew.

"Hello?" The mysterious accent sounded over the line.

"Yeah, is this Alex? The guy who showed up at my door last night mentioning my birth mother?"

"My name is Alex, yes. I'm assuming this is Kat?"

"Did you make multiple house calls last night?" Him acting as if I was calling to chitchat frustrated me. "You have some explaining to do."

He drew in a quick breath. "The necklace. It did something, didn't it?" Genuine worry, as if he hadn't wanted this anymore than I did, filled his voice. It cooled some of my anger.

"Yes, and I can't get the damn thing off. Since you seem to already know about it, you should have no problem explaining it to me. I want answers."

"Good, because I want to give them to you. That's all I've wanted since I found you. I would've told you everything last night if you'd only let me in." He went quiet for a beat and then lowered his voice, as if he was wary of the answer I'd give. "What did it do?"

"Oh, it only made ice come out of my hands, among other things." Angry sarcasm filled my voice.

"And you had no control over this?"

"I just told you ice came out of my hands, and you're asking me if I had control over it? I don't even know what to do with that. How long will it take you to get here?"

"A few minutes at the most. I'm nearby."

"All right. Knock like a normal, civilized human being when you get here this time."

After hanging up, the silence of the apartment overwhelmed me. Even though Alex didn't make me feel uncomfortable, I didn't want to be foolish. I was still inviting a stranger, who could easily over-power me, into my home. I grabbed the largest knife from the knife block that sat on my kitchen counter—because having absolutely no experience or training in physical fighting and self-defense, I figured this would be a good idea. At best, this Alex guy might think twice about potentially attacking an insane woman waving a knife around.

I put on my headset and updated Nicole. "He's on his way."

"Good. Don't let him leave until you have answers. Talking about your birth mother might do you some good."

"All I care about is getting this necklace off."

"Fair enough. Be safe."

My mad knife-wielding skills were probably not what she meant. "I already have the app up on my phone, and it's in my pocket."

"Okay. I'll be here collecting pixie wings to craft a Font of Healing robe. But I'll be calling you to check in, and if you don't answer, my next call will be to the police."

"Of course. I wouldn't have it any other way from my overpro-tective best friend." A respectful three light raps sounded at the door. "That's him. Gotta go." Halfway to the door I had to backtrack to pick up the knife from my computer desk. My fingers curled around the handle so tightly that my knuckles turned white, but I didn't feel any more prepared for my visitor.

CHAPTER 5

J opened the door a crack, keeping the knife visible in front of me.

Alex's eyebrows rose at the sight of the knife. "Whoa, I'm just here to talk. You invited me, remember?"

"You don't need to come in. You just need to tell me how to get this damn thing off."

Alex shook his head and shrugged, regret in his eyes. "I won't be able to remove it either."

"Then what good are you?" Heat swelled in my chest. No, not in it, on it.

Alex eyed the amber stone. "Let's sit down and talk. I'll tell you everything I know, and then you can decide what to do. You need to calm down or it may do something again."

My neighbor came up the stairs and went into his apartment. A few doors down, a group of friends sat in lawn chairs drinking and talking. People were milling about the courtyard. The last thing I needed was for someone to see fire burst out of my chest or worse, hurt someone. I stood back and opened the door wider. "Come in."

There he stood, just inside the front door of my apartment, me pointing a knife at him and wearing bright green plaid pajama pants with the fancy dark purple blouse I'd worn to the hearing and a possessed necklace around my neck. I don't know what I expected him to do or say, so I just stood there until his lips started to twitch into a grin.

"What's so funny?" I thrust the knife in his direction a couple of times as if to emphasize the seriousness of the threat I posed to him.

"You called me because you learned that you can make ice shoot out of your hands, and it's a knife you choose to defend yourself with? A weapon that you clearly don't know how to wield properly."

"I can wield it just fine, thank you." Pointy end goes in, twist, repeat. Nothing to it.

Before I even knew what happened, he had my wrist in one hand and the knife in the other. Apparently, there was a little more to knife skills than I thought.

"I'm going to go put this away, because you're far more likely to hurt yourself with it than me." He turned and slid the knife into its obvious spot in my largely unused knife block. "Now, with that taken care of, let's sit down and talk. You called me, remember? I don't mean you any harm. Trust me, this is not my idea of fun."

Alex moved from the kitchen into the living room. I only had two seating options: a chair and a sofa, both made of the same blue material and identical to most of the other furniture in this apartment complex. Years ago someone must have made a killing selling all the landlords in the area on buying the cheap furniture in bulk. A TV stand and coffee table made out of particle board completed my living room décor.

Alex chose the chair, leaving me with the sofa. If he wanted to hurt me, he could have done so several times by now. The only person with answers was him, so I crossed my legs up under me on the sofa and gave him my full attention, although I had no idea what he could possibly say that would make sense of what had happened.

"How much do you know about Meglana, your real mom?" The uncertainty in his dark yellow eyes gave the distinct impression he was stalling, trying to figure out how to tell me something difficult.

"First of all, she's not my real mom. My real mom died in a plane crash with my dad six months ago. I just want to get that straight right now." I didn't continue until he nodded to show he understood. "I know next to nothing. That's the first time I've even heard her name." Having her name so casually given to me by a stranger left me with an odd hollow feeling, like the name should mean more to me than it did. "Sometimes I think I have a memory of her from when I was really young, but for all I know it's just my imagination. To be honest, I haven't ever really given her much thought other than trying to find her a couple of times out of curiosity. As far as I'm concerned, though, she gave up any rights to my thoughts when she abandoned me."

"Wow, so you really don't know anything." He rubbed his palms on his black jeans, which did not inspire much confidence. "I guess that makes sense, especially since she gave you up for your protection. I suppose it would defeat the purpose if you had much information about her."

"What do you mean, for my protection?" My parents had always insisted they didn't know anything about why I had been given up for adoption, so I had never heard anything about it.

"I didn't know your mother particularly well, at least not as well as my father did. He died trying to protect her. She put you up for adoption to protect you from the same people who ended up killing her. Or at least that's my understanding."

"She was murdered?" A cold wave went through me. Murder happened to other people, strangers on television, not people connected to me.

"Yes, a few weeks ago."

"Why? And why tell me now? I never knew this woman." Despite her status as a stranger in my life, an odd sense of finality accompanied the declaration of her death, a sadness at knowing she would forever remain a stranger.

"Right before he died, my father made me swear to deliver the necklace Meglana left you. When I said he died protecting her, that wasn't strictly accurate. He did try to save her, but it was the wounds he sustained in making sure I got the necklace that ultimately killed him."

My mouth fell open. "Jewelry? Your father died over a piece of jewelry? My mother thought a necklace was that important? We clearly had nothing in common." What kind of person cared that much about jewelry?

"It's not the necklace that's important, it's the stone. It was your mother's, and she left it to you."

"So it's what, a family heirloom? One that causes ice to form?" For someone who was supposed to have answers, he sure wasn't giving me the information I needed. I'd already mourned one mother; I wasn't doing that again for someone I'd never even known.

Alex took a deep breath. "This is the part where I tell you that what you really need to know about your mother is that she was a mage."

My mother had been a gamer? Maybe we did have something in common after all. But that didn't seem relevant in the moment. Maybe the necklace was some super-advanced prototype, some cool new peripheral for a game. I wished I could take it off and look at it. "I don't understand. Why would someone kill her? She put me up for adoption when I was two years old. If she did it to protect me, does that mean she spent the last nineteen years fearing for her life?"

"Your mother was an extraordinarily powerful mage. I do know she had a lot of enemies and was paranoid someone from Elustria would kill her."

Elustria? Must be a foreign game. I couldn't recall Elustria ever crossing my radar before.

"I have to say, you are taking this a lot better than I thought you would."

I apparently put on a much more confident air than I felt. "None of this makes any sense. So you're telling me my mom was killed because she's a powerful mage and someone from the game she was playing killed her?"

Alex's forehead crinkled in a confused look, completely changing his appearance. "Game?"

"Yeah, you said she was a mage."

Understanding dawned on his face. "You think that I meant a mage in some sort of game? No, let me try this again. Your mother was from Elustria. It's a parallel world, a different dimension or realm if you will. She was a mage, which means you are too. She came to Earth to work on something, some studies for her magic, I'm not sure, but someone murdered her."

My mind whirled. An actual magical realm? That was insane. What kind of sick joke was this? Yeah, physically assaulting women wasn't his idea of fun, just coming into their homes and mind-fucking them. What a jackass. Here I thought he had some actual information about my birth mother, and all he wanted was to fuck around with my emotions. I rose to my feet, ready to tell him to leave.

"My father protected her, or at least tried to. We're from Elustria too, except we're panther shifters, not mages. Our magic isn't nearly as strong. We pretty much shift between panther and human form and can heal quickly, but that's the extent of our abilities."

Great. A furry. "You're a panther shifter?"

"Yes. I spend most of my time in panther form. I'm only in my human form now so I can speak with you."

The orange flier from earlier came screaming to the forefront of my mind. He had to have known about the panther sightings, trying to make a plausible story, as if that little tidbit would make me believe him. "You're expecting me to buy that you can shift into the form of a panther, that my mother was a magical mage-person from a fantasy realm who was murdered, and you magically found me to deliver a necklace?" The incredulity in my voice should have been enough to send him packing.

"Yes." He nodded. "That's exactly what I'm telling you."

"You expect me to believe this because a necklace made me a little cold?"

"A little cold? You said ice formed."

Maybe it did, maybe it didn't. It could have all been my imagination. I got like that sometimes in-game, my imagination running wild with me; it was part of the fun. The fire could have been started by a spark from the pliers rubbing against the chain or something. "This is ridiculous. I don't know what kind of kicks you get out of lying to a girl about her birth mom, but I really think you should leave now." I pointed to the door, giving him space to squeeze between me and the coffee table.

"You think I'm lying to you?"

"No, I totally believe that there is a magical realm out there that I'm from and that you're just here to deliver a necklace some moronic woman thought was worth dying for. That makes way more sense than believing that I've just stumbled upon a creep. Now get out of here." I went to the door and opened it a crack, hoping he'd get the message. My hand curled around the phone in my pocket, ready to push my panic button if needed.

Alex stood but made no move for the door. "Wait, it's not just a necklace. It's a talisman. It holds your mother's magic. That's what you felt when you wore it. That's what caused the ice."

"Oh, it's a magical talisman, not a necklace. That makes everything so much more believable." I dropped the sarcastic tone. "Please leave."

"How can I prove that what I'm telling you is true?"

I shut the door and crossed my arms over my chest. "Well, if you're a panther shifter, then shift."

Alex looked around. "I'm not sure there's room."

"Stop making excuses."

His jaw set in a firm line as he moved the chair, coffee table, and sofa to create a little clearing for himself. He stood in the middle of it, and in the space of time it took me to blink, an elegant panther appeared looking up at me, as if it were just an overgrown house cat.

The shock prompted a yelp from me. The distinct knowledge that I had a predatory cat in my home that could shred me to pieces in mere seconds sent my body shaking with adrenaline.

In another instant, Alex stood before me again, fully clothed. He grabbed my shoulders and rubbed my arms as if I shivered from cold. "You're fine. I wouldn't hurt you. When I'm a panther, I'm still me, even more me than I am now."

My mouth froze and a flush of embarrassment overcame me. I didn't feel at all in danger with him, but the situation shocked and overwhelmed me. "So it's true? All of it?"

"Yes, that's what I've been trying to tell you." He steered me back to the sofa, and this time he sat next to me.

"So what exactly am I supposed to do with this knowledge?" My eyes darted around the apartment, as if I might find answers, but never focused on any one thing until I caught Alex's yellow gaze, unchanged from when he'd taken the form of a panther.

"Honestly, I don't know. I'm just fulfilling my last promise to my father. The magic in the talisman is strong. If you want my advice, I suggest you go to Elustria, to the Magesterial Council. If you can already form ice with it, then you should probably have some training on how to use it."

This had gone from finding out the truth about my birth mother, to learning about an entire world I never knew existed, to a discussion of me moving to said world. I was supposed to be farming pixie wings right now with GreyMist. I was wearing green plaid pajama pants for crying out loud. People don't find out they're the daughter of a powerful mage and that they must go to some magical, mystical world to learn how to use a powerful magical force while wearing green plaid pajama pants. That didn't happen.

"If you like, I can escort you to Elustria. It seems like the right thing to do. I don't think you'll be able to find out how to get there on your own. I'd like to leave tonight. The sooner I deliver you to the Magesterial Council, the sooner I can go back to my life as a panther." He stood with a hand on my arm, a light pressure urging me to rise, as if I was going to walk out the door with him right now.

"Are you insane? I'm legitimately asking here. You just told me the craziest story I've ever heard—and I'm a gamer who relaxes by reading fan fiction—and you expect me to just up and leave with you? Now I get it: you're a panther shifter. This whole story you told me is clearly true based on the evidence, but this is my life here. Before yesterday, I didn't know the first thing about my birth mother, and now you're not only asking me to accept what you say as truth, you're asking me to leave behind everything I know because a woman I never knew left me a magical necklace."

"I know it must seem that way to you, but you really can't stay here. I'm not convinced you're safe. I delivered the necklace to you because I made a promise. In my judgment, the thing should have been destroyed, but it wasn't my call to make. Your mother wanted to keep it out of the hands of whoever thought it was worth killing for. I don't know what she expected you to do with it, and I don't know who your family is, so the best I can come up with is delivering you to the Magesterial Council. They'll know what to do. They can look up some extended family or someone for you to stay with. Or they can probably figure out how to get the necklace off, and you can come back here and continue on with your life. It really doesn't matter to me."

"If it doesn't matter to you, then leave. You've been nothing but trouble since I laid eyes on you." I knew it wasn't exactly fair, but the truth remained that my life was a whole lot simpler before he came knocking on my door.

"You really want me to leave?"

"Yes. You've done what you came here to do. I'm releasing you from any further obligation you may feel. I'm a big girl. I can take care of myself. I'm certainly not running off with you tonight." I stood to shoo him to the door.

"I can't stick around here and wait for you to change your mind."

"Good. I don't want you to. I'll figure out how to get the necklace off myself."

"What if the person who killed your mother comes looking for you?"

"And how do I know you're not the one who killed her?" It sounded obstinate and petty even to me. I just wanted him out. I hadn't even decided what I was doing after graduation—I wasn't about to take on a whole new world at a moment's notice. Magic? A fantasy world? That wasn't for me. I was just an ordinary girl trying to get through life on my own as best I could. I finally had a little bit of normalcy in my life; I couldn't give that up now.

"I see." A shadow of hurt clouded his eyes. "If you still think I'm the type of person capable of doing something like that, then clearly we would not make good traveling companions. I wish you the best of luck, Kat, and even though you didn't know her, you have my condolences for your mother's death. I can see myself out."

True to his word, he nodded and left the apartment. I secured the deadbolt as soon as the door closed. When I turned around to face my living room, the furniture still sat askew with an empty space where the panther had taken everything I thought I knew about myself and obliterated it. Yeah, that was one man I could do with never seeing again.

I lifted the talisman from my chest. It appeared innocuous, peaceful even. The amber gave no hint to the trouble it had caused. If what Alex said was true, this was the last relic of the woman who had given birth to me and abandoned me. Had she really done it for my safety? The overwhelming comfort of the possibility that I hadn't been abandoned after all, that a woman existed who had simply loved me enough to do what was best for me, brought a light mist to my eyes.

I closed my fist around the stone and brought it to my lips. Power seemed to suffuse me, radiating out from the stone, and filling every cell in my body. Not so ordinary after all.

CHAPTER 6

*B*efore I could even begin to process what Alex had told me, I had to contact Nicole. I believed her when she said she'd be checking in on me. If I told her the truth, it would only make Nicole sure I was losing it. She'd seen what the necklace did when I opened the quest in-game. Nicole would probably believe that my birth mother worked in gaming peripherals and the necklace was some advanced prototype. The ice was caused by its interaction with the game and the fire was from the pliers stripping some wire and sparking or something. That story would work.

All I had to do was lie to my best friend.

The truth was unbelievable, though. If I told her the truth, she'd either think I was delusional or lying. I couldn't lose her friendship. A believable lie was the best option.

Instead of calling, I logged into the game and entered a voice chat with Nicole.

"So, how was it?" she asked before I had a chance to say hi.

"Interesting." That seemed like the most appropriate adjective that was truthful without being too truthful.

"Interesting how?"

"Apparently my birth mom worked in game development. The necklace is a prototype of a new peripheral. It interacts with the game and causes the spells in the game to have little real world displays to make the game more immersive."

"Wait, your birth mom works in peripherals? How cool is that? Do you think you can score me one of those?" Nicole's reaction was exactly what I hoped for. As long as the words were tumbling out of her mouth on waves of excitement, she wouldn't be bothered with anything else. "There's been rumors about a couple of studios working on something like this for a while, but I didn't know they were this far along. I mean, if they're letting prototypes out of the lab, it's got to be less than a year to market. But what about the pliers bursting into flames? That wasn't part of the game."

"Apparently delicate electronics don't like it when you take pliers to them. It must have sparked or something and started the fire."

"It's weird that they'd let a prototype that volatile out into the world. And why can't you get it off?"

Trust her to go digging around my well-crafted ruse. "That was just me being a fumbling idiot. Alex showed me how to get it off."

"So what was he like? How does he know your birth mom? Are you going to meet her?"

"No, she's dead." I debated telling her more, but murder would only bring more concern from Nicole. A murdered birth mom would get me a resounding round of the "Get Thee to Therapy" chorus. I may have been willing to admit that therapy would help before, but I didn't know how I could ever go to therapy now. I was pretty sure honesty was necessary for the therapeutic process to work, and I couldn't broach the truth with anyone.

"I'm sorry, Kat. That's got to suck. You finally find her and she's gone."

"It's not so bad. This way I can't be disappointed by her, you know? Really, I'm fine with that. Now I don't have to go through issues of guilt over getting to know her and replacing my parents and that whole mess. It's good." Even though she couldn't see me, I nodded, as if trying to convince myself.

"You are an expert at feeling guilt, so that's a minefield you've sidestepped."

"Besides, best-case scenario if she were alive is I'd like her and then have to eventually deal with her death sometime down the road. I've done enough of that. No more getting to know people just so I can lose them. I'm only keeping our friendship because we have a sacred pact that I'm dying first."

A guttural sigh came through the headphones. "That's a whole other barrel of issues that requires professional help." Nicole didn't approve of my swearing off personal relationships. "Back to my questions. What about the guy? What connection does he have to your birth mom? What was he like?"

"Alex was nice." Heat rushed to my cheeks as I remembered the sleek panther that had stood in my living room. I wished I could tell Nicole about that. She'd love it, but I couldn't go there without telling her the whole truth. "He didn't know a whole lot about my birth mom. His father knew her and asked him to do this. He said she had given me up because she thought I'd be better off. That was nice. It wasn't like she didn't want me. Alex was very understanding. It was nice that he was the one telling me all this."

"Sounds like you might want to see this Alex again." Nicole's voice carried a bit of teasing, but I knew better than to let her entertain that thought. She was almost as obsessed with my love life as she was with getting me to therapy. I should have known better than to talk about him to her when the picture of his panther form was still so fresh—and hot—in my mind.

"Uh-huh. Moving on. Don't you have some pixies or something that we're supposed to be killing?"

"Don't think you can distract me, but yes, we do. I'm still like fifty pixie wings short of what I need to craft the robe."

Slaughtering pixies in-game was just the distraction I needed. In the last twenty-four hours I'd discovered that my mother was a murdered mage, that a whole other magical world existed parallel to ours, and that I didn't have a scholarship for next semester. Bad news always came in threes, so I was good for now, right?

CHAPTER 7

*T*he next morning, I decided to skip class to take a three-day weekend. Between a magical necklace I couldn't control or remove and my looming financial crisis, I didn't have the mental space to get anything from my lectures.

So far, the necklace had only acted up when I got frustrated or when I read through a quest in the game. Since it had formed frost when I did a quest dealing with ice magic, maybe I could find a quest that would get the necklace to come off. It was a long shot, but I couldn't think of anything else to do.

This early on a Friday, Nicole wouldn't be online yet. Once she got out of class, we'd delve into solving my scholarship problem together, which meant if I wanted to do any digging around for a possible way to get the necklace off, I needed to do it now.

The first thing I did was check my in-game mail for the daily quest. A part of me wanted to believe that yesterday had all been my imagination. The necklace had interacted with a daily quest before, so this would be the perfect test to see if it would do it again.

Instead of the daily quest, an Aquanight Gem waited for me in my mailbox. My heart rate increased and all thoughts about yesterday fled. I had begun to think these Aquanight Gems were a myth. No one I knew had gotten one yet. Magical Games, Inc., the company that created *Wizards and Fae*, had a promotion where players were selected at random to receive these gems that started an epic quest line. Complete the quest line and you could win some actual real-life prizes, like a trip to the Magical Games, Inc. headquarters in Canada, convention tickets, or exclusive art. More importantly, the prizes could be exchanged for their cash equivalent. This could be the answer to my financial problem.

But before I could get started, I needed supplies. I got my box of toaster pastries, popped some popcorn, and grabbed a few cans of soda. That should do me for an all-day binge session. Munchies covered, I curled up in my chair and took a deep breath as I started the quest line, praying that the necklace would behave.

GreyMist: Want to voice chat?

My eyes darted to the clock. I'd been at this more than six hours and hadn't even realized it. I put on my headset and started a private voice chat with her. "Sorry about that. You weren't on earlier, and I don't want to talk with anyone else. You're never going to believe what happened."

"What? Did Alex come back over last night or something?"

Great, I'd successfully driven Alex from my thoughts for several hours and here she brought him right to the forefront. "No, nothing like that. I got the quest, the Aquanight Gem."

"Oh my god, are you serious?"

"Yep, I've been working on it for a little over six hours now."

"Do you need any help?"

"No, it's all in individual instances, so you can't help." The game didn't allow for two people to be in an individual instance at once.

"That's brutal. How are you doing?"

"Better than I thought. I should be able to crack this tonight."

"That fast?"

"There's not a lot of farming or grinding involved. It's mainly just skilled battle. When you got the skills, you got the skills. What can I say?" That's right, I was bragging that my lack of an actual life meant that I'd spent hours a day, every day, honing my skills in this game that wouldn't serve me anywhere else in life. I may not have a career plan or any future prospects, but damn, I could one-shot more baddies and defeat more bosses than most people in-game.

"Have you told anyone else in the guild?"

"No, I don't really want anyone knowing. It's too much pressure, and I feel enough as it is."

"Well, let me know if there's anything I can do. I'll leave you to it. I don't want to distract you. You tell me the moment you finish, okay?"

"You got it. We'll chat later." I took off my headset and focused my attention back on the quest. I was determined to finish tonight. Call me superstitious, but everything was lining up just right. My spells were hitting while I was dodging and keeping my armor up. Every time the game had to make a decision, it came down in my favor. Lucky streaks like this were rare, and I wouldn't risk losing it by leaving and logging back in later. I may not be able to control my mother's actual mage power, but I was Serafina, Dark Sorceress, and I would complete this quest.

Two hours later, I stood before the demon Hades, just me, him, and two dozen of his minions. This quest line was randomized, so no two people got the same encounter. That meant no website had a guide for this fight that I could study like I would before entering battle with my guild. I'd have to be alert and on top of my spells, cool downs, and buffs. I took a deep breath and fully entered the chamber where he waited for me. The usual trash talking commenced, a good twenty seconds of him telling me how he was about to eviscerate me, dismember me, and curse me to eternal darkness.

Not if I had anything to say about it.

As soon as he finished his little monologue, he hit me before my spells had even unlocked. My entire body tensed. I couldn't afford to be a millisecond off my timing. I hit him with everything I had, taking potions at all the right times, eliminating his minions en masse before focusing all my attention on him. For a good twenty minutes we battled, my health bar getting dangerously low several times before I could heal. Just when I got him down to five percent health, the dude healed all the way up. Dammit, I refused to lose this fight. This one thing had to go right for me.

Ten minutes later, I feared my finger cramping. I had him down to one percent health, but he had me down too. At this point, I'd used up all of my magic, and it wasn't regenerating fast enough. That left me with my lame wand. His hands conjured a giant ball of dark magic that would definitely kill me, but it had a cast time of at least a few seconds. If I could hit him with my wand enough times, I just might be able to kill him before he could finish his spell. I mashed the button for my wand as fast as I could, leaning toward the screen.

"Come on, come on." His health bar diminished. The big ball of dark magic was half a second away from hitting me. His hands drew back to cast, and I willed my finger to move faster. His hands dropped to his side, and I held my breath, waiting for the killing blow, but it didn't come. He teetered from side to side and fell to the floor, dead. I'd killed him.

"Yes!" I jumped to my feet for a little victory dance. I had done it. The rarest quest in the game and I'd beaten it. At that point, I didn't even care what kind of prize I got. Immediately the title "Hades Killer" showed up below my name. Everyone in the game would know what I had done.

When I calmed down enough to sit relatively still, I put my headset on to tell Nicole. "I did it! I beat it."

"For reals? Are you kidding me?"

"No," I said with a smug grin on my face that I'm sure she heard.

"Oh my god, how was it?"

I controlled my excitement so I could talk without tripping all over my words. Not only had I done something few people in the world would ever accomplish, but depending on the prize I won, I might have solved a big chunk of my tuition problem. "It got pretty tense at the end. He was literally casting the spell that would've killed me when I took him down with, get this, my wand."

"Your wand?"

"Yeah, my magic was depleted."

"You are the luckiest girl in the world."

"Luck had nothing to do with it. It was all skill." While luck had played a major role in the entire quest line, I wasn't about to admit that, not when this gave me massive bragging rights.

"Uh-huh. So what happened next?"

"I got the title 'Hades Killer,' but other than that, not much else happened. Oh wait, I have some new in-game mail."

When I opened the letter, fireworks went off in the background.

Congratulations, Serafina, Dark Sorceress! You have defeated the mighty Hades. In recognition of your achievement, you are cordially invited to the headquarters of Magical Games, Inc. You will receive detailed instructions on claiming your prize at the email address associated with your account.

"I won! I actually won the trip to headquarters!"

"That's awesome! That's the best prize they have."

"I know. I'm hoping the cash equivalent will be substantial. This could really help with tuition."

GA Casper: Congratulations on beating Hades!

"Hold on, a game admin is messaging me."

GA Casper: This is Casper Rothian, the creator of Wizards and Fae. *May I join you in a private chat?*

"Shit, it's Casper. He wants to chat." Saying the words out loud made it seem even more unreal.

"Well go!" Nicole disconnected.

An invite to a private voice chat appeared on my screen. I almost knocked over the soda sitting on my desk in my haste to click "accept."

"That's better," a male voice said. "Congratulations! I'm the creator of the game."

"Of course I know who you are, Casper. I mean, Mr. Rothian."

A soft chuckle sounded in my ear. "No, Casper's fine. According to our records, your name is Kat Thomas?"

"Yeah."

"It's been a while since someone beat the Aquanight Gem quest." His voice sounded exactly the same as it did in the interviews I'd seen with him.

"I didn't realize you actually spent any time in-game."

"Not as much as I'd like. Unfortunately, a lot of business stuff comes up once you move out of your garage. But I got a notification that someone had beaten the quest line, so I thought I'd jump in-game and congratulate you personally."

Fans, myself included, loved Casper for precisely this reason. "Thank you so much. I've been a fan of the game for a really long time."

"I can see that. As you know, you've won the prize to come visit us at our headquarters here in Canada. I actually wanted to chat with you to see if you could come this weekend."

"This weekend? As in, tomorrow? That's a little soon, isn't it?" Did no one plan things in advance anymore?

"Do you have any plans that can't be changed? The thing is, I really like to be the one to meet the winners myself, give you a nice tour of the campus, show you some exclusive work we've been doing on the new expansion. The weekends tend to work out well for these things because I'm able to pull some people in to give you a nice show without taking them away from their work. This weekend is the last one that I'm not traveling for a while."

"That sounds amazing." It was literally a dream come true, but it was time for me to get my life back together. The mature choice—the correct one—was to take the cash and apply it to next semester. "But I actually wanted to get the cash equivalent instead."

"Oh." Casper's voice hesitated. "I didn't expect that."

A day ago, I wouldn't have either. "I need the money more than I need a cool trip."

"Well, I have no problem giving you both."

I hesitated. "That doesn't seem right."

The silence thickened in my headphones. I didn't know why he'd make that kind of offer or why he seemed to care. Weren't there corporate rules and legal stuff he had to follow?

"Kat, I didn't want to have to tell you this way, but I know who you are. I knew your mother."

My entire body froze. How could he possibly have that information when I didn't even have it twenty-four hours ago? Did Alex tell him somehow? Weakness seeped into my entire body. The entire situation was surreal. Nothing in my life made sense anymore. Maybe he meant my mom. "My mother?"

"Yes, I knew Meglana. I think it's important that we meet."

I tried to brush off the strangeness. "I don't know why. I never knew her."

"I think you may be in danger."

My mind reeled. How had my life turned completely upside down in the space of just a couple of days? Whatever drama surrounded my birth mother, I couldn't get sucked into it. I needed to focus on school and graduating. Now that I knew I at least had the cash equivalent of this trip coming, that was a little less to worry about. The necklace hadn't acted up again, and for all I knew, maybe it had all been some hallucination or something from all the stress. I needed reality, and that meant focusing on schoolwork and getting the rest of the money together for graduation, not chasing after my birth mother's ghost. "I really can't meet you this weekend."

"I'm sorry to hear that. I'm sending you an in-game message now.

If you change your mind, reply to it. I really do hope to meet you soon. And congratulations again on winning."

Casper disconnected from the chat, leaving me hollow and confused. His message appeared in my in-game mail.

Congratulations on beating the quest. I hope to see you this weekend. Like I said, I'll throw in the cash equivalent as well. I promise the tour of the Magical Games campus alone will be worth it.

"So what did he have to say?" Nicole asked.

I hoped my voice wouldn't betray my utter confusion. "Nothing much, just congratulated me on winning."

"Was he as cool as he seems at all the conventions?"

"Yeah, he seemed nice." I couldn't handle the revelation that Casper knew my birth mother. I needed time and space to process it. "I'm sorry, I gotta go."

"Are you all right? You sound weird."

"Yeah, I'm fine, just a little overwhelmed."

"If you say so. I'm here if you need to chat."

"I know, thanks. See you online tomorrow."

"Yeah, you'll be strutting that new title around. Good night."

"Night." I logged out of the game and fiddled with my birth mother's talisman. My mind finally caught up to what Casper had said. How on earth did my mother know one of the most famous computer game designers in the world? More importantly, how did Casper know I was her daughter? It made no sense. The game had my legal name, but nowhere was that name connected to my birth mother. If it had been, I would've discovered her identity long before now. One person might have the answers, and he was the only person I could talk to about any of this. I got my phone and re-dialed Alex's number.

"We're sorry, but the number you're trying to reach has been disconnected."

Dammit, he'd been serious when he said he would leave me

alone. Great timing for him to choose to listen to me. In that moment, I felt more alone than I ever had in my entire life, even more so than when my parents had died. At least then I'd had neighbors and a support group to talk to if I had wanted it.

Therapy sounded like a good idea, but I couldn't exactly walk into a counselor's office and find the help I needed to cope with the fact that my mother apparently came from a magical dimension, was murdered, and left me with a magical necklace I had no idea how to control. Just holding it, knowing now what it was, filled me with an energy unlike anything I'd ever known before. This one relic was the only thing I had left of my mother.

Maybe I should try to find out about her. I was sure Alex could give me more information if I could only find a way to contact him. I tried calling again, even though I knew it wouldn't work. The other option was to take Casper up on his offer. If he had known her, he could give me answers. But did I want them? Was I prepared for them? If I found out the truth and it turned out to be as fantastical as Alex had said, I wouldn't be able to go back, and that thought scared me. For so long I'd been putting all my energy into just keeping my head above water, and I feared any waves of change. They could pull me under and drown me.

I made it an early night. Lying in bed, I stared at the picture of my parents, the loving faces so familiar and comforting. What would they want me to do? The only thing they had ever wanted was for me to be happy.

I clasped the amber stone with my hand and felt the energy surge through me. According to Alex, it was my mother's power. It pulsed through my hand. Twice I'd been told I was in danger. My mother had left me this talisman, but it hadn't been strong enough to protect her. Was I strong enough to take hold of this new identity? The faces of my parents told me I had the strength to do anything. I wished I could believe them.

CHAPTER 8

*W*ith my eyes closed, I kicked off the covers. I must've accidentally tapped the thermostat too hard. My skin was slick with sweat. I rolled over and spread out my limbs, trying to cool down. No luck. I'd have to get up and adjust the temperature.

When my eyes opened, I was startled by the sight of a purple ball floating in my bedroom. My hand flew to the talisman, the source of the heat flowing through me. The mysterious glowing orb hovered suspended in the air. This had to be a dream. I closed my eyes, willing myself to wake up, but when I opened them again, I jerked at the sight of two yellow eyes glowing in my bedroom doorway. A snarl erupted from the giant cat as it leapt into the air and caught the orb, pinning it to the ground.

The beast took up much of my room. I scrambled out of bed and ran for the living room, away from the animal. The pained shrieks of the giant cat following me. The fear of being attacked from behind compelled me to turn around. The purple orb had followed, and the cat swiped at it with its claws out, releasing a scream as sparks flew from the ball. The purple of the orb glowed brighter and pulsed more intensely with each contact.

"Stop it, stop it!" I screamed as if that would have any effect. It was like watching two guys fight at a bar and all I wanted was for it to stop. All the energy in my body seemed focused around the talisman, and a stream of electric blue lightning burst out of it, striking the orb. Identical blue lightning shot from a wall socket and hit the orb at the same time. My computer popped, and the streetlamp that shone into my living room from the balcony extinguished. Not even the digital clock on my stove produced light. The only thing I could see was two yellow eyes shining at me, and then even those were gone.

"Shhhhh!" A man's voice. Alex grabbed my shoulders the way he had the other night. "We have to go. Whoever sent that tracker orb will be here soon, and you need to be gone when he arrives."

"What? No, no, I need to call the police." My hands shook as I thought about where I'd left my phone.

"The police can't help you. They won't even believe you. Now come on. Get dressed and let's get out of here."

Before me stood the only person who could possibly help, and I couldn't let him disappear again. I nodded and felt my way back into the bedroom. I grabbed my cell phone from the bedside table, next to the picture of my parents. The light from the screen illuminated the room enough to find a pair of jeans, a long-sleeved shirt, and some shoes. I dressed quicker than I ever had in my life.

"All right, I'm ready." I had my car keys, driver's license, credit card, and cell phone. I should be fine until I could come back. On the way to the car, I threw my hair up into a ponytail. "So where are we going?"

"Right now we're going to get you away from here, and we should probably get you something to eat. Doing that lightning magic had to take a lot out of you."

The amber stone produced the magic as it had before. It didn't seem like I'd done anything, but now that he mentioned it, the adrenaline that had kept me going receded, leaving hunger and exhaustion in its wake. "You're right. Would you mind driving?"

We stopped next to my car, and I held out the keys to him. His doubtful eyes darted between the car and the keys. "I don't know how to drive."

"What?" I dropped my hand to my side. How had he gotten here? My mind flashed to the panther that had stood in my apartment. An animal like that could run wherever he wanted.

"I can't drive. Come on, we can talk all you want in the car." He climbed into the passenger seat, and I took my spot behind the wheel.

I pulled out of the parking lot and headed to the freeway. Occupied with the mundane task of driving, the reality of what just happened settled over me. My hands shook on the steering wheel, fear catching up with me. I gripped the wheel harder, willing my hands to still and took a few deep breaths. Forcing myself to concentrate on the road ahead, I pushed down the fear. I wanted an explanation, but my low blood sugar didn't help in steadying my emotions. Talking should wait until I could reason better, so we rode in silence. At the freeway entrance, I pulled into a twenty-four-hour diner connected to a gas station.

"No." Alex shook his head. "We should get a little farther away before we stop."

"How far?" With each mile that passed, it seemed less likely that I'd return home soon.

"It just seems too risky to stop at the exit for the town you live in."

He had a good point. I nodded and got onto the freeway headed north. The next three exits didn't look promising, but the fourth had a restaurant with the lights on and seemed sufficiently far from my home. Even if it wasn't, I'd concentrated so hard on the road that I started nodding off, so it would have to do. Despite my fear, I couldn't shake the exhaustion consuming me, and the road lulled me to sleep. Only hunger pains kept me awake.

A bored-looking waitress showed us to a booth. After the darkness of the road, the artificial light seemed unnaturally bright. Only one other table in the restaurant sat occupied.

"Can I start you off with anything?" She looked at each of us without really seeing, simply a movement to indicate we were to speak now.

"I'll have water," Alex said.

"I'll take a coffee." I looked at my menu when the waitress left. "I can't remember the last time I was this hungry. Do you know what you're going to get?"

"Nope," Alex said from behind his menu.

I went back to looking at the menu, as if we were a couple just out for a bite. Alex seemed like a normal, good guy, and it was easy to forget that he wasn't even from this world. Come to think of it, if what he said was true, I wasn't from this world either, or at least my blood wasn't. The strange floating ball back at my apartment didn't seem like it came from Earth. Between that and seeing Alex become a panther right in my living room, I had to start accepting that Elustria was a real place.

"Here you go." The waitress set Alex's water and my coffee down along with cream and sugar.

"What'll you have?" she asked as she pulled a little notepad from her apron.

"The ultimate breakfast," I said. Normally, that would be an insane amount of food, but I seriously doubted it would be enough to dampen my hunger.

"Steak and eggs," Alex said when the waitress turned to him. "And can you make the steak as rare as possible?"

"Sure."

"Thanks."

We handed our menus to the waitress, and she left us alone. The coffee warmed me to my core, seeping into every part of my body. The copious amounts of sugar and cream leant it a sweet taste that made it difficult to not drink so fast that I'd burn my mouth.

"Is that helping?" Alex asked, peering at me with concern. I must look a mess.

"Yeah, it is. Thanks." My gaze darted to the table to escape the scrutiny of his yellow eyes. Under the bright fluorescent lights, I got a good look at his hands for the first time. What I could see of his palms were an angry red. Blisters dotted the rough skin. "Your hands!"

He glanced at them. "They'll be fine."

I reached across the table to turn one around so I could get a better look. "This is bad." The blisters must have come from that floating ball.

"Trust me, it looks a lot worse than it is. My claws took the brunt of the damage. Shifting so quickly after a fight like that sometimes has strange consequences."

I didn't believe him, but if he wanted to be tough in front of me, fine. "What was that thing back there?"

"A tracker orb. A mage or sorcerer must've sent it. Someone's looking for you; my guess is whoever killed your mother."

Talking about it brought back the fear in cold waves. I cupped my hands around the coffee mug, leeching as much heat from it as I could. "And how did you know to be there? How did you even get in?"

"I saw it go into your apartment. It can travel through walls. I jumped up to your balcony and got in through your sliding glass door. You should really keep it locked."

My mom used to tell me the same thing, but I never thought someone would put forth the effort to climb onto a second-floor balcony to break in. It didn't seem logical. After tonight, I didn't know how much of a role logic would be playing in my life anymore. "I tried calling you, but your number was disconnected."

"I don't keep a phone. That one was just a cheap temporary one." He paused and cocked his head. "You tried to call me?" Something between pleasure and intrigue danced in his eyes as the left side of his mouth lifted slightly.

The in-game events that had prompted my call felt like they'd occurred a lifetime ago. The adrenaline rush had probably skewed my sense of time. "Yeah, I had a weird experience. Someone contacted me saying they had known my mother."

The hint of a smile left Alex's mouth as if it had never existed. He leaned forward, concern knitting his eyebrows together. "Who?"

"Casper Rothian, the creator of an online game I play. The whole thing was strange. I completed this quest and won a prize to come to the game's headquarters. He came on and talked to me, congratulated me for winning, and asked me to come this weekend, as in today. When I told him I couldn't do that, he said he'd known my mother and that he thought I was in danger." For the first time, it occurred to me that the whole quest line could have been a setup. Every encounter had passed too easily. No one got that lucky. "Do you think he could be connected with that orb thing?"

"It's not likely. A tracker orb is used to find someone. If he was talking to you, he probably already knew where you were."

True. Besides, if Casper Rothian wanted to kill me, I'd be dead, even if he didn't have magic. The man had enough money to do whatever he wanted. "But how would my mother know a game designer?" The last few days seemed to bring an endless stream of questions and no answers.

"I don't know, but for him to have known her and to know that you are in danger, he has to either be a mage or sorcerer from Elustria. A mage more likely."

The waitress appeared with our food. At the smell of hot pancakes with eggs, hash browns, bacon, and sausage, all other thoughts left my mind. I didn't even wait for her to finish setting down Alex's plate before digging in.

"Oh my god, this is delicious," I said with a mouthful of pancakes.

"Take your time. There's no use choking." He ate his rare steak in a much more dignified manner, but I didn't care. All I knew was that this was food, it was delicious, and I needed to get it inside of me as quickly as possible.

Once I'd taken the edge off my hunger, I slowed to a more

respectable speed that allowed for conversation. "So you can eat human food?"

Alex nearly choked on his eggs and took a drink of water. "Of course. When I'm human, I'm human. My senses are slightly better just because I'm more used to it in my panther form, but when I'm a panther, I'm a panther, and when I'm human, I'm human."

"And what about your clothes? How come they're not affected by shifting?" In books, shifters always ended up naked when they became human. Not that I wanted to see Alex naked, but it did trigger my curiosity.

"They're enchanted to work with shifter magic. They were a gift from my father, so they may have been enchanted by your mother."

"What was she like?" A vulnerable yearning entered my tone that I resented.

"I didn't really know her. According to my father, she was a genius. She would have to have been to attract him. He liked intelligence and power." A bitter aftertaste trailed his tone.

Through all this, it'd been easy to forget that he lost his father too. And he had actually known his father. "I'm sorry for your loss."

Alex shrugged and glanced out the window for a beat before looking at me again. "Thanks, but we weren't close. I hadn't seen him in years."

His words left an awkward tension in the air. I ate a few more bites, but that didn't help. I had to change the subject. "So why can't you drive?"

"Never had a reason to learn. I spend most of my time as a panther. I can easily go years without shifting into a human."

"Years? Doesn't it get lonely?" I may be a loner, but the thought of spending all that time away from humans was incomprehensible.

"That's how I like it. You'll find a lot of shifters are the same. I'm not a pack animal, so I don't have much use for other people. Wolves and the like are a different story. A lot of us come here to stay in our animal forms or to escape all the crap that goes on in Elustria."

I hadn't given much thought to the existence of other shifters living on Earth. A part of me had just assumed that Alex was the only one, that he'd come here to find me, and that was it. The thought seemed incredibly egotistical now that I ran it through my mind. "Other shifters are here? Are there a lot?"

"Oh yes. I don't have an exact number, but there's a large population of us. One of the royal families in Europe is made up entirely of wolf shifters."

"Wouldn't something like that get out?" How would that escape the ubiquitous gossip sites and paparazzi?

"Like I said, when we're in our human form, we're basically human. Shifters are some of the most common people who come to Earth from Elustria, been doing it for hundreds, maybe thousands, of years now. The sorcerers regulate portals between our worlds and don't want to reveal magic to humans, but they don't have a problem with shifters coming through as long as they're an animal that's plausibly found on Earth, so no dragon shifters or the like."

"There are dragon shifters? Like actual dragons?" For the first time since the attack, I smiled.

"No. There are dragons, and then there are dragon shifters. But yes, both do exist in Elustria."

That I had to see. "If you wanted me to go to Elustria with you, you should've led with that."

Alex grinned. "Really? You seem to have a hard enough time dealing with me. I'd hate to see how you'd react to a dragon shifter. Anyway, they're pretty rare now."

He may have had a point about my reaction to witnessing a dragon shifter, but I still wanted to see one. "Why are they rare?"

"Shifters all fall along a certain magical hierarchy if you will. In order to produce offspring that are the same type of shifter, a shifter must mate with their own kind or a person with equal or greater magic. Dragon shifters fall at the very top of the hierarchy. They can only mate with each other or with sorcerers. Too much inbreeding is a bad thing. Since their mating options are limited, their population has naturally shrunk. There are also a lot of superstitions based in ancient prophecies surrounding dragon shifters. It makes people wary of them."

This sounded better than any game or book I'd ever consumed. I wanted to hear everything. "You mentioned sorcerers before. How are they different from mages?"

"I'm not the best person to ask. Like I said, I don't get involved much in Elustria, but the short of it is that mages need to have an external magical object in order to perform their magic. Their skill comes from study and practice. Sorcerers, on the other hand, are made of magic. It literally flows through their veins like blood does through ours. They're generally more powerful than mages. That's how they maintain control in Elustria."

"So when you said my mother was powerful, it was because she worked at it?"

"From what I understand, she spent her lifetime in study. My father greatly admired her."

Only a thin sheen of syrup remained on my plate. The food had adequately beat back my hunger without leaving me stuffed. "So how much time do we have to kill? When do you think it'll be safe to go back?"

Alex's eyes widened momentarily before he slowly shook his head. "You can't go back. Whoever sent that orb will come looking for you, and they're not going to stop until they find you. The only way you can ever go back is if the threat is eliminated."

Despite the large meal, my stomach felt like an open cavern. "I might've grabbed a few more things if I'd known I wasn't coming back." Actually, I had my phone and a credit card. I couldn't think of a single other thing that I actually needed. The picture of my parents that I kept by my bed was also stored on my phone. I wore Meglana's necklace, and it was the only thing I had that wasn't replaceable. I couldn't figure out which was sadder: having to flee my home and my life or realizing that it made little difference because I hadn't built a life for myself at all. "So where do we go?"

"We need to get you to the Magesterial Council in Elustria."

Alex's use of the word "we" went a long way in making me feel better about this entire situation. "Then let's go. You were going to take me the other night."

"That was before an assassin sent a tracker orb into your apartment, a tracker orb that saw me. Whoever is coming after you now knows that you have the help of a shifter. They'll be expecting you at one of the portals we use. It's too risky. I don't have any way to contact a sorcerer to try to get another one opened without tipping off the assassin."

My options seemed to be shrinking. "What about going to see Casper? If he knew my mother, he might know of a way to get to a portal. You said he might be a mage." The thought of Casper Rothian being a mage made me admire him even more. *Wizards and Fae* may actually be based in reality.

"If he really did know your mother, he probably is. She wouldn't have associated with a non-magical being," Alex said.

"It sounds like he's our only option, and he seemed open to helping me. He told me he thought I was in danger." Within hours of his warning, that orb had entered my apartment.

Alex bit his bottom lip, looking past me as he thought it over. "It's worth a try. If it turns out he's an ally, I'll leave you with him."

That last part brought me up short. The comfort I'd felt at his use of the word "we" quickly evaporated. I'd gone from possible friend to troublesome human to be passed off in record time. "Wait, so you're not going to help me figure this all out? You bring all this trouble into my life and then bail?"

Alex fidgeted, squirmed like a little kid forced to sit still when he wanted to run. "I don't get involved in mage business. I feel obligated to safely deliver you to your own kind, but after that, I'm shifting back."

So that's how it was. I wanted to snap at him that he could just go ahead and leave then, but reason urged me not to be dumb and impulsive. I didn't know how things would go with Casper, and Alex knew more about this stuff than I did. If nothing else, it'd be nice to have company. "I can look up the address of Magical Games on my phone, but I don't have a way to contact Casper." He had only contacted me in-game, and I couldn't access that inbox from a phone.

"Is it within driving distance?" Alex asked.

"I think so." I couldn't remember which province the headquarters was located in, but I felt certain it was on the western side of Canada.

"Then we'll drive through the night. Once we get there, we'll find some way to contact Casper and see what he knows."

"And when you say we'll drive through the night, you really mean me."

Alex smiled in a way that hinted at a laugh. "Yes, but I'll stay awake in solidarity." His smile melted. "We should get a move on. I don't want to stay in one place for too long. It'll be a lot harder to track you without the orb, but the magic that necklace released was pretty powerful. It's possible for someone to track it."

I paid for the food, and the waitress gave me a to-go cup of coffee. I wished I could sleep, but even if I could have taught Alex to drive, my car was far too temperamental for a beginner.

As I headed north on the freeway, the talisman around my neck glowed pleasantly, seemingly in approval of our plan. I concentrated on that, hoping it would settle the nervous fluttering of my stomach as I wondered what on earth I had gotten myself into.

CHAPTER 9

*A*ccording to my phone, we'd make it to the headquarters of Magical Games, Inc. by midmorning, assuming I could stay awake the entire way there. I needed to talk to prevent myself falling victim to the lulling effects of the road passing by in the darkness.

"So how does this tracking thing work? Could someone really know where I am because of the necklace?" If so, it didn't really matter where we went since I couldn't get the thing off.

"I'm not entirely sure, and it's not like there's one blanket answer. The rules are completely different for a sorcerer than a mage. A sorcerer would be more likely to trace the magic within the necklace. Mages are closer to your idea of witches. They need something —a wand, talisman, some sort of magical object—in order to perform spells. There could be a mage who has figured out how to track the talisman. For all I know, it's been tracked since before your mother died. Whoever it is could have been waiting for me to deliver it to you." Alex sat relaxed, looking straight ahead at the road, as if he hadn't brought danger into my life.

"Gee, thanks. Could've sold it to a pawn shop, but no, come knocking on a college girl's door and turn her life upside down.

That's a much better use of your time." Bitter sarcasm dripped from my voice.

Alex glanced my way, and his eyebrows rose at my tone. "There was a concern that you'd be able to be tracked anyway. Mages all have a magical spark inside them. You have one passed down from your mother. It was only a matter of time before you were found. After your mother was killed, the natural assumption was that whoever killed her might come looking for you. You could have been left defenseless. That talisman saved your life earlier."

The little thing had come in handy, but I wasn't convinced that all this had been inevitable. "And how do you know for sure that I'm her daughter?"

"Oh, I'm sure." His answer came quick and sure. No further explanation seemed to be forthcoming. That was the most confident statement I'd heard him make thus far. Something had him convinced that I was Meglana's daughter.

"How can you say that?"

"I doubt the talisman would work for anyone else. The reaction it had when you were threatened was telling." This statement lacked the confidence his earlier assertion had held. His certainty didn't spring from that reason.

"But that only happened a few hours ago. What had you so convinced I was her daughter before?" I took my eyes off the road for a moment to see if I could figure out where his hesitance came from. Nervous eyes darted to the side and met mine then focused quickly back on the road. "What is it? What aren't you telling me?"

"The talisman knows who its rightful owner is. It led me to you. It wouldn't make a mistake."

"Led you to me? How do you know it didn't mean to take you to the girl next door?"

"Oh, I know."

His insistence only made me more curious. "But how? Did a voice speak from the heavens? You're turning my life upside down, attracting a magical assassin to me, and all because you have a feeling that the talisman led you to my door?"

Alex grimaced. "It's more than that, all right? The talisman is attracted to you. I wore it around my neck as I searched, and I can't describe it perfectly, but it clearly knew who you were and sought you out. Any time I veered, an overwhelming sense of loss engulfed me. When I saw you for the first time, I've never been so attracted to another person in my entire life."

"Wait, so you're basing this off of being attracted to me?" Anger and shock had me wanting to slam on the brakes, but that wouldn't help anything. "The appropriate response to attraction is asking someone out, not telling her she's the daughter of a murdered mage and is now being hunted."

"You don't get it." Alex shook his head. "It's not a normal attraction, believe me. It was magical in origin. Every part of me called out for you. Every instinct said to go to you. The talisman practically jumped off my chest toward you. And I'm not stupid. That night I met you wasn't the first time I'd seen you. I made sure the talisman wanted you and that my feelings came from it before I showed up at your door."

Not a lot of wiggle room for me in that story. Having a mother of magical origin I might be able to cope with, but the whole being hunted thing really had me wishing he'd made a mistake. "Okay, so it's me. Let's just go with that. What is it the people who killed my mother want?"

"I don't know. Does it matter? I may not know a lot about humans or mages, but it's my general understanding that murderers are not open to reason."

He had a point. Even if I knew what they wanted, it's not like I could convince them to leave me alone. With that depressing thought, I settled in for the drive. Hours slipped by with nothing but the radio playing. The only thing keeping me awake was the fear that if I stopped, whoever had invaded my apartment would find me. If I could give back the necklace, I would. All I could hope was that Casper would have answers for me.

The sun lit the sky with pinks and purples as we approached the Canadian border. Red brake lights shone in front of me, and I slowed to a stop. "Shit."

"What?"

"I forgot about the border. I don't know if they'll let us by." With everything going on, I'd completely spaced that driving into Canada wasn't like driving to a different state.

"What do you need?" Alex asked.

"I don't know, but I don't think they allow you to cross with just a driver's license anymore, and you don't strike me as the type to carry a passport." I didn't have anything else with me, except maybe my student ID in the glove compartment.

"See, you humans complicate everything."

"Oh yeah, I've never heard of an animal killing another who strays into its territory."

"That's what I'm talking about: it's simpler, none of this paperwork and crap you all have to deal with."

We really were from two different worlds. The line inched forward, and when the minivan in front of us was waved through, I put on my most charming smile for the border patrol officer. Her hair was back in a bun with frizzy flyaways, and the bags under her eyes weighed down her entire face.

"What brings you into Canada?" Boredom leaked out of her tone into her posture as she peered at me.

I probably should've spent more time thinking of answers to potential questions while waiting. Would fleeing a magical murderer qualify me for asylum status? Probably not. "I'm going to the headquarters of Magical Games, Inc."

Her eyes narrowed and she looked further into the car. "On a Saturday?"

"Yeah, I won a contest, and they preferred I come on the weekend. I've got class on Monday." It wouldn't hurt to throw in that I had a compelling reason to return.

"ID, please." The woman held out her hand expectantly, and I gave her my license. She spent all of two seconds looking at it. "I'm going to need more than this. This driver's license doesn't prove your citizenship. You need a passport or birth certificate."

"I'm sorry, I thought I just needed a driver's license. I'm just coming over for the day. I'm a student, see?" I handed her my student ID. "I've got to be back for classes on Monday anyway. I'm not going to jeopardize graduation over trying to illegally stay in Canada. Can't you just make an exception this once?"

The officer returned my driver's license and student ID. "I'm sorry, but there's no provision in immigration law for uninformed students to just hop across the border and hop back over. You're going to need to turn around."

I looked up at her with the most pathetic, pleading gaze I could muster. "Please, this is really important. It's a once-in-a-lifetime opportunity."

"Then you should've been better prepared." Irritation replaced boredom. "Now just drive through here and you can make a U-turn and come back with proper identification."

This couldn't be happening. I couldn't go back to my apartment to get sufficient identification. I looked to Alex, frantic. My eyebrows rose waiting for him to come up with some brilliant solution. Did he have some kind of magic that could be useful here?

"You heard the lady, just turn around." I shot daggers at him with my eyes. He in turn pointedly stared at my chest. It took a second for me to realize that he was looking at the talisman that had started to feel a little warm. Better not let it feel too much panic. Right now all the officer wanted me to do was turn around, but I was pretty sure if my talisman decided she was a threat and killed her, I'd have much bigger problems than ID.

I took a deep breath, trying to calm myself before the talisman did anything to worsen our situation, and followed the officer's directions to make a U-turn. A few miles down the road, I pulled into the parking lot of a gas station. "So what do we do now?"

"Now we wait for you to calm down so that talisman stops glowing. You have to learn to control your emotions."

In through the nose and out through the mouth I breathed, willing my panic to subside. "And then what?"

Alex's yellow eyes twinkled. "And then we storm the border by force."

CHAPTER 10

"Storm the border by force?" Panic rose inside me. Alex certainly wasn't normal, but so far he hadn't struck me as completely crazy.

The corners of his lips twitched while the rest of his face remained sober except for a little twinkle in his eyes. "Maybe my choice of words was extreme. We can just cross the border if you prefer."

He made it sound like the easiest thing in the world, like the whole episode at the border had never happened. "But we can't cross the border without proof of citizenship. Didn't you hear her? And even if we could get my ID, you still don't have any. The border is not a 'plus one' situation."

Alex smiled and tapped his head with his index finger. "Thinking like a human again. You're going to have to stop that. The world is not as it seems to you. You're talking about human rules. I'm not. Last time I checked, border patrol has no authority over panthers crossing the border."

I wanted to slap the arrogant gleam from his eyes, but not only did it make them a little cuter, he was also my only hope at the moment. "Okay, so you shift to a panther and go across the border, and then what, cause a distraction for me to drive through?"

"No, you're going to ride on my back across the border."

"And leave my car?" I knew she wasn't exactly enviable, but she was all I had.

"This is a great honor I'm doing you. Shifters aren't pets to be ridden. We only extend the privilege to a select few."

If the thought of riding on his back with him in panther form wasn't alarming enough, the idea of leaving my car behind was unthinkable. "No, that won't work."

"Why?"

I grasped for something more rational than my love for my car. "Because we cut across the border and then what? I'm supposed to ride on your back the entire way?"

"I don't have any problem with that, but if it bothers you, we can always acquire a car on the other side."

I narrowed my eyes as I stared at him. "Is 'acquire' a shifter euphemism for steal?"

He tipped his head side to side and sucked in a breath. "You could say that."

Dammit, the little smirk that played on his lips was entirely too charming for someone who had just suggested committing grand theft auto. "I know I'm not a model citizen, but I'm certainly not a thief."

"I understand. I'm sure that argument will be persuasive to the assassin who shows up to kill you."

I turned away and gripped the steering wheel, frustrated by my circumstances, the lack of options, and Alex's insufferable knack for being right when I wished he wasn't. "Fine."

"Why don't you drive down that dirt road and see if there's a place you can park out of the way?" He pointed to a barely visible road off to the side of the gas station.

The farther we traveled, the more the car bumped and jostled as the road degraded into little more than muddy potholes. The forest on each side of the single lane stood too thick to penetrate with the car. If the road continued to deteriorate, I feared we'd get stuck. After a few more minutes, I saw a small clearing on the right and pulled into it. The trees thinned just enough for me to squeeze the car through into a clearing hidden from the road. Alex didn't waste a second once I'd parked.

"Grab what you need and let's go." He exited the car and waited for me to join him. For some reason, leaving the car actually hurt. I had nothing left. Leaving my apartment had been bad enough, but that at least was a rental. This car was mine, free and clear. I locked the doors and saved our GPS location to my phone so I could find her later. Then I popped my phone out of its case and placed my license and credit card behind it and popped it back in. That way I wouldn't have to worry about one of them falling out of my pocket. That done, I placed the key in the wheel well. If someone wanted to steal her, I'd rather they not break a window to get inside, and I didn't want to risk losing the key on this trek across the border.

"I'll be back." I kissed my fingers and touched them to the windshield. Once everything settled down, I hoped I'd find my baby in working order.

"You humans bestow a great amount of value on inanimate objects," Alex said from the other side of the car.

"All I have left is a cell phone, ID, a credit card, and the magical necklace that destroys things, which is slightly less cool when you consider that it's also the reason I've had to give up everything else." I stood in front of him, daring him to tell me I didn't have reason to be upset.

"Yes, sad, little human discovered that she is the heir to one of the most powerful mages in the world and therefore has to leave behind a rather unimpressive vehicle."

Normally I wouldn't let an insult like that slide, but my ear had caught on the word "heir." I hadn't even considered my situation in those terms, but if I was getting all the downsides to being Meglana's daughter, there had to be an upside somewhere. I'd never known her, so it couldn't appear crass. "Did she leave me some sort of inheritance?" Maybe that could help pay for tuition if I ever got back to school.

"You're wearing it around your neck."

Definitely not what I wanted. The piece of jewelry increasingly seemed to be more of a curse than anything. "See, trust funds, that's one area where we humans have it figured out better than you magic folk do."

Alex shook his head and smiled. "You can educate me more later. Let me see the map."

I opened the app on my phone and handed it to him.

He nodded. "I'll be able to take us in the right direction."

Very reassuring. I'd hate to end up back in the U.S. "How exactly is this going to work?" I had never so much as gone horseback riding.

"I'll shift, and you climb onto my back. Wrap your arms around me and lie on your stomach. You should be able to grip with your thighs if you need to. I'm not going to let you fall off or let anything hit you. Just relax and you'll be fine. We won't be able to talk once I shift, but I'll be able to understand you, so if you need anything, just say so."

That all sounded easy enough, but I still worried that I'd fall off. "Just remember that you have me on your back."

"Trust me, I won't forget. You ready?"

I nodded, and he stepped back and shifted into a panther in front of me. The sight was more magnificent than before. It didn't shock me as much, and it definitely didn't scare me. It left me with a sense of awe. He jerked his head in the direction of his back to signal to me to climb on.

His size made it a surprisingly easy fit, more comfortable than I would've expected. The dark fur felt just as velvety as it looked. I wrapped my arms around his chest and rested my cheek against the back of his neck. Once I was settled, he took off. His graceful strides resulted in almost no movement for me. For the first time since waking up, my body relaxed. It'd be so easy to drift off to sleep.

Within a few minutes I had lost all sense of direction amid the undifferentiated trees. Alex, though, continued his sure movements, apparently harboring no doubts about the route we traveled. Every nerve in my body prickled on high alert. At any moment a border patrol officer could stop us. A girl riding on a panther's back would make for an interesting sight. My real fear should be for Alex. If someone saw us, he was likely to get shot.

No physical characteristics appeared to mark the divide between the United States and Canada. I couldn't tell if or when we had crossed the border. Alex simply continued onward, appearing to have the situation under control.

The sun beat down on my back, heating it to an uncomfortable degree. The air no longer held the crisp chill of morning. I must have fallen asleep. Alex's back was more comfortable than I could have imagined. I wanted nothing more than to continue my slumber, but Alex had stopped moving beneath me. I opened my eyes to a vibrant blue sky, devoid of all traces of the pink light of dawn. When I turned my head, bright yellow eyes peered at me over a black velvet shoulder. I took the hint and slid off Alex's back, stepping away so he could shift.

"Did you sleep well?" he asked.

"Yeah, how did you know?"

"The way your weight settled on me. Plus, you had an adorable little snore."

I wanted to deny it, but how would I know? "You didn't have to let me keep sleeping, but thanks. How long has it been?"

"A few hours. Based on the map you showed me, we shouldn't be too far away."

I looked at my phone, and my jaw went slack when I saw how

much ground Alex had covered. The GPS showed our destination as only an eight-minute walk from our current location. "How did you do that?"

Alex brushed it off, like I had complimented him on breathing and walking at the same time. "I have an excellent sense of direction. Shifters are faster and have more endurance than Earth cats."

Even with magical animal instincts, his accuracy after seeing the map once, hours ago, amazed me. Stashing my phone in my pocket, I followed his lead, trusting him to get us the last of the way there.

"So do you have a plan?" Alex asked as we walked. "I doubt they're just going to let you in."

"Yeah, I'm not too worried." I had no idea where my confidence came from other than a determination that I hadn't abandoned my apartment, my car, and my life to be thwarted by a gatekeeper.

A little security hut sat at the entrance to the Magical Games, Inc. campus, manned by a lone security guard. The parking lot beyond sat almost completely empty. My only hope lay in the fact that Casper had seemed desperate to meet me. If I could convince someone to contact him, or even let me log into the game so I could reply to his in-game message, I felt sure he'd see me. Besides, Casper struck me as the workaholic type. He probably regularly stayed in the office on weekends.

Alex and I walked straight up to the security hut, probably looking like a couple of crazies. It occurred to me too late to check my morning breath, but I didn't have any gum or mints anyway. The security guard stepped out of his little building, a slight paunch stretching out his gray polyester uniform. "I'm sorry, folks, but I'm gonna have to ask you to turn around. This is all private property."

"Oh, we know. We have an appointment." I ambled right up to him, attempting to appear as if I belonged.

The guard sighed, clearly having a super interesting show or game to get back to in his little hut. "I don't have any appointments down for today. Without an employee ID, I can't let you through."

"You don't understand, Casper Rothian invited me here himself. I won an in-game contest and he asked me to come here this weekend. My name is Kat Thomas. If you just call up to him, I promise you, he'll want to see me." I kept my voice nice, not letting frustration or anger enter into the mix. This guy was just doing his job.

"I'm sorry, but I can't call Mr. Rothian any time a couple of kids try to get in here." His fat cheeks pulled his mouth down into a frown.

"I can prove it." I pulled up the email on my phone that congratulated me for winning and turned it so he could see. Security guard Rick—based on the name tag I had just noticed—took the phone from me and read over the email.

"These kinds of things are always arranged in advance." He shook his head, eyebrows furrowed in frustration. "No one's told me about it."

I waved my hand in dismissal. "It was all really last minute. I only won last night, as you can see from the email, but Mr. Rothian said he was traveling soon, so he wouldn't be able to meet me for months if I didn't come this weekend. I told him I didn't know if I could make it for sure, and he promised me that if I made the effort to get here today, that he'd see me. Just call him, and he'll confirm."

When Rick handed back my phone, the wariness had left his face. "It is true that Mr. Rothian is traveling a lot. But still, he would've had a secretary leave your name with me."

Alex spoke up. "I'm sure one little call isn't going to hurt anything. If it turns out we're not telling the truth, you have my word that we'll turn around and head right back in the direction we came from."

Rick still seemed unconvinced. "I don't care about that, kid. I'm not bothering Mr. Rothian for anything. He fires people who interrupt him. You know how these temperamental tech people are."

Casper, while beloved by fans, did have a reputation for being intense in his work. Time to take matters in a more drastic direction. I pulled out my phone and navigated to The Codex, the largest fan site for *Wizards and Fae*. Typing furiously with my thumbs, I didn't even look up as I spoke. "Fine, I'll just take to the forums. I'm sure the rest of the players will love to find out how this contest is just a scam. And Rick is R-I-C-K, right? Let me ask you, Rick, have you ever been the target of an angry online mob? Don't worry, most of the ire will come down on Casper. You know how us Internet folk love to find out what our online heroes are really like. Turns out Casper likes to put on a good face for the cameras and at conventions while treating the players who made him wealthy like crap. I get that. In fact, I'm pretty sure one of my guildmates is a reporter. I'll make sure to send him the link to my post."

Rick held up his hands in defeat, shaking them as if to alert me to stop. "All right, all right, just hold on a sec. Let me go make a call so we can figure this out."

I smiled and looked up from my phone. "That sounds like a good idea, Rick. And if I were you, I'd make sure that I didn't accidentally call the police instead of Casper. Nothing like the image of a fan in handcuffs to really get the online mob frothing."

Rick retreated into his hut and picked up the phone.

"Impressive," Alex whispered to me. "His face paled rather quickly once you got going."

"Just showing some of my good old human ingenuity. If there's one thing that would bother Casper more than being interrupted, it's bad PR for his game." Out of the corner of my eye, I saw Alex smile for a fraction of a second.

Rick quickly emerged from the hut, this time holding two guest badges. "I'm so sorry, Ms. Thomas. Please accept my apologies. Mr. Rothian is very eager to see you and asked that I go ahead and take you and your guest up to reception myself." He handed Alex and me each a badge then led us to a waiting golf cart.

CHAPTER 11

The golf cart hummed along around the corner of the main office building. Apparently, the parking lot entrance was not the front of the campus. Before us stood an enormous fountain with statues of giants, elves, and wizards, perfectly recreating the login screen of the game. My inner geek emerged, and all thoughts of the talisman and assassins fled. Without even thinking, I turned to Alex, holding out my phone to ask him to take a picture of me with it, and stopped at the sight of his yellow eyes staring at me in amusement. Even if he knew how to work a camera phone, I doubted he'd take kindly to my request. I put my phone away, but not before surreptitiously snapping my own blurry selfie with the fountain.

Rick stopped the golf cart right outside the front doors. The parking lot on this side of the building was more crowded than the one we had initially seen. Sitting in the spot closest to the front was a bright yellow sports car. According to a press interview, Casper had bought it when the game surpassed five million subscribers.

When we got inside, a perky receptionist greeted us. "Mr. Rothian is expecting you. Please, follow me." Her smile revealed the whitest teeth I had ever seen, and her ponytail swung with a cheery little clip as she twirled to her left, expecting us to follow her.

"Turns out you did good, Rick." I nodded in the security guard's direction as we walked off. No need for him to worry that I'd go through with my threat.

We followed the swaying ponytail to a nearby elevator. When the doors opened, Alex and I stepped inside while the receptionist swiped her ID then pressed the button for the fifth floor. "Someone will be there to greet you. Have a great day!" She waved and twirled back in the direction from which she'd come.

Once the doors closed, I realized the elevator was a replica of a lift from the elven capital city in the game, complete with the same soundtrack. Translucent, sparkly blue and green walls surrounded us, and the buttons for the floors resembled mother-of-pearl. I wished I was here under different circumstances. Casper had been right; I would enjoy the full treatment. Maybe we'd be able to get the necklace off and I could take a tour. Deep down, I knew that wouldn't be the case. The elevator dinged and the doors opened, revealing a nearly identical bright-eyed receptionist to the one who'd met us downstairs.

"Welcome! Mr. Rothian is expecting you. If you'd follow me right this way?" She gestured with her arm to the left as we exited the elevator and followed her. I'd never seen anyone so perky at their job, but I guess I'd be perky too if I got to work somewhere like this.

I had expected that the floor with Casper's office would look like a regular, boring office building. I couldn't have been more wrong. Just like the elevator and entryway below, the hallways here were exquisitely decorated with art from the game. The conference rooms we passed were a fascinating mixture of state-of-the-art technology and old-world fantasy. Frosted windows were etched with epic battle scenes from the game. I couldn't resist reaching out to touch one, the smooth yet bumpy texture of the glass leaving me in even more awe.

The receptionist halted in front of the door to a corner office. She knocked and, without waiting for an answer, opened the door and gestured for us to enter. After we crossed the threshold, she closed the door behind us, leaving us alone with the red-headed man I recognized instantly as Casper Rothian, creator of the biggest game franchise in the world.

Casper stood, and a smile lit up his face as he walked around his desk with an outstretched hand. I didn't know anything about fashion, but even I could tell the dark navy suit he wore wasn't off the rack. It fit his trim body perfectly. While some tech billionaires took to jeans and a hoodie, Casper had always bucked that trend for a more professional look. Everything in his outfit was immaculately put together from his pocket square to his shined shoes to the ruby cufflinks I noticed as I shook his hand. "Kat, so good to see you. I'm happy you were able to make it after all." He released my hand then turned to Alex. "And who is this?"

"My name is Alex. I'm a friend."

As soon as their hands touched, Casper's eyes narrowed curiously. "A shifter? I'd guess you're one of the cats."

"You're correct." Alex didn't elaborate. Something about him seemed on edge, as if he didn't entirely trust Casper or the situation we found ourselves in.

Casper focused his brown eyes on me as he leaned back against his desk, crossing his ankles and folding his arms across his chest. I didn't know if it was because he wanted to address me directly or if he felt uncomfortable beneath Alex's scrutiny. "I take it since you brought along a shifter, this isn't you simply wanting to redeem your prize."

"You're right, although now that I've seen the place, I really would like a tour sometime." A nervous smile pulled at my face, but Casper didn't match it. His face settled into a serious, determined expression.

"Why did you come? What's happened?" He eyed the amber stone on my chest then resumed eye contact.

The abrupt change of tone brought back the events of last night. "Someone tried to kill me."

Casper uncrossed his arms and ankles, stepping forward with a sense of urgency. "A sorcerer?"

"Something magical. I woke up to an orb floating in my bedroom. Alex seems to think that whoever killed my mother is coming after me."

Casper nodded. "We better get out of here. I have somewhere safe I can take you. That talisman of yours is giving off enough power to potentially be tracked depending on who's trying to kill you." Casper strode back behind his desk and picked up the phone. "I'm going to be leaving ahead of schedule with two guests. I'm making my way to the roof now. Meet us there." He hung up and didn't miss a beat, striding to the door and motioning for us to follow. "I have a helicopter on the roof. It'll take us to a safe location, one with protective enchantments."

I started to follow, but Alex caught my arm while keeping his eyes on Casper. "Wait, we don't even know you."

Alex had a point, even though I felt as if I did know Casper from the years spent following his career and watching his promotional videos and interviews. But all I knew was his public persona. That man, while he had always appeared authentic, could be a PR creation.

Casper had already opened his office door, but stopped to look back at us. "No, you do not. However, it seems like the only thing you need to know is that I'm not trying to kill you. I'm a mage and a friend of Meglana's."

The man made a good argument. I glanced at Alex to see if he accepted this and found him looking at me. I shrugged. "I don't really see a better option."

Alex nodded, and we followed Casper out of his office.

When we arrived on the roof, the helicopter blades were spinning to life, and we had to duck into the wind they produced. Casper led the way and ushered first me and then Alex into the cabin. The second the door latched behind us, the helicopter took flight. I don't know what I had expected, perhaps the type of helicopter news stations used, but this one was clearly designed for the comfort of its wealthy owner. Cream-colored leather seats looked and felt every bit as luxurious as you'd expect for a multimillionaire, or was it billionaire? I didn't quite know where Casper stood in the monetary hierarchy.

"It shouldn't take long to get to our destination. We can speak more freely there, where I'm assured there are no eavesdropping ears. In the meantime, enjoy the scenery." Casper gestured to the large window on my right. Indeed, the landscape passing below us was breathtaking but hardly a suitable distraction from the more exciting topics at hand, especially after my years in Montana. I'd had my fill of snow, trees, and mountains.

"Why the helicopter? Why not just teleport us?" Alex's question tore my attention from the window, and I looked over him to Casper. As cool as the helicopter was, teleporting sounded far more interesting.

"The use of any magic opens us up to the possibility of being tracked. The place I'm taking you to is something of a magical island, meaning there's no teleporting in or out. It's completely self-contained. Think of it like the magical version of an air-gapped computer." Casper looked out his window, ending the conversation. I doubted Alex understood the computer reference.

After hours of travel, I'd made it. I was sitting in a helicopter with Casper Rothian, my idol…and the man who had revealed less than twenty-four hours ago that he had known my birth mother. My worlds collided in strange ways. Now that I was with him, I didn't want to waste any time. "You said you knew my mother."

Casper held up his hand. "Not now. Wait until we land. I promise you, I'll tell you everything you want to know once I'm assured we're safe."

We flew in silence. Last night I'd gone to bed blissfully unaware of the full extent of the danger which threatened me. It seemed ludicrous that a full day hadn't passed since then. Staring out at the scenery, my mind wandered to all that had happened. My financial problems seemed far away, but if Casper could get me to the Mages-terial Council and get the necklace off, then I could return to school. I needed to remember to get the cash equivalent of my prize. I hoped Casper would honor my request. I doubted showing up at his office today counted as redeeming the trip. Without the necklace, the danger should pass. I could get a new apartment and go back to normal, right?

"Ah, here we are," Casper said, pulling me from my thoughts.

Outside my window, a giant stone structure materialized through the misty fog of clouds. "It looks like a fort."

"That's what it was back when this area of Canada was colonized. It had been abandoned for ages before I bought it. It has the advan-tage of being in the middle of nowhere yet a quick commute by heli-copter. I call it the Armory."

The pilot landed us so softly that I barely noticed. Casper pulled a small box from his pocket and opened it to reveal a ring that he put on his right ring finger. Before I could get a good look at it, the pilot opened the door for us to exit, and I realized for the first time that he must be magical too. Casper didn't strike me as the type to trust humans when he made such a big deal about the secrecy of the Armory. My suspicions of the pilot were confirmed when he headed to a glowing circle in the ground and promptly disappeared.

I could hardly believe my eyes. Seeing a person disappear produced the same unsettling feeling as seeing a limb bent in the wrong direction. "What did he just do?"

"Teleported. You're about to do it too," Casper said as he led us to a different circle. The idea of teleporting both scared and excited me. The analytical part of my brain screamed that this was madness. Teleporting was not something that could or should be done. What exactly would happen to my body? According to the science fiction I'd read, I'd be disintegrated into lots of tiny bits and then re-materi-alized on the other end. That hardly sounded safe or sane. So far, my track record for successfully producing magic that I could control was zero. This seemed like an awfully big first step with a giant downside should it not work properly.

"I'm happy to use the stairs. It's healthier."

Even Alex eyed me in a manner that clearly conveyed how full of shit he thought I was.

"There's nothing to worry about." Casper held out his hand invitingly. "Teleporting is perfectly safe, I assure you."

"I'm sure it's safe when you know what you're doing." Casper knew me as Meglana's daughter. In his world, mages were probably teleporting from the time they could walk. I'm sure he meant well, but I doubted he knew the level of my ineptness.

"It's also easy. As long as you're in the ring with a mage who has been to your destination, you can use it to teleport. That's how your friend here is going to be able to come along. If even a non-mage can use the teleportation rings, trust me, you can too."

According to Casper's tone, saying that even a shifter could do it was tantamount to saying that the village idiot could figure it out. I noticed Alex's jaw tighten at the insulting tone. Nice to see that bigotry was alive and well even in the magical world. I took Casper's hand but also held my other one out to Alex as a peace offering. Plus, I needed his support. Something about him saving my life made me inherently trust him.

"All right, when you get into the ring, there's really nothing you need to do, but it does help if you close your eyes and keep your mind blank, especially the first time. If you hold on to where you're at too tightly, you'll just stay here and not teleport."

"So the worst that can happen if I do it wrong is that I stay here? There's no chance of half of me ending up somewhere else?"

Casper chuckled. "The magic that's used here is incapable of causing you physical harm. You either stay here, or you'll end up at our destination, completely whole. Those are the only two options."

I nodded and stepped into the circle with him. As soon as my second foot hit the ground and my eyes closed, my whole body felt as if it were being sucked through a tube, compressed and pulled so tightly that my skin tingled. I wanted to open my eyes to see what was happening, but I feared they would pop out of my head. Safe my ass.

As suddenly as it began, the sensation ended, and I stood just as I was before it started, only much warmer.

"Welcome to my home," Casper said.

I opened my eyes to find myself in the most magnificent place I'd ever seen.

hile the headquarters of Magical Games, Inc. had been impressive, the Armory was pure luxury. We had teleported to the entryway of a grand living space. Rough-hewn stone walls appeared as if they hadn't changed a bit since the last soldiers had abandoned it long ago. Despite the cold walls, the space had a remarkably warm and cozy feel to it. To our left sat a living room, and in the far corner a fireplace was carved from the stone and already housed a leaping, crackling blaze. The furniture was all brown leather and inviting with fat cushions. Thick, plush cream carpet covered the floors, and in the middle of the seating area a low maple table sat with intricate carvings all along the top. From this distance, I couldn't make out if the etchings were some foreign language or artistic in design.

Directly across from us a spiral staircase led to the floor above. An iron banister with detailed patterns of leaves, trees, and flowers carved into it twisted upward. To my right stood a library. Bookshelves covered the entirety of the walls, overflowing with books whose spines would make a collector's heart leap, all leather and cloth, nothing appearing to have been produced within the last century. The chairs in this area were the same brown leather except for a giant throne-like chair sitting behind an ornate desk. The throne chair looked as if it had been carved from a solid piece of wood and not a single part of it had escaped the artist's touch. Rich red velvet upholstery formed a back and seat cushion which were embroidered with gold thread mimicking the designs carved into the wood.

The desk was every bit as imposing as the one in Casper's office, but in an entirely different way. I could picture a king banging his fist on it as he ordered his men into war. Thick legs were carved in the shape of an animal's head that was completely foreign to me. It had the nose of a fox, the mane of a lion, and the curled horns of some type of goat. Without being told, I knew this wasn't the product of an artisan's imagination: I was seeing a creature from Elustria.

Little balls of light floated in the air, casting a warm glow throughout the space. Three hung suspended above us. When Casper stepped forward, one of the balls of light followed. What an ingenious creation, but I doubted it had much to do with energy conservation, though it seemed like a brilliant solution.

Alex and I followed Casper to the living room, much to my disappointment. The sight of all those books had driven away thoughts of anything else, and I wouldn't have minded getting a closer look at the desk's animal carvings either. In this new environment, I naturally gravitated toward Alex, the man who had saved me, and we sat together on the sofa while Casper took one of the chairs.

"You can relax. I assure you that you're perfectly safe here." Casper's sharp brown eyes penetrated me, giving me his full attention, as if he willed me to relax. He steepled his hands in front of his face with his elbows resting on the arms of his chair, and I got a better look at the ring I'd noticed earlier. The design was incredibly simple, but I'd never seen anything like it. A thick gold band held a dark red stone, maybe a ruby, in the shape of a pyramid, the edges and point glinting in the light of the fireplace, seemingly sharp enough to cut glass. "I see you have your mother's talisman." He nodded toward my necklace, and in that moment, I knew the ring was Casper's talisman.

I looked down at the amber stone resting on my chest, peaceful and serene as if it hadn't caused all kinds of trouble for me. I fiddled with it, running it up and down the chain. "Alex delivered it to me. I didn't know anything about my birth mother, never even really wanted to. This has all been one hell of a shock."

Casper focused on Alex. "So you knew Meglana?" His eyebrows rose in surprise.

"Not really. My father worked with her."

"Ah." Casper nodded in understanding. "She would find value in a shifter, someone who can sniff out magic, give her warning of an approaching enemy."

Alex didn't say anything more, didn't reveal that his father died in her service. I wondered at the motivation behind his silence.

"So what can you tell me about my birth mother?" I asked. Casper was the only one of us who seemed to have known her. I wanted to know why she would have left me with something so dangerous and nothing else, not a note or anything.

"Meglana was an extraordinary woman. She was the most powerful mage of our generation." Admiration lit Casper's eyes. His face relaxed when he talked about her, as if he remembered something pleasant.

"Then how did someone murder her?" So far nothing I'd learned about Meglana made sense. If she had been so powerful, I'd think she could've protected herself.

"Her strength made her a target. Sorcerers are naturally stronger than mages, and her strength threatened them. They were after her for years. It's why she hid you."

I wondered if he had known her when I was adopted or if he heard the story from her later. He would have been very young, assuming the age he claimed as a human was correct. "I don't understand why she wouldn't have given me a note or something. Why find me after all this time only to leave me with a dangerous neck-lace and no explanation?"

Casper's eyes sharpened. "The talisman isn't dangerous. It won't hurt you." As if the thought that Meglana's talisman was anything other than wonderful offended him.

"It started a fire in my apartment. In my book, that qualifies as dangerous." I didn't have whatever sentimental connection to Meglana and the talisman that Casper did.

"What were you doing when the fire started?"

I shifted in my seat. This would sound stupid, but at the time it had seemed reasonable. "Trying to remove it with pliers." My words came out sheepish and timid.

Casper's eyebrows rose. "Pliers?"

I exhaled in acknowledgement of how dumb it sounded. "Yeah, I haven't been able to get the necklace off. I thought I might be able to pry one of the links open. It didn't work. I got frustrated and threw the pliers into the sink. That's when they burst into flames."

Casper chuckled. "Your frustration made the reaction of the talisman more intense. The flames were to protect it and you. It doesn't want to leave you vulnerable, so it'll attack whatever tries to remove it." He made it sound like that amber stone had a mind of its own. That didn't make it sound less dangerous. My face must have said as much, because Casper added as an afterthought, "Your mother would have charmed it to behave that way."

Every time the talisman had done something, it had been to protect me or it. The only exception was when it first formed frost. Other than that, it had tried to prevent me from removing it, which was freaky, but it also saved me when that floating orb had come into my apartment. When the border patrol agent had stood in my way, the talisman responded again. Hearing Casper explain it made me feel even more stupid. "Well, it didn't come with an instruction manual, which would have been helpful."

"I can only guess that Meglana wasn't aware her end was near. If she'd had the time, I'm sure she would have given you some instructions. But she didn't leave you with nothing. She knew I'd find you." Sitting across from me was the same calm, confident man who regularly addressed fan conventions and the press. Nothing seemed to faze him. He had an answer for everything. It was easy to believe him and get wrapped up in his assurance that all had worked out according to plan.

"How?" Everything had seemed like pure chance. When Meglana gave me up for adoption, *Wizards and Fae* hadn't existed yet. Casper, at least the human Casper, would have been a complete unknown.

"That's a more complicated conversation." Casper skimmed right over my question. I could only assume it had something to do with magic that I wouldn't understand. "Why don't you tell me what happened that changed your mind about accepting my invitation? You said someone tried to kill you. Walk me through exactly what happened."

"I woke up last night to a glowing ball floating in my room. The stone on my necklace had warmed to an almost unbearable heat. Luckily Alex was there and fought off the orb thing. I ran to the living room and the necklace short-circuited or something. It hit the orb with enough electricity to cut the power to my building. Alex told me I was in danger and that whoever sent that orb would be by soon to kill me, so we left. Since you told me you knew Meglana and you had made the offer, I came to your office." This story sounded so unbelievable, even to my ears. Things like this only happened in movies and books, not in real life.

Casper's gaze shifted to Alex who had stayed quiet throughout my explanation. "Do you think it was a tracker orb?"

"Yes. It didn't attack, but it had strong defenses." I wondered at the life Alex had led that he knew these things. Were tracker orbs common in Elustria? It didn't seem likely.

"Did the magic from the talisman destroy it or did it get away?"

"Kat destroyed it." I appreciated that he made it sound like I did something other than scream off in the corner while he fought it.

"The burst of magic would've been impressive if the thought of her not being able to control it wasn't so scary."

Casper pursed his lips. "The talisman is aware of its rightful owner and is trying to defend you, Kat. That's to be expected, but the strength of its protection is unusual. Though, I should say I'm not surprised given who your mother was."

I sure didn't feel protected by the necklace. If Alex hadn't been there, I'd probably be dead by now. The orb would have left and whoever controlled it would have come for me. "It's terrifying not being able to control it. I'm scared I'm going to hurt myself or someone else."

Casper's eyes softened around the edges in sympathy. "I understand, although you are in no danger yourself from the talisman. As long as you wear it, it will not allow your power to hurt you. But, if you like, I can remove it for you."

The relief that poured through me at his offer had me melting into my seat. Without even realizing it, I'd held my body and muscles rigid with unease. "That would be wonderful."

Casper stood, and I followed suit. The ring on his right hand glowed as he passed his palm a few inches in front of the medallion. "Your mother placed quite a few defensive charms on it. She took great care to protect you."

He leaned closer and murmured words in a language I didn't understand. A powerful energy passed between us as if the magic of both our talismans was a tangible thing. My heart raced beneath the amber stone as I smelled Casper's expensive cologne and tendrils of magic tickled my chest. His hands came around to the back of my neck, and his fingertips lowered to the chain, but just before they curled around it, with a great whoosh of air, he was gone. A giant zapping noise filled the air as if a thousand mosquitoes flew into a bug light at once followed by a crash.

Casper lay huddled against the wall on the other side of the room cradling his hands. The chair that had sat behind him was overturned and thrown to the side by the force of his body flying backward.

Alex rushed to my side, rubbing my arms in a comforting gesture I enjoyed too much. His close proximity calmed my nerves and took the edge off the situation. "Are you all right?" The concern in his eyes was palpable. I hadn't felt anything at all other than a rush of air as Casper flew backward, but the experience so shocked me that it took a moment to form a coherent thought.

"Of course she's all right," Casper said as he struggled to his feet, his face pale as he continued to cradle his hands. "The stone's protecting her." He moved his gaze from Alex to me. "If you didn't want me to take it off of you, you could've just said so."

The bottom fell out of my stomach at his accusation. "I'm sorry. I do want it off. I didn't try to hurt you." Guilt overcame me. The amber stone had betrayed me, and now it appeared as if I wished harm on one of the few people capable of helping me. With every second that passed, I regretted more and more ever putting on the necklace.

Casper relaxed, his face softening in response to my obvious distress. "No, no, of course not. Don't worry about it. It appears it doesn't want to leave your neck and will not do so until commanded to. We'll try again later." The last traces of distress had left Casper. Other than the overturned chair, no evidence of the mishap remained.

Alex had a different idea. "I think we should take her to the Magesterial Council. Perhaps they can remove the necklace."

"Perhaps." Casper nodded. "I need to go get my hands looked at. Allow me to show you to some guest rooms so you can rest. You've both had quite a journey." Casper gestured to the stairs, and I saw the angry red marks on his hands, much like the ones Alex had sustained after fighting the tracker orb.

Up the magnificent spiral staircase we went. Up close, the detail in the cast iron banister left me in awe. I wanted to believe that the delicate carvings of trees, flowers, and ivy were made by magic. The thought that a human could perform such intricate work was too unbelievable. The texture of the leaves and velvety flowers were so masterfully rendered that the cold feel of iron beneath my hand shocked me.

We got off the stairs at the first landing even though the staircase appeared to ascend another three or four floors. Casper led us to two adjoining bedrooms. "Please, rest yourselves. There should be food waiting for you as well. If you need anything, there are communication orbs next to the beds. Now, if you'll excuse me." Casper nodded his head and walked away with such authority he looked like he was walking into a board meeting, not down the hall of his own home. The air lightened without the weight of his presence.

Alex followed me into my room, and after having grown used to his comforting presence, I didn't mind. He walked past me and scanned the room as if he were looking for threats. The room was as comfortable and luxurious as the rest of the house, but a table in the sitting area with a platter of food caught my attention and didn't let go. Last time I'd eaten had been at that twenty-four-hour diner right after we fled my apartment. Not only was it past time for me to eat but after being denied for so long after the feast at the diner, my stomach growled with the ferocity of a bear.

Without bothering to say anything to Alex, I dug into the platter of fruits, cheeses, breads, and meats. I didn't notice the taste of the food, only that it filled the cavernous pit of my stomach. Something about that attack on Casper must have drained me. Out of the corner of my eye, I saw Alex retreat through the door that presumably connected our rooms. He returned a moment later carrying his own platter and joined me at the table.

"You can have some of mine too. Eat as much as you want." Alex nudged his food in my direction.

Not needing another word of encouragement, I picked my favorites from among his platter and added them to mine: a hard white cheese, pieces of candied fruit, a hunk of sourdough bread, and some type of smoked meat with a gamey flavor I couldn't place. "Aren't you hungry?"

"Yes, but I'm not picky. I'll have whatever you don't. I might shift and go hunting outside."

The thought of him hunting outside, his black, velvety fur contrasting against the untouched snow, was alluring. "I bet you're anxious to get back in your panther form."

Alex shrugged, but I could tell by the way he moved in his human body that he was antsy. "I don't understand why Casper isn't taking you to Elustria. It doesn't make any sense."

Really, I didn't want to go to Elustria. At least here I was in my home world. Elustria seemed infinitely far away and foreign. This was the first time I'd so much as left the United States, and Alex wanted me to leave the world. It wasn't something I could agree to easily. If there was a way to fix this problem here and get me back home, I was all for it. I had to figure out how to pay for my last semester so I could graduate. This was merely a distraction from my real life. To Alex, going through a portal to Elustria was the most natural thing in the world, but what if I got stuck there? I'd be in a strange world surrounded by magic. On paper, that sounded cool, but the reality left me scared. I should've been excited at the prospect of a magic world like the one I was used to playing in, but there was a reason I played video games. The danger there was safe, the perfect escape for someone like me who didn't want to face life. I felt pathetic and weak, but if Casper could get this necklace off, then the person looking for it would leave me alone, and I could get back to my life. "He may know something we don't about who's trying to kill me. Maybe it's not safe," I said.

"If that's the case, then he needs to tell you. You have a right to know." He took a bite of meat, but that didn't occupy him for long. "I don't like this. A mage has been murdered and her daughter is under threat and untrained. You belong with the Magesterial Council, and Casper should take you to them."

"I'm sure he has his reasons. Besides, I don't see a better option unless you have one." I needed something to go right, and I didn't appreciate Alex poking holes in my plan.

"I don't trust him." An irritated, defensive edge entered his voice, as if I was his to worry over. I appreciated the concern. "I hate the thought of leaving you here with him."

My heart lurched. "Do you have to go so soon?" Anxiety laced my voice. We hadn't known each other long, but he had saved my life. I'd left behind everything, and while I felt like I knew Casper, I wasn't as comfortable around him as I was Alex.

Alex met my gaze, as if he was thinking of how to respond. After a moment in which I thought my heart would pound out of my chest, he gave me a warm smile. "No, I can stay for a little while."

I released the breath I'd been holding. I couldn't mentally cope with losing the security of Alex's now familiar presence. My life had changed too much, too quickly.

After I'd eaten as much as I could without puking, I climbed into the four-poster bed and snuggled under the covers. Without a word, Alex stood and shifted into his panther form. He paced in front of the bed a few times before settling on the floor, facing the door. My protector.

Between Alex's protection and the talisman's, I should have felt like the safest girl in the world, but I couldn't help an uneasy feeling that true safety would be a long time coming.

CHAPTER 13

$\mathcal{A}$ ball of light glowed above me, brightening as I fully woke. The light stretched until I saw the empty floor at the foot of my bed. The absence of Alex jolted me upright. The rest of the room remained exactly as I had left it.

A tiny marble sat on the bedside table next to my phone. That must be the communication orb Casper had spoken of. Not having had the best experience with magic, I filed it away as a last resort. I hadn't the faintest idea how to work it.

I needed to find Alex. He'd talked about leaving me here with Casper, but I didn't think he'd do it, especially not while I was asleep and without saying goodbye. He could be out hunting, but again, that didn't seem likely. Muffled voices came from the other side of the door that connected my room to Alex's. I breathed a sigh of relief. Now that I thought about it, it seemed obvious that he'd be in there.

I grabbed the last few pieces of fruit from the food tray and went to the door. I pressed my ear up against it, trying to get an idea of what I'd be walking into. What little I could hear definitely sounded like Alex and Casper. I don't know who else I expected, but they sounded neither angry nor particularly happy. When I entered, they both looked up from where they sat talking in Alex's sitting area.

Alex stood as soon as he saw me. "Did you sleep well?"

"Yeah, I did." I was surprised dreams hadn't interrupted my rest, or at least none violent enough for me to remember. "How long was I out?"

"You slept right through the night. It's early morning now."

Transforming into a morning person was at least one good side effect of this entire ordeal.

"Alex and I were just discussing how to proceed." Casper kept his seat, and Alex resumed his. There were only two chairs in the room, so I sat on Alex's untouched bed facing them. The tight tone of Casper's voice led me to believe that their discussion had been strained at best.

"We should take you to the Magesterial Council," Alex addressed me. "They are in the best position to help you. They have the resources to get your mother's talisman off. They'll be able to find any surviving family you have, if that's what you want. Most importantly, they can protect you."

"You don't know what you're talking about." Casper waved a dismissive hand at Alex. "You're a shifter who's spent his entire life Earthside. Things aren't as neat and clean back in Elustria, and it's certainly not safe for her to travel there. A sorcerer assassin killed her mother and is now hunting her. The sorcerers control and monitor the fabric between our worlds. We can't take her through a portal until I'm assured of her safety."

"The fae make black-market portals all the time. We can have them make a portal right to the gates of the Council." Alex faced Casper, and once again, I was removed from the conversation.

"Yes, and they're mercenaries. They'll take our money for a portal and then turn around and sell us out to someone else. For all we know, this assassin was sanctioned by the Circle of Sorcerers. If that's the case, there may be a bounty on her head or on that talisman. A fae could create a portal and then kill us as soon as we step through, or lie, which is not at all out of character for the fae, and actually make a portal that takes us right to the Circle of Sorcerers. If I could create a portal I would, but the reality of the situation is that we're dependent on others. I only ever travel through sanctioned portals, and we can't risk that until we know more about who's trying to kill her."

"Don't mind me. I'll just sit here and let the two of you fight it out." Alex and Casper turned to face me, surprised by my forgotten presence or my outburst or both. "The two of you would do well to remember that I'm an actual person, and it's my decision what happens to me. Just because you two know more about the situation than I do doesn't mean you get to decide my future."

They both looked at me expectantly. This was the part where I had to make a decision, but I still didn't know what was best. I trusted Alex, but Casper was right, he hadn't been to Elustria in a long time. While I technically had just met Casper, I felt like I knew him. He was one of the richest men in the world. Combine his wealth with his magic and I didn't doubt that he had the resources to keep me safe. Casper's plan sounded logical while Alex's sounded like the quickest way for him to get rid of me and back to his life. I didn't blame him, but I needed to do what was best for me. "I think it's best that I stay here for now. I can always decide to go to Elustria later."

Hurt flashed across Alex's eyes so quickly that I wouldn't have noticed if I hadn't kept my eyes on him. I hated being the cause of it, but this wasn't about him. I hoped there wouldn't be tension between us now.

"Excellent." Casper smiled, genuinely pleased with my response. "I'll let you freshen up and eat some breakfast, and then you can join me downstairs."

When Casper stood to leave, I noticed his attire had changed. Gone was the contemporary power suit he'd worn in his Magical Games office. Now he wore a dark forest-green shirt which appeared to be made from a thick, soft material. The black pants looked both foreign and familiar at the same time. The material seemed to be some type of leather and could possibly have come from an animal that didn't exist on Earth. His calves were encased in shiny black boots. The most striking difference was a red robe he wore. Gold thread embroidered it in a similar pattern to the throne chair downstairs. The robe had to have some significance; I doubted he'd wear something that so obviously clashed with his red hair unless it held importance. He turned and left the room, the robe billowing slightly behind him.

"How are you feeling?" Alex didn't touch the breakfast food in front of him, concentrating entirely on me. The lines around his face showed his concern more than his eyes or his words did. Tension appeared in those lines, as if he could only relax when assured of my well-being. I didn't understand why he cared so much. I was nothing more than an assignment to him, a promise to his father, one he had fulfilled already. The sensation of having someone care was familiar and foreign at the same time, like when you come home after a long trip away and find your home exactly as you left it and realize you're the one who's changed. It had been a long time since someone had cared, and while I liked the feeling, I hadn't grown accustomed to it.

"I'm fine. I just want to get this necklace off so I can move forward." I scooted off the bed and took Casper's vacated seat.

"I still think the best way to do that is to go to the Council."

I sighed, trying to figure out how to explain it to him. "It's different for me than it is for you, Alex. I've never been to Elustria, and while it seems completely normal to you, the thought of leaving this world behind scares me. Everything in my life has changed in little more than a day. My entire identity has been toppled, and I'm left to rebuild it. I've abandoned everything, and the only thread of my life I have left is the familiarity of at least being on Earth. Casper knew my birth mother, and right now, that has to be enough for me."

Alex was silent a moment and then nodded, resigned to my decision. "Yeah, you're right. I'm just antsy to get moving."

A pang of loss went through me at Alex's apparent desire to be done with his mission and therefore with me. We didn't know much about each other, but he was the one who started this entire thing, and he'd saved my life. The stress of this situation had forced a stronger bond than two people normally made over the course of a couple of days. Logically, I knew all that, but that didn't make any difference. I'd miss him when he was gone.

"You've done what you said you would. Don't let me hamper your plans." I wondered if my eyes betrayed how much I didn't want him to heed my words.

"No, it's nothing like that. I just…" His voice drifted off, and I realized I wouldn't get an answer. He took a bite of Danish. I could see the thoughts racing around in his head, and I wished he'd give voice to them. After he washed down his bite with a gulp of water, he spoke. "You know I can't stay here forever, right? I don't belong here in this skin. It's time for me to shift back, but I want to see you safely to Elustria."

"And I'm not sure I ever even want to go to Elustria. I certainly don't want to be forced to make the decision. If Casper can get the necklace off, then I can make the choice of my own free will." I didn't like choices being made for me. If I went to Elustria now, forced by the talisman, then it would always be a bitter place for me no matter how wonderful it may be. It would doom any chance of me liking it. Staying here with Casper didn't close any doors the way going to Elustria would. I may not be brave enough to step through those doors right now, but I might want to someday.

Alex leaned toward me, his yellow eyes fierce. "I just want you to be safe. That's what I promised my father. I don't like Casper. I don't want to leave you in his care."

"I can take care of myself." The words sounded absurd even to me, sitting across from a man who had saved my life. "Or at least the talisman can take care of me. I'm not saying Casper's the most sociable guy, but he's not going to hurt me. Even if he wanted to, the stone wouldn't let him. I know you don't venture into the human world much, but Casper Rothian is extremely famous. This isn't some recluse who lures girls to his remote cabin in order to dispose of them."

"I don't like the way he treats you." Alex leaned back and shifted in his seat, as if he couldn't quite contain his disgust.

I racked my brain to figure out what he was talking about. The only thing I could come up with was Casper's response after he tried to remove the talisman. "You'd be short with me too if you'd just been thrown across the room trying to help me."

Alex shook his head. "No, I wouldn't."

The sincerity of his words hung thick in the air between us. I didn't know how to respond, so I excused myself to go shower. When we met back in his room to go downstairs, the air had cleared, but his sincerity still hung around my heart.

CHAPTER 14

I grabbed a croissant and orange to eat on the way and walked to the door. Alex beat me to it, holding it open for me. Having a personal protector was pretty nice. We'd made a lot of progress since our initial impressions of each other.

Walking down the hall, I tried peeling the orange, but couldn't get it started. Alex saw my obvious ineptness and stuck his hand out in invitation.

"Thanks," I said as I handed him the fruit.

In one swift motion, he carved a line down one side of the orange. If I'd blinked at the wrong moment, I would've missed it. I couldn't believe what my eyes had seen. "Did you just make your nails grow?"

His lips quirked as he contained a smile. "Shifter trick. If I start to shift then stop, I can get my nails to shift just long enough to cut something."

"Handy." That was the kind of practical magic I could find use for. Much more practical than making things combust.

He finished peeling the orange and handed me one half. Sweet juice exploded in my mouth. In a few bites I had eaten the entire thing, and Alex handed me the second half. I swallowed the last of it as we met Casper in the same living area we'd been in yesterday.

I still couldn't believe that I was in the home of my idol. I'd worshipped Casper for years. To find out that he was actually magical and had known my birth mother was easily the coolest thing that had ever happened to me. It took all my self-control not to geek out around him. I wished I had met him under better circumstances. I wanted to be picking his brain about the game and how he created it, not stressing about this talisman and the person who killed my birth mother.

"Good, you're here." Casper spread his arms in greeting. "Glad to see the clothes fit. My people had to guess your size."

"They're great. Thanks." The drawstring pants and tank top that had been waiting for me in my room were comfy. After a full night's sleep, refreshing shower, and a normal breakfast, I felt up to doing whatever I had to in order to return to my life.

Casper sat at the end of the sofa, kitty-corner from the chair he gestured for me to take. Instead of taking one of the other chairs, Alex stayed standing. "You're welcome to shift if you like," Casper told him. "Given that you're on Earth, I assume you enjoy spending most of your time as a cat."

"I'm fine, thanks." Alex's voice lacked genuine gratitude. Everything Casper did seemed to irritate him. I couldn't understand why.

"Suit yourself." Casper didn't appear the least bit perturbed by Alex's attitude. He focused his dark brown gaze back on me. "It occurred to me last night that the talisman may be staying on you because you are not communicating with it. From what you described, the magic you've done thus far has seemingly been from the talisman itself and outside your control."

"That's right. It's like it's something happening to me rather than something I'm doing." That's why it scared me so much. Instead of feeling powerful, I felt powerless.

"You haven't bonded with your magic the way a mage typically does. This could be causing a miscommunication, so I thought we'd start with something that should be a bit familiar. It was the ice spell that first activated for you in-game, correct?"

"Yeah."

"Good. We're going to recreate that. Now, I want you to sit, close your eyes, and relax with both hands flat on the arms of the chair."

I leaned back and shifted until I was comfortable and took a deep breath. I'd already done this before, so at least I knew this kind of magic was possible.

"I want you to feel the power of ice flowing through you. Picture water forming into ice, picture your hands forming frost beneath them." I felt the talisman come to life and my hands turned cold. "You're doing good. In your mind, I want you to say 'glaze ice' and picture ice under your hands."

As I repeated the words in my mind, power surged through me from the talisman. Shocked, I opened my eyes. Frost covered the arms of the chair and crept down toward the seat. "I don't get it. I don't know how I made that happen. Was it picturing it or saying 'glaze ice'?"

"The visualization exercises allow you to more easily make the connection to your magic since you haven't been raised with it. Same with the verbalization. Think of it like training wheels on a bike."

That made a certain kind of sense—if uncontrollably shooting ice from your hands were anything like learning how to ride a bike. In my experience, it wasn't. "But I don't feel anything."

"You don't feel the energy of the talisman?"

I thought back to all the times magic had occurred. Each was preceded by a feeling of energy in the talisman, but it had no clear edges, no distinct beginning or end. "Sure, but it's not something that can be controlled. I can feel that the heat is on because I'm not freezing, but that doesn't mean I know how to control it."

Casper chuckled. "I know that sounds like a reasonable analogy to you, but the magic is part of you. A more apt analogy would be throwing a tennis ball. You can probably chuck it pretty far, but you don't feel the strength that goes into the action because your strength outweighs the task at hand. It's the same here. The issue is not one of having too little power but of having too much."

My only option was to trust that he knew what he was talking about. "What if it really is different for me because I wasn't raised as a mage? I've never performed magic before. Maybe it's something that you grow out of if you don't learn how to do it early enough."

The idea that it might be too late scared me. Not that I particularly wanted or needed to learn how to use magic, but I did desperately need to get this necklace from around my neck. Until I could do that, I would have no options for the future.

"You're not the first mage to be in this situation."

"I'm not? There are other people out there who find out as an adult that one of their parents was a mage and bequeathed them a dangerous talisman?" I didn't think I was special or anything, but come on. I doubted this was an everyday occurrence.

"No, nothing like that, but there are people who don't find out that they're a mage until reaching adulthood. We call them latent mages." Casper eyed Alex where he stood to my right and then focused back on me and changed the subject. "As I said, I want to try something new. We do this type of training with children to help them learn how to control their magic. Go ahead and stand and move your chair to the edge of the room and come back."

I did as he asked, and when I turned from pushing my chair to the side, Casper drew back his hand. The split second before the red light emerged from it, I instinctively knew what he intended. The talisman reacted before I could even think of what to do, producing a shield of ice that held against the fiery red whiplash coming from Casper's hand. In that same moment, Alex shifted and released a vicious snarl as the red light disappeared.

Casper held his hands up in a sign of surrender. "I'm done. There's no need for that, Alex. My strike wouldn't have hit her even if she hadn't reacted. As you can see, she did exactly what I thought: she used magic to produce a shield."

"It's all right, Alex," I said.

He growled and shifted back to human form. "What the hell were you thinking?"

"As I said, this is a tactic we use with children. Animals may eat their young on occasion, but I assure you, mages do not endanger their children."

Hatred poured off of Alex. My presence seemed to be what kept him from attacking, though I liked to think that Alex was simply the bigger man. "What could she possibly learn from that?"

"When children instinctively reach for their magic, it teaches them how to do it in the absence of a threat."

I didn't create the shield at all. That would've required some kind of thought. "But it was just the talisman. I didn't do anything."

"That's because we're not done. Now, I want you to think back to the moment when I raised my hand. You knew it was coming, and because you knew what was coming, so did your talisman. Summon those feelings, that bit of fear you felt, but instead of thinking about protecting yourself, think about attacking. I pose a threat to you, and you must eliminate me. How do you do it?"

My stomach shifted uneasily at this turn of events. Fighting computer monsters was one thing, but I'd never been a violent person. "I'm not comfortable with this. I could kill you without realizing it."

Casper chuckled and shook his head, banishing the thought. "Your talisman will protect you from imminent threat, but it's not going to kill me. Besides, I have defenses of my own."

I looked to Alex and he gave me an encouraging nod. Apparently he was all for experimenting with magic if the target was Casper. I closed my eyes and tried to summon the apprehension I'd felt when I'd realized what Casper was doing. The thought flitted through my mind that I should learn how to do this with my eyes open at some point, but for now, I was all about baby steps.

"Good, your talisman is glowing. You've activated your magic.

Now you need to command it. Say or think 'ice arrow' and picture shooting an arrow made of ice out of your hand."

I visualized an ice arrow shooting from my hand. *Ice arrow*, I thought, willing it to form. I opened my eyes. A sad little ice arrow flew a few feet from my hand then dropped to the ground.

"Good!" Casper said, sounding far more impressed than my pathetic result warranted. "Use your emotion to fuel it until you've built the confidence to call on magic at will."

I took all the frustration I felt at my situation, channeled it into my command to make an ice arrow, and flung out of my hand. An arrow crashed into the wall opposite me, the ice shattering into a thousand pieces.

"Yes, that's it!" Excitement lit Casper's expression. I hadn't expected it to work so well. In the face of Casper's encouragement, I didn't have time for my success to shock me. "I'm going to move about the room," Casper said. "I want you to try to hit me. Don't worry, you won't hurt me."

"Are you sure?" I asked, uncertain. The arrow had shattered like glass. I didn't want Casper to take this small victory to mean that I actually had control over the magic.

Casper didn't seem to share my doubts. "I'm positive. Hit me."

I took aim, but my arrow didn't even make it three feet.

Casper cocked his head to the side, doubting my sincerity. "You can do better than that. Hit me."

He seemed sure, so I put more effort into my next attempt and came close to hitting him. He moved out of the way just before my arrow reached him. I got more into the game, anticipating Casper's movements, but I still wasn't fast enough for my arrows to land.

"I'd think a gamer would be better at this." Casper smiled as he taunted me and dashed around the room.

"Oh, we're playing like that?" My competitive spirit stirred to life. The next arrow hit its mark, or it would have if Casper hadn't deflected it with his magic.

"That's what I'm talking about! You got this. Hit me."

Casper feinted left in front of Alex and then darted right, but I'd already cast left. The arrow penetrated Alex's shoulder, pushing him flat on his back. A strangled yelp escaped his mouth before he clenched his jaw against the pain.

"Oh shit." When I got to him, the water drenching his shoulder was tainted by a pink swirl of blood that quickly darkened to red. I didn't know what to do. It was supposed to be a stupid game. It didn't seem real that I could shoot Alex, cause actual pain. "I'm so sorry."

"It's all right. It wasn't your fault," Alex said through gritted teeth as he glared at Casper. If it weren't for the blood steadily streaming from his shoulder, I thought Alex would attack Casper right then.

"Let me look at it." Casper knelt down beside me. He placed a hand over Alex's shoulder, and I couldn't quite tell if Alex's grimace was from pain or a desire to avoid the touch. Casper muttered a spell that melted the arrow then dried the area. "How is that? Better?"

Alex looked at his shoulder and nodded. He stood and moved the joint in slow circles, wincing in pain. Blood oozed from the wound, but it seemed slower than before even though the arrow no longer blocked the blood flow. "I should be fine."

"No, you're not fine. I shot you." Alex acted as if he'd skinned his knee falling off a bike.

"Shifters might not have much magic, but we do heal quickly. With the arrow gone, the healing process will proceed even faster now." The fabric of his shirt had already mended itself. I assumed it must be part of the enchantment Meglana placed on it.

No matter what Alex said, I couldn't escape the fact that I'd shot him, the person who saved me. Even accidentally, it shouldn't be possible for me to do something so horrible.

"Alex, I'm really sorry." I kept my hand on his cheek, trying to convey how horribly I felt, how concerned I was for him, how much I cared. He withdrew from the touch and struggled to his feet.

"Like I said, it's not your fault. Don't worry about it. Accidents are bound to happen. It's not like you did it on purpose."

"He's right, Kat," Casper said. "Why don't you take him upstairs to get some rest? I'll have some food sent."

My stomach growled at the mention of eating. Doing this much magic had drained me, and now that the fun of the game was over and the panic from hurting Alex had receded, fatigue was all the remained. A nap sounded heavenly, but I didn't want to stop or show any sign of weakness. Sure, my body was tired, but I was more tired of being beholden to this necklace, held captive to a power I couldn't control.

"I don't need rest," Alex said petulantly. Any other time he'd jump at the chance to get away from Casper.

"Yes, you do," I said. He wouldn't listen to me. Even though I wanted to continue working, I tried the one tact that was most likely to get Alex to concede. "And even if you don't, I need to eat and relax." I stared him down, meeting his gaze with a fierceness I hoped communicated that I'd carry him upstairs if I had to.

His eyes didn't back down and his face didn't relax, but he muttered, "Fine."

Careful to bury my smug smile, I walked with him upstairs. I wanted to get Alex to his room, and then I would go back downstairs to continue working with Casper.

"Don't think you're just going to ditch me up here," Alex said once we reached the landing. "You really do need to take a break and eat. Using magic is like using a muscle. It takes energy. Eating will help."

A stone capable of devastating harm remained firmly around my neck. An assassin hunted me and may be able to track any attempt at escape through a portal. The only two people capable of helping me were fighting. I was attracted to a shifter I couldn't possibly have a future with, and I had to come up with enough money for tuition and rent next semester. But sure, eating would help.

CHAPTER 15

*A*lex's knee bounced under the table in my room. I had to restrain myself from stilling it with my hand. We didn't have that kind of relationship. He'd insisted on eating with me, but so far he hadn't touched the food in front of him. "You need to eat for your shoulder."

"My shoulder's fine." Alex's voice was grim. He didn't want to talk or eat.

"Someone once told me that magic, such as the magic to heal, is like a muscle that you need to feed." I took a bite of sandwich to prove my point. Alex grunted in acknowledgement but without humor. The worry I'd tried to hold at bay came surging forward. Was he mad at me for the shoulder? Maybe he was putting on a front to spare my feelings. "I really am sorry."

That startled him enough to wipe the grim look from his face. "You've got nothing to be sorry for. It was an accident."

Nothing in his tone or demeanor made me think he was lying, but something clearly bothered him. "Not just for your shoulder. I'm sorry you got dragged into all this."

Alex shrugged. "I'm sorry my hair is black."

Had I heard him correctly? "What?"

"Oh," Alex looked at me with wide-eyed innocence. "I thought we were apologizing for things that aren't our fault."

I threw a piece of bread at him that he caught easily, and a ghost of a smile flitted across his face too quickly to reach his eyes. "There's no need to mock me. Something's bothering you."

Alex shifted in his seat and looked to the side before looking back at me, considering whether or not he should answer. Whatever it was, he thought I wouldn't like it. "You don't find it weird that he's keeping us confined to our rooms and that living area? Why aren't we eating in a dining room? This place is huge. What is he doing with the rest of it?"

His first instinct had been right, I didn't like it. This attitude was tiring. "Maybe the man likes his privacy. We're basically two strangers who have crashed his home. He's extended a great deal of hospitality." Now that he mentioned it, it did seem a little strange, but tech billionaires like Casper liked their privacy. The fact that he was a mage would only make him more protective of his privacy. Who knew what company secrets or confidential new projects he had here? "You're determined not to like him no matter what."

"That's not true." Alex was quick to take offense, but I could tell from his voice that it was a lie.

"Then what is your problem with him? You two have a difference of opinion on how to proceed. I made the decision. If you have a problem, it should be with me." Irritation at him and the entire situation fueled me, and I was on a roll. I couldn't hold back. "Maybe you should grow up and learn how to move on when things don't go your way." I was tired of this attitude from him. If all he was going to do was complain, he might as well not even be here.

"Perhaps I should leave," Alex said, his voice so soft I had to strain to hear it. He stood and took a step toward the door, but my seat was in his way and he stopped, unwilling to shove past me.

My heart lurched. I may have been thinking the same thing, but that was the anger talking, not me. I may have known of Casper longer, and he knew my mother, but Alex felt more like a peer than Casper ever could. Whatever the right answer was, I was out of my league. "Please don't." The words came out in a whisper. It was all I could say without betraying even more of my feelings and my weakness to him.

Alex's face jerked back as if my words had hit him. Then he shook his head, his face softening some. "No, I didn't mean for good. I think I'll go for a hunt. I'll be more agreeable after I've had some time as a panther."

I nodded and moved my chair aside for him. Hunting could at least get out some of his aggression. His path cleared, Alex didn't go immediately to the door. He stayed where he was, looking down at me. Warmth spread over me at his gaze. There was a tenderness to it. I couldn't be imagining it. Whatever I felt between us, he felt it too.

The moment passed, and Alex left. I stared at the shut door for a second then went back to eating, but much of my appetite had fled. I wanted to watch him hunt. His velvety black fur would be a stark contrast to the white snow that surrounded the Armory. Under normal circumstances, I would call Nicole, but how could I talk to her? I couldn't exactly tell her about my conflicted feelings toward a panther shifter or my failed attempts to learn enough magic to take off a necklace.

I wanted to get back to my life. It might not be much, but it was mine. This whole thing had served as a wake-up call. I'd do better, rededicate myself to school, go to therapy, but to do all of that I had get out of here, away from Casper and mages and panther shifters who consumed my thoughts. Taking a deep breath, I forced my mind to calm. When my mind was as still as I could make it, I focused all of my thoughts on the chain releasing from my neck. With my eyes closed, I reached up to remove it. Every fiber of my being willed it to come off, but nothing happened.

My frustration came out in a loud groan, and I jumped up from my chair. I didn't have time to take a nap or relax. I needed this damn thing off of my neck. Only one person could help me with that, so I went downstairs searching for Casper.

CHAPTER 16

I found Casper sitting in the living room with his back to me, speaking with a man whose face appeared in an orb that floated at eye level.

"It looks like you have a visitor." The man nodded to me and then his face disappeared and the orb shrank to the size of a marble.

Casper grabbed the communication orb and put it in his pocket as he stood and faced me. "I was wondering if you'd come back down now that Alex has left."

After so much time with Alex, I had feared it would be awkward to be alone with Casper, but he seemed to shine in the absence of competition. The charming, lovable founder of Magical Games, Inc. and the creator of *Wizards and Fae* stood before me. The only difference between the Casper I knew and the Casper I'd seen in the media was that this one continued to wear the clothing and robes of Elustria. He wore them with authority, as if they were his natural habitat and the clothes he wore to work were merely a costume.

"I have a lot of work to do. I can't afford to waste time. I tried to remove the necklace again, and it won't budge."

Casper smiled. "That's the attitude. You're so like your mother.

113

Let's take a little break from the talisman and go into the library. I've seen you eyeing it."

I'd come downstairs prepared to do the work necessary to remove the necklace. Although he was right about me wanting to see the library, I wanted to get this all over with even more. Casper, however, didn't wait for an answer. He led the way to the library and took a seat in the throne chair behind the desk. Perhaps focusing on something else would ease my frustration and ultimately help matters. My curiosity won out, and I curled up with my legs under me on one of the brown leather chairs. The library had a cozy feel lacking in the rest of the building. Sliding wooden doors closed behind us, hiding the room from view with a gesture from Casper.

"I thought we'd take this time while Alex is gone to talk about things I can't while he's here," Casper said with an affable smile. "Don't mistake me, I like Alex, but he's a shifter, and I can't reveal all the secrets of the mages to him. It would go against the oath of my order."

"Your order?" That sounded like some sort of secret society. It didn't surprise me that there were things Casper wouldn't want to talk about in front of Alex, but given that I couldn't remove my talisman or do much else, I don't know why he wanted to talk to me about mage secrets. If he was willing to talk, though, I was willing to listen. It felt like I would never understand this magical world.

"Yes, I belong to the order of the Dinathion, the same as your mother. It's an ancient order of mages. I'm a descendant of that bloodline. It's why I wear these robes: they're to signify my order. I don't choose to wear a color that clashes so harshly with my hair."

The red of his robes did clash in an unattractive manner with his red hair. It only worked because of the confidence with which he wore it. "So is that how you met my birth mother?"

"Yes. I knew her through the order and we became friends because of our mutual desire to improve the status of mages. We didn't see much of each other, but she helped build this operation that made it possible for me to find you." Casper nodded at me.

Affection for my mother shone in his eyes. He had a great amount of respect for her.

"I don't understand what you mean by 'this operation.' I also don't understand how you found me." I was missing something in all this. Ever since I'd discovered the magical side to Casper, I had gotten the sense that it was more than just a descriptor of who he was. The identity of a mage held purpose for him, and from everything I'd gathered about Meglana, it held the same for her.

"Ah, yes. I believe it'll be easier to show you. Time for a tour." He slapped his hands on the armrests of his chair and stood, gesturing for me to precede him out of the door. "I'll take you to the heart of the operation." He led the way to the teleportation ring we had arrived in.

I stepped into the circle with him and closed my eyes, remembering back to the instructions he'd given me the first time. My body was squeezed tight just as before, tighter and tighter, the pressure building until it released all at once, and I opened my eyes to find an enormous room that could very well be in an entirely different building.

Casper made a wide sweeping gesture with his arm, pride filling his features. "Welcome to the map room."

My eyes couldn't make sense of what I saw—a strange mixture of the technological and the archaic. My mind wandered to a discussion I'd seen online about the blurred line between advanced science and magic. In front of me hung a giant map of the world covering every inch of the wall. Little dots glowed and extinguished on it like fireflies, but it wasn't an electronic screen as I would expect at the headquarters of Magical Games, Inc. Instead, the map was a woven tapestry that appeared ancient. My mind couldn't reconcile the fabric with the lights that moved about it.

In front of the tapestry were four long tables, two on each side of the room, equipped with the latest computers as well as items that appeared more magical in nature. Two women whispered around a computer with the man who had spoken to Casper through the communication orb earlier. One of the women looked up from the conversation when we entered and nodded toward us. The other woman and man glanced at us and then went back to talking.

"What is this?" I asked, my eyes wide as I tried to take in everything.

"This is the heart of the Armory, and it's thanks to your mother. She's the only person I've ever known whose ambition rivaled my own, but I'm not embarrassed to admit that on my best day I couldn't compete with her. She helped set up all this. The map tracks latent mages."

"Are latent mages like me common?" I didn't know which answer I wanted. The thought of more people like me out there living normal lives was comforting. However, my mind couldn't wrap around the idea that the magical world intertwined so deeply with the mundane. The magic had been here all along, and I'd never known.

"Oh yes, although you're a unique case given your provenance."

All my provenance had done was cause problems. How much different would things be if I'd been born to an average mage? If I had a talisman of ordinary power? Would discovering my mage side have been easier then? "How do you find them?"

"I would've thought you'd figured that out by now: the game."

The first time I'd formed ice was while performing the quest line in-game, but that didn't have anything to do with the game. I just happened to be playing after I put on the necklace. Given how much time I spent in-game, there had to be something like a ninety-percent chance the first time my magic would show itself would be while playing. "I don't understand."

"The whole point of the game is for us to identify humans who have a spark of magic. Anyone who has a spark is a mage as long as the spark is strong enough to activate. I'm the one who came up with the idea, but your mother's the one who discovered the enchantment to place on the game. She turned the code into a kind of talisman. That's what the daily quests are. The language in them is designed to trigger the magic, usually through low-level spells. The Aquanight Gem quest line appears to those whose spark has activated through the daily quests in order to give us a better reading on how strong their spark is. Of course, more people than just potential mages get the quest line, but its true purpose is to act as a talisman and reveal our kind who are unknowingly among humans."

"Then why didn't my spark trigger it earlier? Why did it only happen after I got my mother's talisman?"

Casper's lip twitched and he looked away so briefly that I wasn't sure he was aware of the action. "I don't know for sure, but my guess is that your mother stripped your spark and put it into the talisman. The last time I saw her, she'd been researching how to remove a spark or set it dormant. That's why we never found you until after you put the talisman on. Your mother wanted you hidden away. She knew the dangers of the path she was taking, and she didn't want you to be tracked. If she had left you with your spark, someone other than me could've found you."

Every answer Casper gave me only spawned more questions. "But how could she know I'd play your game? And what was so dangerous about what she was doing?"

"There will be plenty of time to talk everything over later. We don't need to cover it all now. This was simply one of many ways she had to find you if and when the need arose," Casper said in the tone you used with kids when you were trying to sell them some bullshit to get them to stop asking questions. Well, I wasn't done with my questions.

"That night I beat the quest line, how did you know I was Meglana's daughter?"

Casper's face softened in memory. "I'd recognize that magic anywhere. It's unique, even in a world of magic. The longer you spend around other mages, the more you'll realize it. Your mother took all her accumulated power and knowledge and put it into the talisman. You see these little flickers of light on the map?" A faint light appeared over Sweden, and another over India, and a brighter light appeared in Mexico. "Your light made it impossible to see anything else. It was nearly blinding. I knew then that it was you. Maybe that was just hope, wishful thinking. Once I tracked you from one of our terminals, there was no mistaking the magic."

The three people huddling around one of the terminals took turns eyeing me. The attention was unnerving, especially since I didn't understand the source of their fascination. Casper noticed and walked me over to the trio. As soon as they saw us approaching, they focused squarely on us.

The brunette had large blue eyes and an easy smile framed by her soft curls. The other woman was slighter but all harsh lines and sharp angles: from her bleach-blonde pixie cut to her high cheek-bones and the firm line of her lips. Between the women towered a man who seemed the perfect mix of the two. His dark hair was cropped short, and while he shared the build of the blonde, his face had the welcoming expression of the brunette. All three of them wore the same type of clothing that Casper did underneath his robes. I couldn't quite put my finger on what made them different. I suppose there was no reason the clothing they wore couldn't be from Earth, except I knew it wasn't. It gave me the same feeling as steampunk: a familiarity with reality, but not quite genuine.

"Kat, allow me to introduce you to Sadie, Analise, and Mikael, sometimes collectively known as the triplets, even though they're just siblings. They were here the night you were discovered." He spoke about me as if I were a country claimed in the name of mages everywhere.

The brunette stepped forward, her hand outstretched. "It's an honor to meet you, Kat. Casper wasn't exaggerating. The night we found you, you lit up the entire wall. I've never seen anything like it. We're all excited to get to know you more. Your mother was a legend, a real freedom fighter."

Her handshake and smile immediately put me at ease. Her sister, on the other hand, gave a barely noticeable nod then pointedly turned and walked away.

"Welcome. Don't mind Analise." Mikael shook my hand, furthering the appearance that he was a balance between both women: welcoming, but not as vivacious as Sadie while not being as curt as Analise.

"We'll see you at lunch when I'm done giving the tour," Casper said, seemingly aware of my discomfort around the strangers. He nodded to the siblings, and they went back to work. On our way back to the teleportation ring, he leaned in so the others wouldn't hear. "Don't let their excitement make you nervous. Their parents were both killed fighting for our cause."

"I'm sorry to hear that. I'm confused though, what exactly is the cause?" Sadie had called Meglana a freedom fighter. It was the most interesting thing I'd heard about my birth mother outside of her being a mage.

"Our cause is the cause of all mages. We're at constant conflict with the sorcerers in Elustria. They don't believe people on Earth who are born with the spark should be allowed to join the ranks of mages. We believe it is their birthright and that no one should deny it to them. The sorcerers are doing everything they can to diminish our power. For millennia they've controlled much of Elustria, and they don't want our numbers to grow. People like your mother and I strongly believe that magic should be available to all those who are willing to study and work for it."

If my birth mother had died trying to bring freedom to her people, that added a new dimension to this whole thing. It also gave weight to the idea that she had hidden me for my own protection. "Were their parents assassinated?"

"Yes. They were killed by a sorcerer assassin while here on Earth looking for ancient artifacts. At different times throughout history, mages and other magical creatures have traveled to Earth. There are magical relics all over the world, such as the talisman you now wear. My talisman is another such relic." He held his hand up so the ring was in clear view. "The sorcerers will stop at nothing to make sure that mages are oppressed and unable to access our full potential. The thought that we might be as powerful as they are scares them. They've gone so far as to send assassins to Earth, train them in physical combat, and kill mages without the use of magic so that we can't track them."

The depraved tactics used by the sorcerers made me sick. My birth mother had died at the hand of one of these assassins, maybe even the same one who killed the triplets' parents. "Do they know who killed them?"

"No, but they've dedicated their lives to making sure their parents didn't die in vain."

And here I was, playing tourist in their home and wanting my mother's necklace removed so I'd have the option to walk away. As we stepped into the teleportation ring, I looked at Analise working at one of the terminals on the far side of the room. If I were her, I'd hate me too.

CHAPTER 17

othing else I saw on the tour was as interesting as the map room. The rest of the Armory was composed of training spaces for newly found mages. In my room after the tour, I tried to ignore the twinge I felt when I realized Alex was still gone. It was probably for the best. I didn't know how much I could tell him about what I'd seen, but I needed to talk to someone. Nicole would be wondering about my absence in-game. Even if I couldn't tell her everything, it would be nice to hear her voice.

I grabbed my cell phone from the table by the bed. I had more than a dozen text messages.

> *I'm assuming you came to your senses and went to the game HQ to meet Casper. That's the only acceptable excuse for you being MIA this long.*
>
> *Okay, I'm getting worried now. This isn't like you to disappear without a word. Let me know if you're okay. That necklace didn't electrocute you or something, did it?*

That was eerily close to the truth. I couldn't tell her everything, but I could tell her something, and I needed to talk to my best friend.

"Kat! Please tell me you did the irresponsible thing and took

Casper up on the trip instead of taking the payout. We can always find ways to get more money, but you can't just waltz into Magical Games headquarters anytime you want. If you didn't, then you have some explaining to do." She wouldn't admit to it, but I heard a trace of worry in her voice. It may have only been a couple of days, but we spoke multiple times a day, every day, no matter what.

"Of course I did the irresponsible thing." I heard a slight release of breath on the other end of the line, the only sign of Nicole's relief. The more I told her, the better. The closer I could keep to the truth, the easier this would be. I already felt wretched for keeping secrets from Nicole. It'd be worse if I left Alex and Meglana out now then slipped up and mentioned them later. "It's actually a strange story. Turns out Casper knew my birth mom."

"Really?" Nicole squealed. "That's crazy. Was it because of her work?"

She meant the game peripheral work I made up to explain the talisman's strange actions. "Yeah. Small world, huh? It's been a crazy couple of days. Alex, the delivery guy"—as if she could forget who he was—"came with me. They all kind of knew each other."

"And how is Alex?" I could practically hear her wagging her eyebrows.

I rolled my eyes. "He's fine. I may be spending some time here in Canada, so don't worry if I'm not online. I'm taking this opportunity to learn more about my birth mom."

"Cool. Hey, do you think it was really a coincidence that you got the Aquanight Gem quest line?"

I couldn't exactly tell her that the magic in my mother's necklace triggered the game, but it was too obviously not a coincidence for me to pass it off. "No, I think Casper set it up."

"Still, you beat it. That's something."

No, it really wasn't, because I felt sure the game would have let me win no matter what, but I appreciated her saying it. It did hurt acknowledging that maybe I wasn't as good at the game as I wanted to believe. It had been my life since my parents died. I wanted something to show for it. "Thanks. That was all me."

Nicole chortled at my arrogance. "You are the best. I'll let the guild know that you're away at headquarters. They've all seen your 'Hades Killer' title."

Realistically, I didn't know when I'd be back raiding in the game. My life seemed to get more complicated with each day. "I understand if they need to boot me."

"Don't be silly. Even if you miss a few raids, the guild is getting a lot of attention for having a Hades Killer in it. Jabberwocky is loving it."

"If you say so."

"I do. He's not going to boot you, and if he does, he'll have to boot me, too." Her voice lowered to a more earnest tone. "Seriously, this is important for you, Kat. Take the time to do what you need to. You've gotten a lot of big information. You need to process it all and learn what you can about your birth mom. And I'm always here for you to process it with."

"I know." That was the problem. I trusted Nicole, loved her like a sister. I could tell her anything, which was why I needed to get off the phone. If I spent too much time with her, I'd end up spilling the whole unbelievable story, and I couldn't put that on her. She didn't need to worry about me losing my mind on top of everything else. "I've got to go eat. I'll try to keep in touch better, but don't worry if you don't hear from me."

"Understood. But you better bring back some great pics of HQ. Get one in front of that statue outside! That thing looks epic."

"It is." I'd have to see if I could stop by and get a picture when all this was over. My blurry snapshot wouldn't cut it. "Talk to you later. Tell the guild good luck on the raid tonight."

"Will do." The line went dead. Even though I couldn't be completely honest with her, the talk had done me good, a bit of normalcy injected into the fantasy world my life had become.

Alex still wasn't back from his hunting trip. I spent much of my life physically alone. I didn't have roommates and didn't want them. It had always been that way, but after the plane crash, I had wrapped my solitude around myself like a warm blanket. Now the thought of being alone unnerved me. If I sat around with my thoughts, I'd go mad. There was too much to digest and work through. I didn't yet know how I felt about the revelations Casper had made, and I couldn't begin to unravel them all and make them fit into the life I had before.

Then I remembered Casper had told the triplets we'd see them at lunch. I'd eaten earlier and wasn't very hungry yet, but I needed to get out of my room and my head. The company would be good, even if I wasn't quite comfortable around the triplets who had such purpose to their life that it put me to shame. I'd had that fire of purpose before, and I had to believe I'd find it again. Perhaps I'd find it here.

CHAPTER 18

J grabbed the communication orb from the table. I'd seen people using these but had never seen someone initiate a call. Figuring it had to be simple, I told it to call Casper. The orb hovered above my palm, and his face appeared, giving me a little satisfaction at the successful use of a magical device.

"Kat, what can I do for you?"

"I was wondering if I could join you for lunch."

"Of course, we would love to have you." The warmth in his voice made me feel welcome, like I wasn't an interloper here. "I'll meet you in the living room in five minutes and take you to the dining room." His face disappeared and the orb floated down to my palm.

This was how my birth mother had lived her life, using orbs instead of phones to communicate, fighting off sorcerers in reality instead of in a game. What would my life have been like had she kept me? I imagined I'd be much like the triplets, raised to believe in a cause and devoting my life to it. It seemed like all my life I had been yearning for a cause. It's why I became a political science major. I had wanted to equip myself to affect change in the world, but my vision had never extended any further than graduation, getting a master's degree, and then law school. It was more schooling than a lawyer required, but part of me had clung to the academic world hoping it would spark some inspiration of what path I should follow.

When Casper and I arrived at the dining room, I was happy to discover that the triplets were the only other people present. Casper hadn't introduced me to any of the other mages who worked here or any of the trainees. Even though I didn't hit it off with the triplets, eating with them was better than having to meet new people.

The dining room was a warm space with the same cream carpet as the rest of the living spaces. Sadie and Mikael sat around a mahogany table with beautiful etchings on the surface. When Casper and I appeared, a smile lit Sadie's face. "Kat, so glad you could join us." She gestured to the seat across from her at the table. I took it, facing her and Mikael while Casper sat to my left. "Analise couldn't come. She's working and wasn't at a good place to stop."

I waved away her explanation. "I understand. Work comes first." It had been a long time since work had come first for me, but despite Analise's obvious dislike of me, I admired her dedication to her cause. However, I had a sneaking suspicion that had I not been present, Analise's schedule would have freed up for lunch.

With all of us seated, Casper used a communication orb to let the kitchen know we were ready to eat. A second later, salads appeared on the table before us along with silverware. We lapsed into an awkward silence as we ate.

When the next course appeared, Sadie broke the silence. "Yours is the strongest talisman I've seen." She gestured toward my amber necklace with her fork. "Have you been able to unlock much of its power?"

"Not intentionally or with any control." I continued to eat rather than elaborate. The white fish and risotto tasted just as good as everything else I'd eaten here. The salad wasn't bad either.

Casper expanded on my answer. "Meglana placed defensive charms on the stone. So far, that's the bulk of the magic she's experienced except for the spell from the game, which she's become somewhat proficient in." He gave me more credit for the frost spell than was warranted and conveniently left out that I'd accidentally shot someone with it.

"Given the way it's reacted so far when I've been threatened, I don't understand how my mother could have been killed." Her death didn't make sense to me when she had a talisman that would defend her. All I'd heard about was her immense power.

"My guess is she was cursed," Sadie said. "It's the only thing that explains it. It would've been a slow death, and she got away to increase the talisman's defenses before dying and passed it on to the shifter who brought it to you. I'd love to know how your mother found it, the history behind it. Once you're able to take it off, I'd like to study it."

"Sadie, don't be offensive," Mikael said, angry disgust filling his eyes.

She hadn't offended me at all, but according to Mikael's tone, he was offended enough for both of us. "I wasn't offended."

"As I knew you wouldn't be." Sadie shot a look of irritation at her brother, an indication of the kind of sibling squabbling that was universal.

Mikael met my eyes for the first time during the meal. "That's only because you don't know enough to be offended, my dear. What Sadie suggested is very offensive. You never talk about removing a mage's talisman, not unless you're a filthy sorcerer. Make a suggestion like that to Analise and you'd quickly find yourself on your back or worse. She won't even tolerate jokes about being separated from her wand."

My ears perked at that. "Wand?"

Mikael smiled at my obvious interest. "We're wand-wielders."

He reached into his left sleeve and pulled out a wand with his right hand. It was small, no longer than his forearm. It looked similar to a thick twig, worn smooth from use. "Most mages use wands. They're made from magical wood that we get from the fae."

"The fae? Is everything in the game real?" I directed my question to Casper. As if wands weren't cool enough, now I find out that another mythical species actually existed.

"No. It's safe to say that Elustria inspired the game, but it's not a replica. There are many magical species in Elustria, and some of them are presented in the game, though not accurately. The fae in Elustria are different than the ones in the game. You can read about them in the library."

"So if I went to Elustria, could I get a wand?" My fingers fidgeted in front of me, eager to reach out and touch the wand Mikael had put on the table. Only the recent discussion of how offensive that would be restrained me.

"You could," Sadie said, "though I don't know why you would want or need one other than as a learning tool in the beginning. That talisman acts like a wand, and I dare say you could spend your entire life studying it and not plumb the depths of its power."

Wands still seemed cooler. I didn't want to admit that it was the power in my talisman that scared me. Maybe if I had been raised as a mage I'd be better suited to wield it, but given my current situation, a manageable wand seemed like a better way for me to do magic. I took a bite of fish and tried not to think about how cool it would have been to be raised with magic. I'd had a wonderful childhood with my parents, and here I was willing to forget all that for the sake of a little magic. "I don't know if I can ever safely use this talisman. I think I may be too old to learn how to use something this powerful."

"That's nonsense. We've trained mages older than you before. No one's ever too old to learn magic." Sadie smiled at me in what I'm sure was meant to be an encouraging way, but I didn't think she realized just how bad my attempts had been so far.

The illuminator that floated above Sadie's head drifted down to eye level. Then it grew to the size of a grapefruit and Analise's face appeared.

"I have a possible hit on a sorcerer. You might want to come check it out. Bring me some food while you're at it." Analise didn't wait for a response. Her face disappeared and the orb shrank back to the size of a marble and resumed its place above Sadie's head.

"Guess somebody's cranky and lonely." The smile vanished from Sadie's face in favor of an irritated scowl.

"You better go, I don't want to have to deal with her later," Mikael said.

"Oh, but I get to deal with her?"

Mikael tilted his head in an effort to solicit understanding. "You know she's having a tough time right now. It wouldn't kill you to be a little extra nice."

"But I suppose it would kill you."

"Exactly." Mikael nodded and straightened. "Or, more accurately, she'd kill me."

That put Sadie's affable smile back on her face, and she stood to leave. "It was great meeting you, Kat. I look forward to talking with you more."

Even her change in demeanor couldn't mask the tension in the air. I had the distinct feeling that I was the cause of Analise's sour mood.

Once Sadie left, Casper tried to assuage my fears. "Don't worry about it. Analise is very devoted to the cause, more than most. She admired your mother greatly, and the news of her death hit her hard. I think meeting you has brought up a lot of feelings for her."

Even though he didn't say so, something about the way he danced around his words led me to believe that meeting me was actually a disappointment. The great mage Meglana had produced a child who was more girl than woman and couldn't so much as remove her own talisman. I decided not to worry about it. I would simply avoid Analise altogether.

"Casper's mentioned you want to learn more about Elustria," Mikael said, changing the subject. "I can help you there. My area of expertise is history. I usually focus on the history of travel between our two worlds, but I'd be happy to answer any questions you have."

"How many different kinds of magical creatures are there in

Elustria?" Since discovering that *Wizards and Fae* struck a passing resemblance to reality, I wanted to know just how much of it was true.

"How many different species are there on Earth?" Mikael's expression lit with the glee of someone who delighted in educating another.

In my mind, I'd always assumed that there were just mages and sorcerers. But now that he put it like that, the idea of life in Elustria being exactly like Earth except for humans who could do magic seemed ludicrous. "That's a fair point. How different is it there than here? Are there other humanoid species?"

"You'll find that things in Elustria are quite similar, just different. There is a new trend I've seen among some human entertainment—I believe it's called steampunk? Elustria is similar to that in look and feel. As far as technology goes, we haven't advanced as far as the humans on Earth have, largely because we haven't needed to. Everyone in Elustria has some form of magic. There are fae and elves. Then there are hybrids such as shifters or centaurs and merpeople. None of these groups individually have much need for advanced technology. We trade amongst each other. For instance, the mages and fae have a close relationship because of our use of their wood in our wands."

"I gather there's tension between mages and sorcerers, but do the different species in Elustria live together?" I liked the idea of walking down the street and seeing an elf or a centaur.

"That's a complicated question," Casper said.

"And it always has been. We go through phases in Elustria. In general, you'll find that our species like to stick together. There has been mixing between sorcerers and mages, and that's led to some problems."

"Yes, sorcerers can't mind their own business and let us tend to ourselves," Casper said. "They hate that we have blood running through our veins instead of pure magic as they do, and yet we've managed to rival their mastery of magic through sheer hard work."

He spoke with passionate disdain I hadn't heard from him before. He and my mother were the people sorcerers hated. Now that I was a mage, I supposed they hated me, too.

"And that hate is what led to Meglana's assassination? They wanted to prevent her from growing too powerful and sharing that power with other mages?" It sounded like tribalism to me, a classic story of one group in power trying to oppress another to maintain that power.

"Sorcerers are elitist snobs who have tried to deny us our birthright for too long." Casper tossed his napkin onto the table and sat back in his chair. "There was no good reason to kill your mother. She left you her talisman because she wanted you to continue her work, otherwise she would've had it brought here. She wanted you to lay claim to your birthright."

My hand curled around the amber stone on my chest. The necklace was so much more than an heirloom. It was a legacy. The grave expression on Casper's face elevated it to the level of a mantle, one I felt ill-equipped to bear. More than ever I wanted to take the thing off, to give it to Analise or Sadie or Casper, anyone who could advance my birth mother's work, ensure that her death wasn't in vain. Yet deep down, I wanted to be her daughter. I wanted to be part of something. Maybe this was the reason I had never found my place after my parents died. Maybe subconsciously I knew my path lay not just somewhere else but in a completely different world.

"I think that's enough for today," Casper said, breaking into my thoughts. "I need to go check on whatever it is the girls are tracking."

Before teleporting to the map room, Casper and Mikael dropped me off at the teleportation ring in the living room. Upstairs, my knocks on Alex's door went unanswered, so I went to my room.

Getting to know Mikael and Sadie and learning about Meglana opened my eyes to the possibilities in front of me. There was something here bigger than me and my problems. That's why I'd gotten into political science, to learn how to work toward something bigger. Those dreams of doing important work died with my parents, but maybe they could be reborn here. Going back to my old life seemed like throwing away an opportunity. Without my scholarship, college was effectively over for me or at least delayed. Here I had the chance to step onto a new path, one with different obstacles and a potentially greater reward. I would never know my birth mother, but I could continue her legacy.

This was exactly the kind of thing I needed to talk to Nicole about. I grabbed my phone to call her and noticed a voicemail notification from Bethany. She was in my Monday afternoon lecture. I played the message in case she needed notes or something. I would need to let her know to ask someone else.

"Kat, where are you? I've been calling and haven't gotten an answer. Some guy came looking for you. He acted like he knew you, but he clearly doesn't, and he just creeped me out. I went by your apartment, but I didn't see your car. I hope you're okay. If you want me to, I can call the cops the next time he comes around. Let me know."

The food from lunch turned to stone in my stomach.

CHAPTER 19

The man who had questioned Bethany had to be the assassin who sent that orb into my apartment. Up until now, the man hunting me—and I'd always assumed it was a man, I don't know why—had been a nebulous thought, a concept more than an actual person. The thought that he had found my friends sickened me. My problems were spreading themselves to the people around me. I didn't know if this guy would leave it at questioning, but I wasn't inclined to think the best of a murderer.

Casper needed to know about this new development. He would know what to do. He would also be better equipped to predict what this man would do next. But before I could find Casper, I had to respond to Bethany. Nothing about this situation was fair for her. I couldn't leave her waiting for a response, worrying about me when I was as safe as I could be.

Talking on the phone with her would be impossible in my state of mind. She might be able to read something in my voice, tell how scared I was, or I might do something stupid and tell her more than I should. A simple text message would do the trick.

I'm fine. I went out of town to visit some friends. Thanks for letting me know about the man.

Should I put that there's nothing to worry about? It seemed people only actually used that phrase when there was something to worry about. I decided not to.

I might be gone for a little while. I'll bum notes off you when I get back :). If this man comes around again, just give him my number.

I didn't relish the thought of him having my phone number, but I'd rather have him calling me than hounding my friends.

The phone rang the moment I set it back on the table. I glanced at the display and saw a number I didn't recognize. My heart sank. I wanted to believe this was Alex, but I still had his number programmed in from the last phone he had used.

A chill ran through me, and I knew that the assassin already had my number. I could do nothing but stare at the phone, its display asking me to accept or decline the call. The harsh trill of the digital ringer sounded unnaturally loud in the quiet room.

It stopped, and I held my breath, waiting to see if he'd done what I thought. The pleasant *bing-bong* of a new-voicemail notification sounded, and I pressed the play button.

"Hello, Kat Thomas. I've been looking for you. I see you've enlisted the help of a shifter, just like your mother. You can't hide forever. I will find you. It'll be better for everyone if you just agree to meet me. It doesn't have to be like it was with your mother. I just need to talk to you, that's all. You can reach me at this number. That shifter friend of yours already got hurt attacking my orb. No one else needs to get hurt, including you."

A click signaled the end of the voicemail, and I ran to the bathroom. Fish and salad came up as my stomach convulsed. The force of my heaves squeezed my ribs as I threw up until nothing remained but the burn in my throat.

After I rinsed my mouth and threw some cold water on my face for good measure, I used my communication orb to contact Casper.

"Yes?" Casper was looking off to the side. When his eyes focused through the orb onto me, he said, "You're paler than the snow outside. What's wrong?"

"I need to talk to you."

"I'll be right there." I nodded and set down the orb. A few seconds later, Casper strode into the room and sat next to me on the bed. He placed a hand on my knee, which under normal circumstances would have made me uncomfortable, but in my current state, the physical touch grounded me.

"I checked my phone, and I had a message from a friend. She said some guy was asking around about me." Casper stiffened, knowing as I did that this was the assassin. "She was worried because I haven't been answering my phone, and she came by the apartment, and I wasn't there. I didn't want her to get worried and call the police or anything, but I also didn't want to talk to her and risk saying too much, so I sent her a text telling her everything was fine."

I decided to leave out the part about telling her to give the assassin my phone number. It seemed inconsequential now. "But as soon as I finished sending the text message, I got a call from a number I didn't recognize. It was him. He left a voicemail." In my head, I could hear his smug voice, and my stomach turned.

"May I listen to the message?" Casper asked.

I nodded, and he grabbed the phone from the table. The ease with which this assassin had found me, had invaded my home, and now called me, shattered my sense of safety. My phone was an extension of me, and he had called it just as if he were a friend. I couldn't fight back, and even if I wanted to give him the necklace, I couldn't.

"You're going to be all right," Casper said when he finished listening to the message. "He can't find you here. I promise."

I heard what Casper said, but his words didn't register; they didn't feel right. I would never truly be safe until I could take care of myself. For years I'd escaped into a world of make-believe that Casper created. I had battled pretend monsters and formed relationships with people I'd never met in real life. Meanwhile, that world had been real for Casper, for my mother, for an entire race of people I belonged to and didn't even know. The danger that hunted me wasn't pretend. If I removed the necklace and handed it over, that danger would not go away. At the most, I could hope that it would no longer target me. That provided little satisfaction after meeting Sadie, Mikael, and Analise. Their parents had been killed just like my mother had, but instead of trying to keep themselves safe, they fought on in the work they believed in.

I may not have been raised by my birth mother, but she had done what she could to pass that belief onto me in the form of a talisman. She had protected me by making sure that I couldn't be targeted while she was alive. And now that I was the target, she'd also given me the power to defend myself, but maybe that power was meant to be used for more than a defense. That was what my mother would have wanted.

"I want you to teach me magic." Conviction steadied my voice, overriding the fear and turmoil in my gut. "I don't just want to learn how to get the necklace off. I want to learn how to use it. And I want to learn what my mother was working on. If it was important enough for her to die for, it's important enough for me to learn. I don't want to rely on your protection. I want to be able to stand on my own two feet." I waited for Casper to tell me how silly I was for thinking I could follow in my mother's footsteps.

"It would be an honor to teach Meglana's daughter magic. There's a lot to learn, but I have every confidence you'll honor your mother's memory."

I hoped so. More than my own life depended on it.

CHAPTER 20

I don't know how long I sat on my bed after Casper left. It could have been minutes or hours. That voicemail shook me up, and then I'd compounded it by making the decision to stay here and learn magic. I'd resisted making decisions for months, and now I'd made a huge one.

A knock on the door pulled my attention. I took a deep breath and went to answer it. Alex stood on the other side of the door, reminding me of the moment I met him four days ago. A split second before he saw me, he appeared relaxed, as if his hunt had done him some good. Once his eyes met mine, he tensed. Something about me stressed him.

"Are you all right? You look pale," he said. The voicemail came rushing back to my mind. It didn't surprise me that I still looked rattled from it. There were residual traces of panic coursing through me.

I opened the door wider and gestured for him to come inside. "I'm fine." We could talk about it later. "How was your hunt?"

He settled into the chair at my table, and I sat across from him. "Good." He nodded. "Relaxing. I feel more like myself when I'm out there. Now why don't you tell me what happened that made you so pale?"

He'd find out eventually. "I got a call from the man who killed Meglana."

Alex leaned forward in his seat. "Have you told Casper? He needs to know."

It was nice to see that Alex could get over his dislike of Casper when needed. "Yes, I had him listen to the voicemail the assassin left."

"So I take it you've decided to go to the Council for protection?"

Not this again. It hadn't even occurred to me after listening to the message to go to the Council. I felt safe here with Casper. There were enough mages here to protect me, and this location was remote and secret. There was no guarantee we could safely travel to the Council. Casper had said we're dependent on sorcerers and fae mercenaries for portals, the very type of people who either wanted my birth mother killed or could be paid off to turn in her daughter as she tried to get through to Elustria. "No. I've decided to stay here and learn magic."

"What? You think you can take on an assassin by yourself? Casper thinks this is a good idea?"

"It's not that, Alex. While you were gone, Casper gave me a tour of this place. I met mages here who have devoted their lives to a cause, people who are freedom fighters, who looked up to my birth mother as a hero. I want to be part of that. I need it. I need something. I've been lost for so long since my parents died. I can learn magic here, get the necklace off, and when it's safe, go to the Council."

Alex looked past me with resignation. "The very things that attract you to this place are the things I'm running from. I don't need the conflict and turmoil in my life."

"You're looking at a political science major. Fighting for people's rights is what I've always wanted to do. I want to be part of something bigger than myself." It occurred to me that I didn't owe him an explanation, but I wanted to give him one. The man had saved my life. For some reason I cared what he thought of me.

"I worry that you don't realize how much bigger than you this is. If you've made your decision, though, I respect that. I think it's time for me to leave." Alex's words tore at something inside me, like he would be leaving with a piece of me. He was the one who had started this entire thing. If it weren't for him showing up on my doorstep, I'd be back home right now playing *Wizards and Fae*, delaying making a decision about life after graduation, chatting with Nicole, and sleeping in my own bed with a picture of my dead parents looking over me. In a weird way, he was the bridge between my old life and my new reality. With him here, it felt like I could keep one foot in my college apartment and one here.

"I'm sorry for your shoulder. I really didn't mean to hurt you." I winced at my plaintive tone. I'd meant it as a simple apology, but it came out like a plea for him to stay. This wasn't like me.

Alex reached across the table and took my hand in his. Where I was frantic energy, he was calm steadiness. "This has nothing to do with my shoulder. I meant it when I told you not to worry about it. I don't blame you. This has turned into something more than I ever could have imagined. It's time for me to go back to my panther form, to get back to the wild. I've delivered your mother's necklace and seen you safely to a mage. That's what I came here to do, and it's done."

Heat spread from our clasped hands, up my arms, and down into the pit of my stomach. I hadn't been attracted to anyone since the plane crash. Alex awakened that part of me, and I didn't want to watch it walk out the door. I met his eyes, and the desire I saw there mirrored my own. We hadn't known each other long, but this wasn't about that. This was raw attraction, the kind that grips you around the middle and steals your breath. He had to feel it. It couldn't just be me.

"You could stay." As soon as I said the words, I wanted the earth to open up and swallow me whole. What was I doing? This obviously couldn't be anything other than maybe a one-night stand on his way out. In the back of my mind, I could hear Nicole's voice asking what was wrong with that if we were two consenting adults.

Wariness entered Alex's eyes, and the air grew heavy with unease. "The thing is, Kat, I can't trust this feeling between us. It's not real. When I wore the talisman searching for you, it reached out to you, attracted me to you. I like you, but I can't know how much of it is from the talisman and how much is from me. I don't like magic interfering with my life. It's why I stay in my panther form."

"Oh." I pulled my hand back from his. "I hadn't realized that, but of course, it makes sense." Yeah, a magical stone drawing a guy to me was way more understandable than him actually finding me attractive. Ugh. Self-pity did not look good on me.

Alex shook his head, looking to the side and then facing me again. "I've really messed this up. I've been attracted to you since we met, since the first time you opened the door to your apartment and snatched that package from me. That's not real, Kat. People don't develop feelings like that in such a short amount of time. It's not fair to you, and it's not fair to me, which is why I've tried to keep it a secret from you."

In his eyes I could see the conflict, the uncertainty, the struggle he'd carried. He'd done an admirable job of dealing with these feelings. I didn't know what to say to that. He continued. "Every instinct in my body tells me to protect you. It's tiring. You're safe here. Casper isn't going to hurt you. My dislike for him probably springs from this magical attraction. I won't have magic dictate my relationships for me. If I wanted that, I could've stayed in Elustria."

I didn't want to hear anymore of how horrible this was for him. "I understand. Thanks for explaining, and thanks for everything you've done." I stood from the table, eager for this to be done now that it was decided. "Who knows, maybe someday we'll meet again."

"Yeah, maybe someday."

There we stood, in the middle of my room, and nothing had ever felt more awkward. "I wish you the best."

"Once you and Casper figure out how to get that necklace off, don't let my attitude dissuade you from magic. You could be great. Take care of yourself."

"You too." We stood in silence until the awkwardness was so suffocating that I thought it would consume me. Then he turned and walked out of the room, leaving me alone.

CHAPTER 21

I didn't have time to think about Alex or how lonely I'd be without him. Mikael and Sadie seemed nice. Over time we could become friends, but friends should really be the least of my worries now. I'd told Casper I wanted him to teach me magic. Catching up on a lifetime of study would take enough of my time.

During the tour, Casper had told me I had free use of the library. My formal study wouldn't begin until tomorrow, but I could do some reading tonight. I needed to focus on something, keep my mind occupied. Walking down the beautiful staircase, I realized that this would be my home for the foreseeable future. I'd have to work out withdrawing from school. It shouldn't be difficult. Without a scholarship, I was headed in that direction anyway.

This was really happening. The decision felt good. At the bottom of the stairs, voices pulled my attention to the right. Casper and Alex sat across from each other in the living room. My calm determination fled and my chest fluttered at seeing Alex still here. He sat with his back to me, but Casper sat across from him and saw me. He stood. "Kat, excellent. Come join us."

Alex's head turned at my name. The awkward surprise I saw there accurately summed up what I felt. I wanted to turn and go back upstairs, but that would only make the situation more uncomfortable. Alex faced forward again, relieving me of the pressure of his gaze. "I was just going to the library," I told Casper.

"That can wait. This conversation concerns you." Casper gestured to the spot next to him on the sofa. His posture made it clear he would not move again until I came.

The only thing that could make the situation more awkward with Alex would be to let him know I found it awkward, so I trudged over to the sofa and sat. The fact that they were discussing me didn't surprise me. It seemed like that was the only thing they ever talked about, and I was tired of it. Taking control of the situation was my best chance at banishing the awkwardness. "I'd appreciate it if you didn't talk about me behind my back. Any decisions about my future will be made by me."

A hint of mirth lit Alex's eyes and the corner of his mouth twitched. Glad I amused him.

"I was just getting some information from Alex before he left," Casper said then turned his attention back to Alex.

"What kind of information?" I couldn't imagine he'd have anything that would be useful to Casper.

"He wants to know more about how your mother died," Alex said. "But like I told him, I don't really know much."

"No, but you know where you met your father," Casper said. "That's all I need. If you can give me directions to that spot, there's a decent chance we can track the magic to where she died."

"And what will that do?" I asked.

"I'm hoping to find clues as to who killed her and what she wanted you to do with the talisman. She might have left a message for us to find. It's a long shot, but we don't really have much else to go on."

Alex caught the wary hope in my expression. "It's been weeks. It isn't likely there'd be enough magic remaining for you to track to the spot where she died."

"It's worth a try, though. Just give me the coordinates, and we'll check it out. There's no harm to it," Casper said.

"And don't you have enhanced senses?" I asked Alex. Maybe he could track his father's scent.

"Not enhanced enough to find what nature has swept away over weeks."

"But between you, the talisman, and Casper's magic, we might be able to do it." My wariness had fled and all that remained was hope. Alex hesitated. This wasn't fair to him. He wanted to leave, and I knew it. He had already given more of his time than he wanted to. "I'm sorry. I didn't mean to assume you'd come. Really, if you just let us know where you met your father, I really think that Casper could track back to where she died." I had nothing to base this belief on, but I felt wretched for manipulating him with my hope and optimism. It was time for him to move on with his life and me with mine.

"I met my father in the middle of the forest. Without landmarks, I doubt I'd be able to give you accurate coordinates. I can take you there, though. I met him in Bolivia. I can show you the general area on a map. Once we get there, I should be able to find the spot."

"Are you sure?" He'd already done enough. I didn't want him to feel pressured.

The corners of Alex's yellow eyes softened as tenderness filled his face. I tried to ignore what that look did to my heart. "Yes, I'm sure."

"Excellent!" Casper stood. "I'll make preparations."

I'd never left the country before this week. In a matter of days I'd become quite the international traveler. "Wait, I don't have a passport."

Casper smirked then laughed. "Don't worry about it. I wasn't planning on traveling through customs." He turned his attention to Alex and gestured to the library. "Why don't you come show me on a map the general area we're traveling to?"

I stayed in place while they disappeared into the library. Did

Casper mean that he would be taking a private plane and therefore would bypass customs? I didn't think it worked like that. More likely he had teleportation rings somewhere in Bolivia that we would use. Traveling around the Armory using the rings was one thing, traveling halfway across the world was another. It should be the same in theory, but there was no convincing my stomach of that.

CHAPTER 22

*A*s it turned out, taking rings halfway across the world really was exactly like taking them from one floor to another. It didn't even take longer. Since Casper didn't have access to any rings in Bolivia, the most convenient option was to teleport into his penthouse apartment in Buenos Aires then take a private plane to Bolivia in the morning. We'd land in a private airfield where money could be depended on to avoid the hassles of customs.

The penthouse in Buenos Aires fit the expectation of what a tech billionaire would buy. The open, modern floor plan was built for cocktail parties and entertaining. The apartment took up the entire top floor of one of the highest buildings in the Palermo neighborhood of Buenos Aires. Floor-to-ceiling windows presented a view unlike any I had ever seen. I could imagine women in expensive, sparkly gowns sipping fancy cocktails next to the windows while men in tuxedos vied for their attention over the sounds of soft jazz from a live band in the corner.

Sadie was the only other person from the Armory who made the trip with me, Alex, and Casper. She walked around the apartment as if she came here somewhat regularly. Casper went to a room down the hall talking on his cell phone while Sadie brought Alex and me bottles of water from the kitchen. Casper had called ahead to his staff to get the place ready for a quick stay. They had cleaned and stocked the kitchen and bathrooms with everything we would need.

"Just wait until you see the roof," Sadie said.

"You might as well show her now. We're going to leave first thing in the morning," Casper said as he came from the back of the apartment, his phone call done.

Sadie squealed and did a little dance while waving Alex and me to follow her. When we stepped through the door onto the roof, I audibly gasped. The rooftop garden was straight out of a movie. I didn't think places like this really existed. Bright pink and purple flowers grew on bushes around the perimeter of the roof. Trees heavy with oranges stood at the corners. At one end was a bar and a pergola covered in ivy. Chairs, loungers, and ottomans with giant cushions formed several intimate seating areas. The seating area under the pergola had a giant TV and to the side was an outdoor kitchen and barbecue area that was bigger than my actual kitchen. The centerpiece was a pool that ran down the center of the roof with an infinity edge on one end. Just looking at it made my knees go weak. No way would I ever have the stomach to swim that close to the edge.

Sadie threw her arm over my shoulders. "I told you it was amazing. Every once in a while Casper will throw a party up here." Every once in a while. Because that's why you buy a place like this when you're a billionaire, to use every once in a while. I'd forgotten exactly how wealthy Casper was. "I'm going to get in the pool." Sadie went to a changing area near the pergola to put on a bikini.

While I was busy checking out the amenities, Alex was at the edge of the roof looking out at the sunset. The rays of the sun bathed the city in pink, matching the flowers around us. The longing in his eyes was unmistakable. "One more day and you'll be back out there past the city limits," I said when I came up beside him.

He turned at my voice and an easy smile lifted his lips. "That wasn't what I was thinking."

"Really?" I looked out over the bright pink clouds that nearly mirrored the flowers around us.

Alex turned back to the view. "Just admiring the beauty of it. I never tire of sunsets. No matter where we go, they're always beautiful."

"Are you going to be okay tomorrow?" I asked him.

Alex looked at me, his eyebrows crinkled in confusion. "What do you mean?"

"Well, the last time you were at the spot you're taking us to, your father died."

Alex shrugged and looked back out over the now purple sky. "It wasn't exactly an emotional time. I hadn't seen him in ages. Panthers don't play a large role in the life of their young."

The death of my parents wrecked me in every sense of the word. When their plane crashed, I lost my center, the sense of who I was. In some ways, I wished their death had affected me as little as Alex's father's death affected him. Trying to place myself in his situation, I shied away. I wouldn't give up the amazing life I'd had with my parents, with the people who had chosen me, even if it meant not falling apart after their death. To Alex, his father's death was more comparable to Meglana's. It bothered me that I would never know her, but it didn't even register on the grief scale next to my parents.

Little stars twinkled to life now that dusk had fallen. The silence sat comfortably between us. I'd miss this when he left. His hand found mine, and when his fingers curled around my palm, I looked at him, wondering if he even noticed what he was doing or if it was merely instinctual. His face turned toward me, and I saw something in his eyes that shocked me. I hadn't been with anyone since my parents had died. Grief takes many shapes and forms, and everyone has their own way of dealing with it. Mine had been to retreat within myself, but I saw lust staring back at me, familiar even after all this time. The energy between us had shifted, and I couldn't figure out when or how. He leaned down and kissed my lips, slowly, delicately, a soft assurance. It only lasted a second, and then he pulled back.

"I'm sorry. I shouldn't have done that," he whispered, his lips just an inch from mine.

I didn't want him to regret it. I didn't. It was stupid. He was leaving, we both knew it, but that didn't make me want it any less. Before I could say something foolish, Sadie interrupted us.

"Hey, you two, come join me." Sadie splashed water in our direction from the pool. "You're going to wish you had when we're back in Canada."

The mood was broken and Alex backed away as he bristled. "No thanks. My kind don't particularly like swimming."

A picture of a drenched panther scowling entered my mind, and I laughed. "So really deep down you're just a big cat."

"Pretty much."

I walked to the edge of the pool and removed my shoes and socks. The winters in Montana were long. It'd been ages since I'd gone swimming. "I'll dangle my feet in, but I don't have a swimsuit."

"I can get you one," Sadie offered, but I shook my head.

"It's not really worth the hassle." The cool water soothed my feet. While it was winter back home, here it was summer, and the warm air felt good on my skin. If circumstances were other than they were, I'd want nothing more than to spend tomorrow up here with a good book soaking up as much sun and vitamin D as I could.

Despite his protestations, Alex joined me, rolling his pant legs up and putting his feet in. "See, some silly human things like pools can be enjoyable."

"Maybe, but this pool has nothing on the ones in nature." Alex's eyes went distant as he focused on some memory. "I've seen waterfalls that would take your breath away."

"I'm sure you have. But this pool has an advantage." I waited until Alex focused his gaze back on me. "No snakes."

"Don't tell me you're scared of swimming in anything other than chlorinated water in concrete?"

"Am I scared of poisonous snakes that can kill me before I even see them? Why yes, yes I am, and I'm not ashamed of it."

"Huh. Scared of something that's more scared of you but you're not scared of an assassin tracking you."

It was easy to forget in the protection of the Armory and now far away at a luxurious rooftop pool that someone hunted me, the same person who had killed my birth mother. "That's why we're here. Tomorrow we should get some answers or at least clues as to what Meglana wanted me to do."

"As long as you remember that this isn't a vacation. I'm worried about what's going to happen to you when I'm no longer here to protect you." Concern lingered in his eyes, but it was the concern of someone who felt themselves responsible, nothing more. It wasn't born of affection or any feelings other than those conjured by the talisman. We'd established that.

"You did the most important thing which was getting me to Casper. He has the resources to protect me. As soon as it's safe, I'll go to the Council and they'll know what to do. There's no use worrying when you've already made up your mind to leave."

There was a flicker of something unreadable in Alex's eyes, and he turned away, ostensibly to take in the view.

"We're all set for tomorrow." Casper's voice intruded behind us. "A druid will be meeting us in Bolivia. I have dinner prepared for us whenever you all are ready."

I wanted to stay up on this rooftop with Alex forever, but the mood was already broken. As we walked back inside, it hit me that this was the last night I'd spend with Alex. After tomorrow, he'd be gone.

CHAPTER 23

A town car drove us from the apartment to an airfield on the outskirts of Buenos Aires. The car pulled right up to a private jet and we boarded with no security checks, no taking off our shoes or putting all of our stuff into little bins. Out of all the perks of Casper's wealth, private air travel was my favorite.

The plane didn't have a crew other than the pilot. It was a different man than the one who had flown the helicopter to the Armory, but I bet he was also a mage. Even though all of Casper's staff, human and mage, probably signed ironclad non-disclosure agreements, I liked not having to watch what I said around a human flight attendant.

The cabin was laid out more like a living room than a traditional plane. Hoping that it would help my anxiety, I opted to sit on the sofa, but my hands still shook as I fastened my seatbelt.

Alex sat next to me and immediately noticed my hands. "Shit, your parents died in a plane crash, right? Are you okay?"

"Yeah, I'll be fine. I've flown a few times since then, for the funeral and stuff. I just need to get through the take off, and I'll be fine." Nothing broadcasted cool calmness more than saying "I'll be fine" twice in two seconds. Alex's hand slipped into mine and gave it a little squeeze.

"Well, if you're not fine, I'm right here."

"Thanks." I let myself enjoy the comfort of his hand for a few seconds, keenly aware that in a matter of hours he'd be gone and I'd be flying back to Buenos Aires without him.

Once the plane leveled out, I relaxed a little and let go of his hand, but I needed conversation to distract me from the irrational fear of the plane plunging to the earth in a massive ball of fire. "Who is this druid who's meeting us? And what exactly is a druid?" There were druids in *Wizards and Fae,* and I thought druids were part of ancient Celtic religion. Good money was on our druid being closer to the *Wizards and Fae* version, but I had learned not to assume.

"It's not just a druid, it's *the* druid. Dorran," Sadie said, in a tone that made it clear I should know who he was.

Alex raised his eyebrows and let out an impressed whistle. "Dorran? How did that happen?"

"He was intrigued when Casper told him why we wanted him."

"I'm amazed Casper even knew how to contact him," Alex said with the same awe someone might use when told a friend had gotten in touch with Oprah.

"Who's Dorran?" I looked first at Sadie, then at Alex. I was more interested in how Alex knew who this person was.

"He's an ancient druid," Alex said. "Many say he's the first druid to ever come through a portal to Earth. Ever since then, he's roamed Earth, going from enclave to enclave, mingling with humans. He's a bit of a mythical figure for both Elustrians and humans. I never thought I'd get to meet him."

The idea of such a famous figure being involved in my predicament made me uneasy. It was weird enough involving Casper. This felt too public, too big. I didn't like the idea of my birth mother's tragedy put on display for others. "What exactly is a druid?"

Sadie answered me this time. "Druids are a race of people from Elustria whose magic is nature-based. They're generally nomadic."

"Are they immortal?" I asked. Alex made it sound like Dorran was thousands of years old. I didn't know if any creatures in Elustria were immortal, but it wouldn't be the strangest thing I'd learned.

"No," Sadie said. "They can be killed, and they age, but if they aren't killed, they can live almost indefinitely. There are some that have turned to stone, literally petrified, in Elustria because they've lived so long."

That didn't sound like something to aspire to. "So this guy must be pretty young if he's still moving around."

"He's old enough that no one remembers his real name," Casper said as he put aside the tablet he had been reading. "I don't even think he remembers at this point."

"It's not Dorran?" I asked.

"Dorran is a Celtic name meaning 'stranger.' It's what the Celts called him when he first appeared, and the name has stuck," Casper said. "Personally, I think he likes the mysterious air it gives him—not that he needs help in that department. You'll see when you meet him."

I couldn't wrap my head around living that long. "What are enclaves?"

Even though Alex had mentioned them, Casper answered me. "They're magical communities that are hidden on Earth. They're in a bit of a gray area. The sorcerers would prefer they not exist, but as long as they keep magic contained to the community, they're left in peace."

Once this was all over, I wanted to see an enclave. An entire community that included magic right here on Earth sounded incredible. "So this Dorran guy wanders the Earth doing random magic. What exactly is he going to do for us?"

"Once Alex takes us to where he met his father, Dorran should be able to take us from there to where Meglana died," Casper said.

"How can he do that after so long?" If Alex's senses couldn't get us there, I didn't understand how this druid could.

Casper looked to Sadie to answer my question. "Druids have

different magic than we do. Because his magic is based in nature, he'll be able to elicit the help of the trees and plants and even the animals to take him to where your mother died. Once we're there, he's going to see if he can get the earth to show us the last moments of her life."

My heart pounded so loud I could hear it. "Wait, you mean I'm going to actually see Meglana die?" Alex took my hand as my breathing quickened.

Sadie eyed Casper uneasily before focusing back on me. "Yes, but you don't have to look. We certainly don't want to upset you, but this is the best way for us to figure out what happened and why your talisman won't come off. We may even get a glimpse of who killed her."

We were basically flying to see a snuff film starring my birth mother. That's not what I'd expected. I hadn't so much as seen a picture of Meglana.

"Hey, are you going to be all right?" Alex whispered as he leaned toward me.

When I looked into his eyes, the rest of the plane and its occupants melted away. I felt like the center of his attention. He wasn't asking just to be nice. A part me wondered if he would overpower the pilot and turn the plane around if I said I didn't want to go through with it.

"I'll be fine. This is something we...I have to do." If this was our best shot at figuring out who killed Meglana and how to control my talisman, then there wasn't any other choice.

Alex searched my eyes for a moment longer, trying to see if I was lying. Finally satisfied, he gave a little nod and sat back in his seat. The rest of the plane came back into my awareness, along with the fact that he was leaving and these types of feelings toward him could only end in heartache for me. I didn't have time for that.

CHAPTER 24

 Ohen our plane landed, a local man with a Land Rover
 was waiting for us on the tarmac. The man dressed
casually, not a customs agent from his appearance. Casper produced
a thick envelope of cash from out of nowhere and handed it to the
man. His jeans and button-down shirt were too finely tailored to
have concealed such an envelope, so maybe he had conjured it from
thin air. With Casper it was hard to tell what was magic and what
was plain old wealth in action.

In exchange for the cash, the man gave Casper the keys to the
Land Rover, and we climbed inside. In this instance, Casper's money
bought us discretion as well as a rental. No one bothered us for
passports. Casper took the driver's seat, and I sat behind him. Sadie
buckled in next to me while Alex took the front seat to navigate.
We'd be relying on his memory for directions.

The drive from the private airfield quickly turned into off-road-
ing. This place was in the middle of nowhere. I couldn't even figure
out where the man who had met us lived. Everything surrounding
the runway was forest. A single-wide office trailer had stood at one
end of the runway, but that was it.

The seatbelt dug into my neck and hips as I was flung this way and that. Alex had found a rough approximation on Casper's phone of where he had last seen his father. We'd drive there, then Alex would give more specific directions until we found the right place. Everything looked the same to me, nothing but forest, but I'd never been the outdoorsy type. "Aren't we going to pick up Dorran somewhere?" I asked.

"We'll summon him once we get there," Casper said, as if summoning people to him was a regular occurrence. Between all the money and magic, I supposed it was.

Next to me, Sadie bounced around as much as I did. I looked to her to expand on Casper's comment. She picked up on what I wanted right away. "Druids can teleport without the use of rings. I can't imagine old Dorran tolerating the drive."

The image of an ancient druid jostled around in this Land Rover made me smile. I wanted to think about anything other than what we were making this trip to see. As uncomfortable as the drive was, I couldn't help wanting it to last longer when Alex said, "You can stop here. We'll walk the rest of the way."

I had not thought this through with my wardrobe choices. Sturdier shoes would have been great. Even though all of my clothes were in an apartment I couldn't go back to, I knew I could have had Casper get me anything I needed. Oh well, at least I wouldn't get blisters from breaking in a new pair.

Alex shifted into his panther form and sniffed at the ground and air. It had been so long since he'd last been here that I couldn't imagine his scent remaining on anything, but maybe other scents would jog his memory. When he started moving, it was at a slow enough pace that we could all easily keep up.

It didn't take long for my clothes to get wet with sweat. The humidity dragged me down and the mosquitos buzzing around didn't help. I kept slapping myself trying to kill the little buggers but never succeeded. How Alex could find nature appealing was beyond me.

"Here, have a drink." Sadie passed me a water bottle from her backpack.

"Thanks." The water made more of a difference than I would have thought. I wanted this little trek to end, but that meant watching my birth mother die. There were no good outcomes here.

After what felt like hours but was likely twenty minutes or so, Alex shifted and declared that this was the spot.

Casper looked around as if something on the plants and trees would speak to him. "This is where your father gave you the talisman?"

"Yes." Alex pointed to the tree in front of him. "I found him here, nearly dead. After he gave me the talisman, I left and didn't see him again. I don't know if he stayed here or went somewhere else to die."

No emotion escaped Alex's lips. He spoke of seeing his father for the last time the way a person would speak of seeing a stranger. Throughout this trip Alex had offered me support. Even though he didn't look like he needed it, I refused to be fooled by this macho act. Besides, even if he didn't want my empathy, he had it, and it wouldn't hurt to let him know. So while Casper and Sadie did whatever it was they did to summon Dorran, I went up to him and slid my hand into his the way he had done with me on the plane.

"Are you all right?" I echoed his question from earlier.

Alex nodded, but he didn't look at me, keeping his eyes trained ahead where they couldn't betray anything. I gave his hand a squeeze. "It's okay that it's complicated."

I knew the way a parent's death made you think, the mental knots it tied you into. Human nature was to turn the deceased into a saint, but that wasn't real. There were still memories of hurtful comments, raised voices in arguments, conflict, and those memories crashed against the grief, making it more painful. I'd loved my parents dearly, so I couldn't imagine how confusing it must be for Alex who insisted there was no love lost between him and his father.

In the ramrod straightness of Alex's back and the squaring of his shoulders I saw my own future. I'd soon watch the last moments of life of the woman who had given birth to me but who had never been my mom. I didn't know her, and she didn't know me, although she might have thought she did. My grief was for an idea, but soon I'd have to see the woman behind that idea. The image would crash against the feelings I already held about her death and would threaten to crumble the wall I'd built around my heart that proved I didn't care about this woman who hadn't kept me.

Behind us, Casper and Sadie stopped talking, whatever spell or communication they had performed with Dorran finished. But it wasn't the lack of voices that caused the silence. The birds and bugs that chirped and hummed all hushed. Even the whistle of the wind in the trees stopped.

A papery thin voice, once rich but now stretched from the stresses of time while still retaining a deep bass pitch, broke the stillness. "So here is the source of all this death."

CHAPTER 25

I turned toward the voice. Dorran stood facing me with a forest green cloak concealing his body and a cowl pulled low over his head. My first thought was that he had to be sweltering under that fabric. Sweat poured down my forehead in a steady stream, but Dorran gave no sign that the heat bothered him. He was a good head taller than me, his back straight in defiance of his age. He held a staff worn smooth from use. At the top of the staff a light green stone about the size of my fist sat suspended in an intricate setting. If he were a mage, I'd assume it was his talisman, but I didn't think druids needed a talisman. Casper was right, this guy loved the mysterious stranger persona. Tendrils of gray hair escaped the cowl and curled softly on his shoulders, but beyond that, his features remained hidden in shadow.

A strange feeling overcame me at the sight of Dorran, as if he had an interest in me beyond what was appropriate for a new acquaintance. It seemed he meant that either I or my talisman were the "source of all this death." The talisman was the more likely culprit. I reminded myself that even though I didn't know Dorran, I trusted Alex, and if he had misgivings about the druid, he would have voiced them.

"Dorran, thank you for coming," Casper said. He walked to Dorran's side, but the druid made no movement to acknowledge him.

"Your proposition intrigued me," Dorran said, still facing me. "I felt the shock of a strong curse weeks ago. From what you described, I think this may be the source of it."

"You knew about Meglana's death?" I asked. Every step I took on this journey revealed a larger world surrounding my birth mother.

"Ah, she speaks." Dorran's voice lightened with his mocking, but I still couldn't see his face. "When a curse that strong hits the earth, it reverberates throughout the planet. All of nature cries out with the pain of it." His words settled around us, the air heavy with their implication. "However, that curse did not happen here. Where have you brought me?" For the first time, Dorran turned away from me and looked at Casper.

In response, Casper nodded to Alex and had him answer Dorran's question. "This is where I found my father. He was with Meglana when she was attacked. She gave him her talisman and told him to get it to her heir. When I saw him, he was near death. He gave me the talisman to give to Meglana's daughter. The last place I ever saw him was leaning against that tree." Alex pointed to the spot, and Dorran went to the tree, placing his palm low on the trunk where Alex's father had likely made contact.

The hair on the back of my arms raised when Dorran's hand touched the tree. The forest floor around us seemed to crackle with energy. Something was happening, but I wasn't sure what. After a few moments, Dorran rose and walked away from our group. It took a minute for us to realize that he meant for us to follow.

Dorran led the way, and as he walked, the forest made way for us, branches and undergrowth moving aside to make our passage easier. The movement of the plants around us to accommodate Dorran left me in awe. I couldn't tear my eyes away from them. I wanted us to come upon a boulder just to see if it would roll out of the way.

By the time Dorran stopped, my shirt was soaked in sweat and my breathing was labored. Even with the magical assistance, the hike was strenuous for a girl who spent most of her time gaming. Alex, I noticed, didn't appear affected by the heat or the physical strain. At least Casper and Sadie were there to keep me from feeling like a complete loser. They were just as winded and miserable looking as I was.

"Here. This is the spot," Dorran declared as he knelt down, placing his hand on the forest floor. "Yes, this is where she died."

Uneasiness crept through my body. My birth mother had died a violent death here. Soon I would see it.

When Dorran didn't move for several minutes, Sadie spoke. "Are you going to be able to show us what happened?"

After another moment of silence, Dorran stood. "The earth is reluctant to show me what happened here. It was a great evil."

"There has to be something you can do," Casper said. No wasn't something he was used to hearing.

"I didn't say I couldn't do it. I said the earth was reluctant. I don't use magic to force my will upon her. This will take a bit of coaxing."

Dorran went to the nearest tree, leaned his staff against it, and knelt down. He placed one hand on the tree and one on the ground. I couldn't hear him speaking, but a hum emanated from him, either from his voice or from his magic. The rest of us stood in silence and watched. Alex moved to my side and took my hand in his. It had become such a familiar gesture that I didn't question it.

Mist gathered on the forest floor. It swirled into the air until there was enough of it to obscure the scenery. The thick fog turned a burnt orange color. There she was, Meglana, my birth mother. It looked like a black and white video projection.

"You don't have to watch," Alex whispered in my ear, but I couldn't tear my eyes away.

The image of Meglana was blurry, her features twisted by the swirling mist into something not quite human. Where her face should have been the mist was completely black. The amber stone on my chest warmed.

"Here, it will lead you to my heir." Meglana took the talisman from around her neck, cupped her hands around it and did something, I couldn't tell what. Her head dipped down to her hands like she was whispering to it. "We can't let him get it." She handed the talisman to someone who wasn't visible. Her voice was distorted like on TV when reporters are hiding the identity of their source. It made the entire tableau strangely impersonal.

With the talisman handed off, she looked behind her. "You're too late. You won't get it now. You failed."

"I didn't fail. I eliminated you, didn't I? That talisman will be easy enough for me to track. Now that I've felt its magic in person, it'll be even easier. It can't hide from me."

The fog went from burnt orange to a dark red hue then, like someone turned on the lights, it turned white and dissipated. My hand went to the stone around my neck. The magic emanating from it had become a constant presence, and it could be leading my birth mother's killer right to me.

Casper was the first to break the silence that followed. "That's it? We didn't learn anything we didn't already know."

"It confirmed our suspicions that he's tracking the talisman." That seemed like a pretty big deal as the wearer of said talisman.

"That's inconsequential. I told you that stone gives off enough magic to be tracked." Casper waved aside my concern like it was nothing. "The Armory has so many protective charms and wards on it that no one can track what's inside."

Dorran stood unperturbed by Casper's complaint. "You asked me to show you Meglana's final moments. That's what you got."

"But what happened to her body?" I asked. I hadn't thought much about it until now.

"That's not what I was asked to show," Dorran answered.

"The assassin likely disintegrated it," Casper said. "If he was powerful enough to kill her, he was powerful enough to hide the evidence."

Given how much time had passed since her death, that was actually a bit of a relief. I didn't like the thought of her body being left here.

"I want to know what killed her," Sadie said. "The specifics would be helpful. We can't get anything from what we saw. She was already cursed."

"Be more specific the next time you ask for my assistance," Dorran said. He was being kind of an ass. "You can't feel the magic through nature's memories, so unless the curse was verbally cast, you wouldn't be able to identify it." That answer seemed to satisfy Sadie, and Dorran looked at me for the first time since we got here. "Now for my payment."

"Ah," Casper said, waving a hand in my direction. "Of course. Go ahead."

Dorran advanced on me. Alex let go of my hand and stepped between us. "What's going on?"

Dorran let out a low chuckle. "No need to worry, friend. I mean no harm. All I wanted in exchange for today's service was to look at the talisman that has been the source of all this disruption. I won't even touch it, just look."

"It's okay," I said to Alex and stepped beside him. "Go ahead and look, Dorran." Really, I wasn't okay with the fact that I wasn't asked about any of this, but it seemed a small price to pay.

Dorran stood toe-to-toe with me and peered at the talisman. For the first time, I got a clear look at his face. He wore a full beard the same dark gray as his hair. His wrinkled skin was probably once a rich, dark brown but had a sandy hue, as if the dust of time had settled on him.

He lifted his gaze from my talisman to stare at me. All of his features paled next to his vibrant green eyes. They were alert and piercing, glittering like jewels beneath his cowl. "It is a part of you. You and the talisman are one."

"I can't get it off." I don't know what compelled me to say that, but Dorran seemed like he might have a solution.

"Why would you ever want to take it off?" he asked in the same tone he might use to ask me why I'd want to cut off my hand.

I wanted to learn magic now, live up to my birth mother's legacy. The fact that I couldn't remove the talisman left me with doubts about my destiny and ability. Under Dorran's gaze, I found myself giving voice to those doubts. "I'm not a mage. It's not who I am. I don't know what I should do, if I should stay here or go to the Council."

"You're not a mage." I couldn't tell if he was stating fact or echoing what I said. "It's not who you are. Do not put your trust in the Council. Trust no one but yourself. Submit to no one. Put your faith in your own gut."

"I don't know what my gut is telling me."

"Yes, you do. You can't remove what is part of you. Submitting to the Council is what an Elustrian would do, but you are not an Elustrian. You are meant for this world."

I tried to process what he was saying. He seemed done, so I said the only thing I could think of. "Thank you."

"That is not what I came here to say." Dorran leaned in and whispered in my ear so no one else could hear him. Sadie and Casper moved closer, trying to listen, but Dorran held up a hand and they stopped. His voice hardened, belying his age. "A great evil was done here. That stone is filled with powerful magic. I have felt it now, and if it is used against this world, I will hunt it and its wielder. I have made a nice home for myself here and will not see it destroyed."

Before I could respond, he turned his face to the sky and stepped back. "We are not the only ones here."

At first I thought he meant that we were surrounded by nature or something, but before I could question him, Alex tensed beside me. "It's him. The assassin. He's coming from that direction." Alex pointed in the opposite direction from which we came.

Sadie pulled out her wand while Casper pulled out his satellite phone. "I'll have the plane ready for us. Dorran, take them to the Land Rover. Sadie and I will follow."

"I am not here for you," Dorran scoffed. "I don't take orders. My only loyalty is to my home."

"We're getting out of here," Alex said to me then shifted. I climbed on his back and, despite what Dorran said about not helping us, when Alex took off running, the forest made way for us.

Alex stretched his panther form to its full length as he sprinted to the SUV. This was a completely different experience than the last time I'd ridden on his back. Between Alex's natural grace and the help provided by Dorran, we flew over the forest floor. We reached the Land Rover and climbed inside, Alex shifting as he jumped in. My first instinct was to lock the doors behind us, but that wouldn't do anything to stop a magical assassin and would only slow Casper and Sadie when they joined us.

"Are you all right?" Alex asked once we were inside. He looked me over for any wounds, but I didn't have so much as a scratch on me thanks to Dorran.

"I'm fine. I'm the least of our worries. You and the others are the ones doing all the work." Given the speed with which Alex could run as a panther, I expected it to take quite a while for Casper and Sadie to catch up with us, but they appeared just a few minutes later. They ran faster than normal, probably because of a spell or something. Sadie had her wand out casting a shield to protect them. It looked like something straight out of a video game. The clear shield distorted the image of the forest beyond it. Sparks of magic ricocheted off of it, but I couldn't see the attacker. Dorran appeared off to the side, performing some type of magic, but I couldn't tell what.

Alex and I opened the driver and passenger doors for Casper and Sadie to jump in. As soon as Casper was inside, he started the Land Rover and drove so fast I feared we'd crash. Sadie kept her shield going around the vehicle.

"Did Dorran help you?" I asked as I buckled my seatbelt.

"No, all he was concerned about was protecting the forest,"

Casper said as he accelerated even more. "He stuck around to make sure none of our spells harmed his precious trees." Ecology was clearly not an area of interest for Casper.

Once we came in sight of the airfield, Sadie dropped her shield. Since we started driving, I hadn't seen any trace of magic from the assassin, but that didn't mean much given my non-existent knowledge of magic. Within minutes of arriving at the plane we were taxiing down the runway. I didn't even have time to be nervous about the takeoff. All I wanted was to be as far away from that place and that murderer as quickly as possible.

CHAPTER 26

*M*y face stayed plastered to my window on the plane, searching for any trace of the man who had killed my birth mother.

Alex brought me a bottle of water from the galley. "Unless he can fly, he's not going to be able to track us up here."

I had visions of the Wicked Witch of the West flying her broomstick outside the window. "So you're saying it's not common for people in Elustria to fly?"

"Not really," Sadie said. She took the seat facing me and Alex. "At least, it's not common for sorcerers."

"So you think the assassin is a sorcerer?"

"It makes the most sense given that he found us so quickly. Either a sorcerer or a mage could have left a charm that we tripped when we came here. The difference is a mage would have had to use teleportation rings or get the help of someone who could teleport them."

Casper emerged from the cockpit and joined us. "I spoke with the pilot, and he says he got enough fuel into the plane after I called him to get us all the way home."

"So we're going back to the Armory, not the apartment?" I asked.

"Yes, I think it's the better choice." Casper made eye contact with Alex. "I'm sorry you're stuck here with us. I know you wanted to leave after you guided us to where you last saw your father."

"I'm all right. I'd like to see Kat back to the Armory."

"You're welcome for as long as you like," Casper said.

I hated that Alex saw me as someone who needed his protection, but when he pulled me close to rest against him, it wasn't protection he was offering, it was support. I didn't want to rely on anybody after my parents died. Everyone would always eventually leave. It made me forget how wonderful having someone's physical support could feel. He may be leaving as soon as we got back, but I would enjoy this while it lasted. There was no use depriving myself now because I'd be alone later.

"I didn't realize a plane this size could go so far without refueling," I said.

"This plane can do it easily. That's the advantage of a corporate jet. This one has one of the longest ranges on the market, and it can almost break the sound barrier. We'll land at an airport near the Armory, and then we'll go the rest of the way in the helicopter."

I liked the idea of being back at the Armory. The fact that the assassin had found us the one time I'd ventured out of it made me feel like it was the safest place in the world. From there I could learn to control the magic of my talisman, and then I'd have more choices.

Dorran had said not to trust the Council, to trust my gut. That should make me feel better about my decision to stay with Casper and learn magic, but Dorran's real intent had been to threaten me if I used the talisman's magic against this world. I didn't know if what came before his threat was truth or just some bullshit before his real message.

Given that the assassin had so easily tracked me outside of the Armory, it seemed like it would be just as dangerous to travel to the Council. Add that to Dorran's warning and it made me yearn for the protective walls of the Armory even more. I wanted to be able to protect myself, and to do that, I needed a place to learn.

"Now the assassin knows I have more help," I said to Casper. "Before this he only knew about Alex."

Casper waved away my concern. "We needed to see her last moments. It was the best chance we had to discover why the talisman won't release from around your neck."

"I guess it's just up to me to learn enough magic to get it to obey me."

"You will," Sadie said. "Don't worry."

I wasn't worried about not learning magic, I was worried about what I'd do once I did. I hadn't known Meglana, but seeing her like that, with her face distorted by a curse, fighting to keep a great power out of the hands of an evil madman, stirred feelings in me I hadn't felt before.

When my parents had died, I was angry at a lot of people: the airline, the pilots, the scheduler who had them working too much, and on and on. But I had known it had been an accident, a result of negligence, not malice. This was different. I wanted to learn magic, not to get the talisman off, but to kill the man who had killed Meglana.

CHAPTER 27

*T*he next morning we were back at the Armory. Once I'd convinced myself that the assassin would not appear in the sky to attack us, it was surprisingly easy to sleep. I arrived at the Armory ready to get to work. Only one cloud hung over me.

Alex stood in my room. It felt like it'd been so long since we'd last stood here, but nothing had really changed. "We both knew I wasn't going to stick around forever."

Maybe I knew that on an intellectual level but certainly not on an emotional one. We'd already said goodbye once. South America had been stolen time. I knew that, but a small part of me had hoped that he'd changed his mind after the kiss we shared. Remembering it warmed my lips, and that warmth spread.

But I had too much to do to get hung up on a guy. The last thing I needed was something romantic, yet all I could think about was how much I'd grown to enjoy our time together. Friends didn't come easily for me, and I didn't want to let this one go. "You're right. I've already taken up too much of your time. You were doing a favor for your father and my mother, and I appreciate it. It doesn't mean you signed up for all of this."

He took a step closer to me. "I don't regret a minute of our time

173

together. I'm glad I was able to be with you in Bolivia. I wish things were different, but I'm a shifter. I can't stay here any longer. It's not who I am."

"I understand, really. I'm going to miss you, despite the fact that you are the one who started all this." I cracked a half smile to let him know I was partly teasing.

"I'm going to miss you, too." He went silent for a moment, debating what he should say next. "I'm sorry for kissing you earlier. It was a dick move when I knew I was leaving." His eyes lightened with a hint of mirth. "But you did shoot me with an ice arrow. Call it even?" He stole my half-smile move, and I couldn't begrudge him the theft, not when it made him look so charming.

"We're even. You'll have to forgive me for not being sorry about the kiss. I know it's different for you." The attraction I felt to him had nothing to do with the talisman. A shadow crossed his eyes, and he looked like he wanted to contradict me, but I couldn't give him the chance. It would only make this more difficult. "I'll always remember you, Alex."

In his eyes I saw a tumult of emotion. I thought he might say something, but the confusion never left his eyes, and he didn't utter another word. He just turned and left.

CHAPTER 28

 he room felt strangely empty without Alex's presence. I still had an hour before I was due to meet Casper. I couldn't sit around with my thoughts. I wouldn't turn into one of those weepy girls. My god, we weren't dating or anything. This whole thing was ridiculous. He was just a guy I knew for a little while. That's it. Sure, I wanted the best for him, but that meant nothing.

My phone had charged during the flight back...home? No, I wasn't quite ready to call the Armory home yet, although it was starting to feel that way. Nicole might be available. We didn't usually talk this early, but since I'd been MIA for so long, she might take my call.

The phone barely had a chance to ring before she picked up. "Kat! How's it going?"

"Good. You wouldn't believe the world Casper lives in." That was a massive understatement. "The man has insane money. You can't comprehend this kind of wealth. He flew us on his corporate jet to this incredible penthouse. I mean, the plane was nicer than my apartment."

175

"That's not exactly a high bar." Nicole had never visited, but she'd seen enough of my apartment from our video chats. "I want pics."

Crap, it hadn't even occurred to me to take any. "Sorry, I'm not allowed to take any. Privacy stuff."

"That sucks, but it's understandable. So who's 'us?' Is Alex still there?" Trust her to take the conversation where I didn't want it to go. Or did I? She was my best friend, and I had picked now to call her for a reason, conscious or not.

"He just left." I tried to keep all emotion out of my voice and failed miserably.

"Did something happen between you two? You sound upset."

"We kissed next to the rooftop pool at the penthouse."

"What? That's great. You haven't kissed anyone since your parents died." Nicole had long wanted me to get out into the dating game. Depression had kept me home alone.

"I know. I had hoped he'd stay longer."

"Ah, I'm sorry, Kat." She sounded genuinely sad for me.

"No, it's nothing. At least I know I'm not dead inside. That's something, right?"

"It is." I could practically hear her resolute nod through the phone. "I'm so glad you decided to go."

"Me too." She had no idea just how much this trip had changed my life. I didn't know how to tell her that I'd made the decision to stay here for the foreseeable future. I'd have to tell her something. I couldn't disappear on her, and the whole truth was out of the question. I hated this. I didn't regret my decisions, but I wished I could share everything with my best friend. "Casper actually offered me an internship, and I'm going to take it." Learning magic from him was kind of like being his intern.

There was a brief silence before Nicole said anything. "That's cool, but are you doing this to avoid having to figure things out with school?"

I couldn't blame her for that assumption. "No, not at all. I promise. It's just all worked out really well. It's been neat seeing all the stuff my birth mom worked on, and it's got me interested in it."

"That's great, but you're a poli-sci major." She had a point. I didn't know what a poli-sci major would be doing as a Magical Games intern, but people changed direction all the time, right?

"I just need a little change, something to get me out of my rut and excited about life again. I think this could be it." That was all true, and I really needed her support. I didn't want to lose her, too.

"Then I'm happy for you. When do you start?"

"Right away. I'm going to withdraw from this semester. I know that sounds hasty, but I really think this is the right thing for me to do."

"If you feel that strongly about it, then I agree. I just want you to be happy. And I wouldn't mind a few sneak peeks of some new tech."

A relieved smile filled my face. "I'll see what I can do, but I don't think violating company secrets makes the best first impression on the job."

"You're probably right. Hey, I gotta go to class now. Catch you later?"

"Later." At least this lie gave me an opening to keep in touch with her. It was a short-term plan, but at least it was a plan.

CHAPTER 29

I pushed aside my sadness at Alex's departure and my guilt over deceiving my best friend. That left nothing but nerves about the path I was undertaking. Those nerves turned to excitement as the time for my first lessons in magic drew closer, and I ate just enough breakfast to make sure hunger wouldn't distract me from learning. Downstairs, Casper waited for me in the library, his head buried in a book at his desk. As I entered, he marked his place with a ribbon and looked up.

"Ah, you're looking quite refreshed. I take it a good night's sleep and breakfast were just the thing after yesterday's excitement."

"Yeah, they were, thank you." I sat in the chair opposite him. Now that I was staying, I wondered more about the way things worked. "How does fresh food appear on my table?" I had assumed in the dining room that someone at the table had summoned the food, but that didn't explain the meals in my room.

Casper sat back in his chair with a little smirk. "Let's see if you can figure it out. Think: how have things gotten from one place to another here?"

The only things I'd seen move from place to place were people, but that was through teleportation rings. There wasn't a teleportation ring in my room. I'd assumed the omission was for privacy. The table, however, did have a circle etched into it with markings on the outside edge. The dining room table had as well. I'd assumed they were decorative. "The tabletop is a teleportation ring?"

"Very good. The markings along the outside of the circles place specific restrictions on them. For instance, the one on your table is restricted to delivering food and other items. You don't have to worry about a person teleporting in."

The thought of someone appearing standing on the table out of thin air was both terrifying and hilarious. Knowing that a person couldn't use the ring was nice, but it still seemed dangerous to have one inside a bedroom. "So anyone can send anything into my room?"

"No. Teleportation rings can only be used to travel to a ring that the mage has been to before unless they are traveling with a mage who has already been to the destination. Only someone who has already been to your room can send items to the ring in your table."

As long as Casper trusted the people in the Armory, there was no threat. I could let the thought of these strangers having access to my room drive me to paranoia or I could trust Casper's staff. I had to trust someone.

One other thing had bothered me as I showered and thought over the events of the morning. "How come my cell phone battery isn't dead? I charged it on the plane, but that just made me realize I haven't charged it once here. I imagine I'm in roaming territory which usually drains the battery."

"The table by your bed charges it."

The thought of modern technology interacting with foreign magic was strange. "That's useful. I'll have to learn enchantment."

Casper chuckled as a grin lit up his face the way it did any time he discussed *Wizards and Fae* with the media. "I'm afraid that's not magic, just some old Tesla technology that hasn't made its way into the mainstream yet, though some companies are starting to use it more. There probably is a way to charge a cell phone by magic, but necessity is the mother of invention, and I've had no need to figure out how it's done."

"Oh." I felt stupid for assuming it was magic. "Why don't you sell tables like that?"

"I have no use for more money." Casper shrugged than leaned forward slightly, catching my eye. "Don't feel bad for not being able to tell the difference. There is a belief that advanced technology is barely discernible from magic. Of course, the people speculating have never seen actual magic like what you're going to learn today. Let's get started by having you choose a book."

The mention of handling the books chased away any embarrass-ment, and I jumped from my seat. I couldn't believe he was letting me touch them. Every spine in the room looked ancient, and I expected an old librarian to jump out at any moment warning me of the destructive nature of the oils in my fingertips. All the titles were in a language I couldn't understand. I settled on a book with blue leather binding that looked small enough to be easily handled. I pulled it off the shelf and took it to Casper.

"What are you bringing it to me for? Open it."

I settled back into the chair and opened the book. Unsurpris-ingly, I couldn't read any of the pages. "Now what?" I looked up at him.

"Read it." He nodded to the book, urging me on.

The letters on the page moved, and I jumped in surprise. The letters snapped back into their original order. "What was that?"

"The book was doing as you commanded it. I told you to read it, and before you could think, you began to read. The letters moved to reassemble themselves in an order which you would understand. But then you lost focus, and they returned to their original places."

"So you're saying I can read anything I want in any language and it'll translate itself into English?" Excitement gathered in my stom-ach. The idea of reading anything I wanted thrilled me. A whole word opened up to me.

"Books from Elustria, yes, unless they've been enchanted not to. Most of the books in here should translate for you. The only restrictions placed on them is that they will not translate for non-mages, so you should be fine. If you come across one that won't translate, just bring it to me, and I can see what the restriction is. Go ahead and give it a try."

I wanted to replicate what had happened, so I simply thought about reading the book in my lap. As before, the letters moved and arranged themselves in place.

The theory of potion making has been studied for centuries, but its most significant leaps were made by the mages of Earth and the fae in the Flamewood Forest of Elustria.

"It says here that the mages of Earth worked on potion making. I didn't think there were officially any mages on Earth."

"There have been different periods of time in which mages have traveled to Earth more freely and openly than we do now. Throughout history, the people whom humans have deemed witches have been mages or innocent victims of religious superstition."

There was quite a difference between those two things. I had a feeling that anyone who had been burned at the stake or hanged was most definitely the latter. From what I'd seen of mages, I couldn't imagine one being killed by humans. "Are there other magical beings on Earth that aren't Elustrian?"

"It's entirely possible there are magical races here that we're unaware of. That's partly why we're so interested in studying Earth. We do know that vampires exist, and they did not originate in Elustria. As far as we can tell, they are unaware of our presence."

Having vampires confirmed to be real and not legend was not comforting. That was one paranormal being I would've been happy to keep as fiction. "How come I didn't have to say a spell to get the words to rearrange?" Questions arose quicker than I could ask them.

"Verbalizing your intent is not always necessary. Having the letters translate themselves is relatively easy, made more so by the fact that these books are all from Elustria and were made by mages. They respond more readily to your commands and intent. Spells are used to help focus exactly what it is you want the magic to do. The more difficult the task, the more likely you'll need to verbalize it. There are some great mages who never have to say a word to perform any type of magic."

"I'm confused. Are you saying I can make anything do whatever I want just by watching it? Except get this necklace off, of course." That didn't sound right.

"Hardly." Casper rose from his chair and walked over to me. He leaned against his desk, echoing the first time I met him. "It's not quite that simple. The study of magic is really learning what it takes to get magic to interact with the world around us in a way that produces the results we want. That sounds complicated, I know, and it is, but we start simple with common spells and potions, charms and enchantments. Many mages never go any further than that. They're content with living their lives in other pursuits. But some mages choose to devote their entire lives to learning the secrets of magic."

I wanted to travel to Elustria to see how this all worked in real life, not just theory. What were the day-to-day activities of mages? How did they interact and relate with the world? All that could come later when it was safe to travel there. For now, I needed to concentrate on learning as much as I could. Mages started learning magic from birth, the same way children learn to speak. I felt like an adult trying to pick up a second language for the first time. The scope of the study overwhelmed me. "So how am I going to learn all of this?"

Casper spread out his arms to indicate the books around us. "First, this library is open for your use. You can read anything you find here. Learning magic beyond the basics is, I'm afraid, a tedious process but one that can be quite exciting and satisfying should you have the passion for it." Casper lowered his arms and pointed to the book behind him on his desk. The book followed his motion, and he gracefully commanded it back to its spot on the shelf.

I followed the book with my eyes, my lips parting in anticipation. "I want to learn how to do that."

"Close your book and think the word 'levitate.'"

I did as he said and the book floated a few inches in the air above my hands. An excited squeal escaped my lips, and the book shot up toward the ceiling, startling me, and then crashed to the ground.

"You need to learn how to control your emotions; it affects the magic, especially when you're learning. Your excitement is what caused the book to shoot in the air, and then your shock broke the connection with it, and it fell to the floor. This is why we practice." Casper stretched out his hand and the book seamlessly followed his command until it was back in its place. "Let's go to the training floor, and you can meet the other two recruits."

The idea of attempting to perform magic in front of others filled me with dread. "Are you sure I won't be a distraction? I don't want to slow down their learning."

"Don't be ridiculous. They'll be excited to meet you. They're beginners, just like you. I doubt you'll be spending much time with them. Sadie and Mikael have both expressed interest in working with you one-on-one. They're fascinated with you, and you'd be wise to learn from them."

That sounded much more agreeable. My time with Sadie and Mikael had been pleasant enough. After Bolivia, I thought Sadie and I might become friends. It would be nice to learn from people who understood my situation. Since I used a talisman that I couldn't control, I didn't relish the idea of any more of an audience than necessary. The other recruits might be new too, but they weren't tied to a talisman that overpowered them.

I followed Casper to the teleportation rings. The room we ported to was a large open space that gave plenty of room to practice. In the far corner, Analise was instructing two recruits on how to shoot fire from wands. One of the recruits was a fair-skinned blonde woman with freckles who was probably in her twenties, and the other was a dark-skinned boy with black hair who looked like a high school student.

Casper shouted across the room, "Julie, Preston, take a break and come say hi to our new arrival."

The small fire in front of Preston disappeared as he walked over, Julie following.

"Julie, do you intend to burn down the building?" Analise said. "Mages are always responsible for the magic they produce." Her entire demeanor and attitude conveyed fierceness. Even her white-blonde pixie cut was all sharp points and edges.

Julie went back to her fire, and with a wave of her wand, it disappeared. Once she rejoined us, Casper introduced me. "This is Kat. She's new and may be joining you on some of your training exercises."

"Hi." I waved at them, not quite sure what to do or say. I didn't know how much of my situation Casper wanted other people knowing, so keeping silent seemed the safest bet.

"It's good to meet you. I'm Julie, and this is Preston. So did you just find out that you're a mage?" Julie spoke softly, as if she would normally be shy, but the excitement of the situation overrode her natural tendencies.

"Yeah, I had no idea." I wondered how the process had worked for them, but I couldn't think of a way of asking that wouldn't invite questions into my own experience.

"Neither did we," Julie said. "To think, if I didn't let my roommate talk me into gaming, I would've never found out."

"How old are the two of you?" I asked.

"I'm twenty-six," Julie said. "I was living in New York City before now, trying to make it in the fashion world. Luckily, magic is a lot easier."

"I'm seventeen and from Liverpool," Preston said in a gorgeously accented voice.

My estimation of him being a high school kid was accurate. His confirmation still surprised me. "Wow, so your parents were fine with you coming here?"

Before Preston could answer, Casper did. "We try not to invite too many minors, but Preston hit our radar and was close enough to leaving home that we decided to approach him. His family was given a memory alteration potion."

"What do you do if you approach someone and they don't want to come?" I'd never considered that possibility before, but it had to happen.

"The same: they get a memory alteration potion. We're pretty good at convincing people, though. A quick search of Preston's screen name showed that he was somewhat of a serial gamer. We wanted to catch him before he moved on to his next game."

"So, do you want me teaching her now, too?" Analise asked in a way that made her preference clear.

"Not right now. I don't know how successful training them together would be since she doesn't use a wand."

"You don't have a wand?" Preston asked.

"She has a talisman. It works the same as a wand," Casper answered for me.

"Oh, like you do," Julie said. "Is it that necklace?"

I clutched the amber stone in my palm, as if to assure myself it was still there. "Yeah, this is it."

Casper's illuminator orb floated in front of him, and Sadie's face appeared.

"Casper, we have something for you to look at."

"I'll be right there. Will you come down and take over teaching Kat? We're on the training floor."

"Will do. Sounds fun. I'll be there in a sec." The orb shrank and resumed its place over Casper's head.

"Analise, continue your lesson. Kat can observe until Sadie gets here." Analise, Julie, and Preston moved back to the corner they'd been in when we arrived.

Casper turned to me. "Sorry to leave you so soon, however I had planned on Sadie teaching you today. She's an expert in talisman magic. She's been dying to get a closer look at yours for a while."

"Don't worry about it. I'm excited to work with Sadie." I didn't understand how Sadie could be a better teacher than Casper when she was a wand-wielder and Casper used a talisman, but I couldn't argue with him. I was probably far beneath his level of expertise anyway.

Casper leaned in and mock whispered, "Watch out for Analise. She'll eat you alive if you cross her."

A stream of yellow lightning shot through the air between me and Casper. The visual was stunning, especially given that there were only a few inches of space to work with, but I felt no heat or anything else from it, purely ornamental.

"I heard that," Analise shouted.

Casper smiled and disappeared into the teleportation ring, leaving me with a fully-trained mage who hated me.

CHAPTER 30

I didn't know how many times I'd have to see someone appear out of thin air for the sight to be less shocking, but it would take several more, at least. Almost as soon as Casper teleported, Sadie arrived in his place.

Her affable smile cheered me. I hadn't been looking forward to spending any time with Analise. Overall, the entire atmosphere at the Armory was welcoming. I had the real sense that everyone worked together toward a common goal, but I didn't think I'd ever feel comfortable with Analise no matter how long I had to get to know her.

"You ready to get started?" Sadie walked in such a lighthearted way that I swear she skipped. No one would be able to tell that only yesterday she'd been running from an assassin.

"Yeah, I was just watching them use their wands to produce fire."

Sadie waved her hand as if that were nothing. "They're wand-wielders. They need different instruction. But don't worry, we'll get there soon. Follow me." She led the way to a room next door that Casper hadn't shown me.

"This is the actual armory. I know we call this entire place the Armory because it was back in the day, but this room here is our armory. We've got a ton of magical goodies that I think you'll like. We normally don't bring new recruits in here this early. In fact, I don't think Julie and Preston have been in here yet, but we're doing things differently." Sadie winked and giggled, absolutely giddy about showing me this room. She placed her hand on the door handle and looked back at me, letting the anticipation build.

When she opened the door with a flourish, we walked into a long, narrow room with shelves that could be found in any utility closet running along each wall. I looked up, half expecting to see flickering florescent lights. Illuminator orbs floated above our heads as they did everywhere else in the Armory. The shelves were packed with boxes and baskets of items I didn't recognize, with no apparent organizational scheme.

The excitement deflated as quickly as it had risen. With the exception of the lights, this room could appear in any building anywhere in the world. When Sadie saw my disappointment, both her arms shot out in front of her and she waved her hands, urging me not to pass judgment.

"I know it doesn't look like much, but I promise you this is the best room in the building. It's a regular Liliana's orb."

"A what?"

"Oh yeah, I forgot that's an Elustrian story. Don't you have any Earth fables, stories about not judging something by the way it looks?"

"Sure." The most amusing thing in the room was Sadie herself.

"Then this is that. I actually envy you being able to see it for the first time. Take this for instance." She reached into a box and pulled out a triangular rock with a hole in the middle and tossed it to me. I caught it but just barely. The smooth gray stone fit perfectly in my palm. It didn't appear to be anything special, just an ordinary rock someone had shaped.

"That's a cloaker."

"This is magical?" I looked at Sadie in disbelief.

"Yes. It eclipses your magic so you can't be seen. Keep that one;

190

we have a ton of them, not that they're superabundant, but they're pretty useless in Elustria."

I shoved it in my pocket. "Why? Seems like being able to hide yourself would be handy anywhere."

"I didn't say it hides you. It hides your magic, makes you appear like a void."

"A void?" I felt like an idiot asking all these questions, but I needed to learn this stuff.

"You know, a void: the absence of everything. It makes you appear as if you have no magic whatsoever. In Elustria, where magic is everywhere, it's practically painting a big red arrow above your head. Even a really bad tracker would be able to find you. Here on Earth, where magic is incredibly rare, they're handy for hiding yourself from, say, an assassin. They're not perfect by any means, since most magic can be countered if you know how, but it's handy nonetheless. You don't have to worry about it here, though. The entire Armory is cloaked."

Sadie was already walking farther down the aisle. "Now, what else do we have that you can use?" She tapped her chin with her forefinger as she scanned the shelves. "Here's a communication orb. You should have one in your room, but you can take this one around with you. No harm in having more than one."

I caught the little orb she tossed to me. "Yeah I'm not really sure how these work. I picked up the one in my room and said 'Casper' and he appeared, but is there more to it than that?"

"Yes and no. Since you're here, the orb knew you wanted to talk to Casper, so it alerted him. While you're here, you'll generally make outgoing calls with the communication orb, but the illuminators that are enchanted to follow you around will receive calls for you. You basically tell the communication orb who you want to speak with and it will contact them. The only trick to it is that you have to actually know the person, otherwise the orb on the receiving end will block the call. For instance, just because I say Raphael Godwin, doesn't mean he's going to magically appear. Can you imagine?"

Judging by the look on Sadie's face, I decided to forgo asking her who Raphael Godwin was. I didn't want to be sidetracked by a tangent about someone who I could only assume was a famous and attractive mage in Elustria.

"Ooh, illusion powder." Sadie grabbed what looked like a mix of dark purple and black glitter in a shaker. "I can't give you any of this, because we don't have much, but if sprinkled on someone, you can make them see whatever you want. As you can imagine, it's not something we want everyone having access to." She replaced the shaker and continued walking.

"And here we have the reason we had to come in here today: a wand. Since I was coming in here to get it anyway, I figured I might as well show you the cool stuff we've got. Now, this wand is just a loaner; you won't want to keep it anyway. We're going to use it strictly as a training tool. The talisman is much more powerful, but I wanted you to have the experience of using a wand just to compare." She handed me a stick that I wouldn't have been able to distinguish from the one Mikael had shown at the dinner table last night. It didn't feel magical—none of these items did. It seemed that holding a magical conduit should feel different.

"Now it's time for some fun," Sadie said. "Let's get out of here and start using magic."

When we left the supply closet, as I would be calling it, I noticed there were no locks on the door, but the handle glowed when Sadie closed the door behind her. Probably another magical object, opening for those allowed access and staying closed for anyone else.

The floor and walls of the room Sadie took me to were all made of some material that resembled gym mats. If they were white instead of green, I'd assume it was a padded room in an old asylum. A few utilitarian chairs sat around the room. Why couldn't magic be taught in a more inviting space?

"I know it doesn't look like much, but when starting out, we need to use one of these training rooms. They have some magical enhancements to make sure you don't accidentally, say, destroy the building."

"Makes sense. Is that what the padding's for?" I asked.

"That and to act as a cushion should you fall or blast someone into the wall. They are enchanted, but the padding's there to prevent harm."

Her answers never seemed to put me at ease. Images of me inadvertently throwing her or me against the wall flashed through my mind.

"Based on what you and Casper have said, you're having trouble controlling the magic from the talisman."

"So far it's only protected me or caused things to happen when I lose control of my emotions. I've done a little with ice and water, but I wouldn't say I had much control."

Sadie nodded. "That's pretty common—not the defensive charms but the emotion thing. The charms on the talisman will only defend you from a direct attack, but they won't go on the offensive. A charm like that would be too dangerous because you could end up hurting a friend with it."

I'd already hurt a friend with magic, no charm required. I wanted to be able to play with fire like Julie and Preston did, but I'd settle for being able to do anything I could control at this point. Before I could even think of defending myself, I needed to learn how to keep my magic from unintentionally harming others. "So what exactly is the wand for?" I asked. The thin stick did nothing but make me worry I'd accidentally break it.

"A wand is a bit easier than a talisman to work with in the beginning when you haven't grown up with magic. You're the first latent mage I know of to have a talisman, and really, a wand is just another form of a talisman. We've found that mages on Earth respond best to a wand. I think it has something to do with all of your folklore around witches. Having a wand seems to make more sense to you. Yours is going to be a temporary tool so we can get some early successes out of the way. I want you to leave this room today confident that you can perform magic."

She was far more optimistic than I was, but I liked her spirit. I didn't have time to mess around. I may be a newbie here, but my situation was different than the recruits. They could take all the time they needed. I didn't have that luxury. The assassin hunting me had shown that he wouldn't slow down.

Sadie pulled her own wand from her sleeve. "In your talisman, the magic is stored in the amber stone. You interact with it to perform different spells. With the wand, the magic is stored in the wood, in little fibers called filaments. When you engage with the wand, you'll see those filaments light up. It's a different color depending on the mage and the wand. So for instance, you'll see that when I do this"—she twirled her wand and frost came out of the tip —"my wand lights up with this purple design." She spelled the word "wow" in ice. With a flick of her wrist it was gone. The purple threads illuminating her wand appeared to form an organic pattern with no rhyme or reason.

"We're going to start with water elemental magic since that's the spell you activated in-game and the one you've already used a little with Casper. With the wand, you'll feel what it's like to exercise more control over it."

"So are all the spells in the game real?" That could prove advantageous. I'd played the game for years. My knowledge of the spells was near encyclopedic, especially for the class I played.

"No, but a lot of them are. It's our way of engaging any latent sparks out there. But we're only focusing on one right now. I want you to hold out your wand and say 'frostline' while giving it a little flick."

I did as she instructed, and to my amazement a line of frost shot from the tip of my wand. Sadie jumped up and down while clapping.

"Exactly! I told you you'd be able to do it. Did you feel how the wand helped channel your magic and directed it the way you wanted?"

194

"Yes." I didn't have to pretend to understand; I actually felt it. It was kind of like how I could feel my arm direct the arc of a ball I threw. "How come it doesn't feel this way when I use the talisman?"

"Oh, it will. The issue you're running into with your talisman is mainly a mental one. Like I said, you put more faith in waving a wand around than you do shooting ice from your hands. The other issue is that the talisman is much more powerful than the wand, so it's harder to control."

"If talismans are more powerful, why doesn't everyone use one?" All I heard was how great my talisman was, yet the triplets all chose wands. The only other talisman I'd seen was Casper's.

"Not all talismans are equal. Yours is exceptionally powerful. Many mages don't have access to a talisman since it's pretty rare to find one more powerful than a wand. Some mages have advanced so far with the wand that they wouldn't want a talisman anyway. A person's wand or talisman is a part of them, a very intimate part. It's why we don't want people touching them, and even the mention of taking one from someone is offensive, as Mikael pointed out. I don't want you to get attached to this wand, so I won't be treating it as if it's yours. Your mother left you a talisman, and in our world, that's a sacred thing."

Even though I hadn't yet developed the ability to use my talisman's power, I could understand what she meant. A sort of bond had already developed between me and the amber stone. I didn't know if it was because my mother left it to me or because it had saved my life. I suppose the reason didn't matter as much as the fact that the bond existed. I could imagine after years of use I wouldn't want to use a wand or another talisman. "Do mages ever use both?"

"Yes!" She clapped her hands together again as if I had said something remarkably clever. "You've hit on one of the big advantages mages have over sorcerers. Sorcerers can only perform one spell at a time. So for instance, if a sorcerer is in a fight, they'd have to first cast a shield and then an attack, whereas a mage could use multiple wands and talismans to cast a shield and an attack at the same time.

It's pretty rare, mainly because most mages don't have a need to develop the skill. Your mother could double-wield."

Performing two spells at once sounded intriguing but not like something I could do. The more I learned about my birth mother, the more badass she sounded. If it weren't for the insistence of the talisman that I was its rightful owner, I wouldn't believe I was her daughter. Already I thought of my talisman as a separate entity with a will of its own, like a pet.

"Try the spell again, but really control it this time. Make a design or do something with it."

I raised my wand and repeated the spell. I drew a heart in front of me and then pulled back my wand arm and flung it forward, shooting a bolt of ice from the tip through the middle of the heart. As soon as the ice went through the heart, the heart melted as my concentration left it. "Wow, this is a lot easier than I thought it was going to be."

"I'm glad you think so. Now try to do the frost spell using your talisman." Sadie took my wand and placed it on a chair.

"The frost came out of the tip of the wand, so why doesn't it come out of the talisman itself?" An amusing image of me pulling my shoulders back and thrusting my chest from side to side to get ice to come out of the talisman filled my mind.

"The frost comes out of the wand because that's what you want— it's where you're channeling it. The talisman channels the magic for you and directs it wherever you tell it to. If you wanted, you could shoot ice out of your elbow using a wand or talisman. It's simply more intuitive to do it with your hands or through your wand, if you're using one."

Holding onto the confidence the wand had given me, I lifted my hand and used the spell to draw a heart again. It looked more like a lopsided oval and was much bigger than I intended. When I sent the arrow through the middle, the heart exploded and the arrow crashed into the wall, summoning flashbacks of shooting Alex. The unwieldy magic of my talisman felt completely different from the wand.

Sadie waved her wand and the shards of ice disappeared before they could hit us. "And that's why we do this in a little practice room. Did you feel how the power of your talisman is stronger than that of the wand?"

"Yes, it's overwhelming. I don't know how I could possibly control it." Using the talisman after the wand was like trying to write with my non-dominant hand. It was awkward and without the fine control I had with the wand.

"That's where practice comes in."

I tried again, this time with less force, and my hand acted more like an ice dispenser on a soda machine, little bits of frozen water trickling out of it and falling to the ground. "I can't feel the intricacy like I could with the wand."

"That's normal. Do it with the wand again to get a feel for it."

I took a step toward the chair that my wand sat on, but Sadie stopped me.

"How about you call it to you magically? Hold out your hand and say 'come, wand.'"

I held out my hand and repeated the phrase, and the wand flew to my hand.

"Excellent. You're beginning to think and act like a mage."

I highly doubted that Sadie was capable of being negative, but I didn't let that keep her words of encouragement from lifting my spirits and my confidence. She celebrated each baby step with me, and by the time we broke for lunch, I felt like a mage.

CHAPTER 31

Discovering Your Magic Later in Life: A Latent Mage's Guide to Spells. The hefty volume of spells sounded exactly like what I needed, but I resented the "later in life" title. Sure, I wasn't a child, but I wasn't exactly middle-aged either.

I'd eaten with Mikael and Sadie who informed me that Casper had left on a short business trip not long after leaving me. They thought it best that I spend the afternoon studying, so after lunch I grabbed *Discovering Your Magic Later in Life* and some other books from the library on Mikael's recommendation and plopped down on my bed to study.

Specificity is key. The new mage may wonder why some things, such as levitating objects, are easy while others are more difficult. The key to directing the magic to do what one wants is to find the exact words or thoughts to command it. For instance, telling an object to "rise" would result in the object standing upright. The proper command if one would like the object to rise into the air is "levitate." Other, more complex tasks require even more specific commands. It is for that reason that spells are often performed, especially in the beginning, using the Cadaran language.

Cadaran is the oldest known language in Elustria. It is what many believe our ancestors spoke when they first emerged out of the great magical orb of Elustria herself. The language is no longer spoken in common use because of its great power. Just as there are nuances in all languages, there are nuances in Cadaran that make it the most suitable language for performing spells. You will find, however, that almost all spells can be adequately performed using whatever language the mage natively speaks.

In this volume, each spell is written out twice. The first occurrence is in Cadaran and is unable to be translated. Directly underneath the spell, it is repeated without a binding placed on it so the reader may translate it into their language of choice. It is recommended that one first try the spell in Cadaran to get a more accurate feel for the spell and achieve an early success.

Some mages choose to perform all their spells in the ancient language, but this is entirely unnecessary and is not encouraged for the simple reason that spells are most easily recalled in one's native tongue.

More theory followed the introduction, but I didn't have patience for that. I flipped through to the spells and got to work.

CHAPTER 32

*A*fter practicing all day, I was mentally exhausted and didn't want to worry about carrying on a conversation, so I opted to eat alone in my room. That might have been a mistake. With nothing but a hearty beef stew to hold my attention, my thoughts wandered.

I pictured Alex in his panther form among the snow. He'd probably already headed back south. By this time, he could be hundreds of miles away. Strange how someone could come into my life for such a short amount of time and completely and utterly disrupt it. In all likelihood, I would never see him again, which seemed strange given all we had shared.

Before I could talk myself out of it, I picked up my phone and called Alex's number, already knowing what I'd hear.

"We're sorry, but the number you're trying to reach has been disconnected."

If Alex were here, he'd be impressed by my progress. It didn't seem fair that he only got to see my magic in a negative light. I missed his support, his protection, his kiss. But he didn't have feelings for me, not really. The attraction had been the product of the talisman, nothing more.

201

The world my phone connected me to seemed so far away. The more time passed, the more I questioned whether or not I'd ever return to that life. Among my notifications was a voicemail from a call I'd missed while practicing. My heart rate increased when I saw the number it came from.

"Hello, Kat. I see you've made some new friends since I last saw you. That was quite the entourage you had in Bolivia. At first, I thought that shifter of yours took you to an enclave, but thanks to this computer you left behind, I see that your new friend is quite powerful. I don't think becoming a wealthy and famous business owner is the way for a mage to lie low. Tell Casper that Marcus says hi." The message ended.

Holy shit. At least now I had the assassin's name. I picked up my communication orb and said Casper's name. Nothing happened. He must still be on his non-magical business trip.

The lightning from my talisman must not have fried my computer as I'd thought. It wouldn't have been hard for Marcus to figure out Casper's identity, especially since he saw him in Bolivia. Since I kept all of my logins and passwords stored in an app on my computer, Marcus had access to everything. Between my email from Magical Games, Inc. about my prize trip and all the articles and sites I had bookmarked about the game, he would have easily found a picture of Casper and put it all together. Marcus may have even figured out how to log in to my credit card accounts and seen my purchases, the early breakfast at the diner on the way to Canada, confirming that I'd headed to Magical Games, Inc. The image of Marcus sitting at my desk, on my computer, snooping around left me feeling violated. My apartment, my home, was tainted now, even more than it had been with the tracker orb.

Casper wouldn't be back until tomorrow. Until then, I'd keep this knowledge to myself. The best thing I could do was study. Marcus would continue his search until he found me. I had faith in Casper's ability to protect me, but for how long? The spells I'd learned today would do little should I ever find myself in trouble. The most beneficial addition to my arsenal had been the magic cloaker from the supply closet, but I didn't even know how to use it.

With the cloaker comfortably in my pocket, I went to the library in search of a book that would tell me how to use it. Waiting until morning to ask Sadie or Mikael would be more effective, but I needed to do something to feel like I was making progress toward protecting myself.

The titles on the spines of the books rearranged themselves as I browsed through them until I saw *Common Magical Objects and Their Uses*. That seemed like the most likely book to help me. Instead of grabbing it with my hand, I pulled it from the shelf using magic. Thinking like a mage, that's what Sadie had called it, and it's what I needed to do. Even with Casper gone and virtually zero possibility of anyone walking in on me, I didn't dare sit on the throne chair. Instead, I cuddled up in one of the brown leather chairs and went to work researching the cloaker.

CHAPTER 33

"at, where are you?"

I jumped at the sound of Mikael's voice, sending the book in my lap toppling to the ground. The illuminator that had lit my reading last night floated in front of me, displaying Mikael's face. Books lay scattered on the floor, and a line of drool slid down my chin.

"Did I wake you?" Mikael asked with a mixed look of apology and bafflement. All sense of time had left me last night as I read, so I had no trouble believing that I'd slept away much of the morning.

"No," I said unconvincingly as I wiped the drool from my chin and sat up. A yawn betrayed me when I opened my mouth to say more. "Maybe. I'm in the library. I must have fallen asleep reading."

"Sounds like a fun night." From anyone else, it would sound sarcastic, but I knew from Mikael's expression and the enthusiasm with which he'd recommended books yesterday that he spoke sincerely. "I'm going to be working with you some today. Do you think you can teleport to the training floor?"

"Sure," I said, determined to do it on my own even if I didn't feel capable. Casper had insisted nothing could go wrong, and I'd successfully teleported with others several times. Even if it took me a few tries, the idea of teleporting on my own excited me, gave me a sense of freedom. "Do you mind if I freshen up and have some breakfast first?"

"No, of course not. I'll meet you in half an hour."

"It's a date," I said, but Mikael's face had already disappeared.

After I placed the books back on the shelf, I realized I should've levitated them there, but I was too tired to think like a mage. I put the cloaker back in my pocket and headed upstairs with *Common Magical Objects and Their Uses*. It had contained information about working both the communication orb and the cloaker, and I might want to reference it in the future. The rest of the books had been for fun. An entirely new world had opened to me full of endless possibilities to discover. I hadn't experienced this kind of rush from learning since before my parents had died.

CHAPTER 34

$\mathcal{S}$tanding in the teleportation ring with my cloaker and communication orb in my jeans pocket and my wand in hand, I took a deep breath, closed my eyes, and envisioned the training floor as clearly as I could remember it. Every other thought fell from my mind. The feeling of being squeezed started almost immediately. Even so, it still surprised me to find myself on the training floor when I opened my eyes. It didn't seem possible to successfully teleport on my first try alone, but there I was, facing Mikael who mirrored my own delight back to me.

"Congratulations! That's your first solo teleport, correct?"

"Yeah, I got it on my first try."

"I knew you would. I can tell all this still confuses you, as if you feel you might not belong, but trust me, Kat, you're a very talented mage. You have as much right to be here as anyone."

"Thanks." It sounded lame and not at all sufficient to express the gratitude I felt for him saying it. I wanted badly to belong here, but the adjustment to not only new people and surroundings, but a new identity, was as difficult as it was exciting.

"I wanted to work with you today so we could discuss the reading you did yesterday," Mikael said as he led me to yet another new room. This one was set up like a conventional classroom with pairs of chairs and desks facing a blank wall instead of a whiteboard. Wands would no doubt act as markers.

"Go ahead and take a seat anywhere you like." I chose a desk at the front of the room, and Mikael pulled a chair around to face me. "From my wake-up call this morning, I take it you took to the reading well."

"It's all so fascinating. I wish learning about Earth was this fun."

A wide grin spread across Mikael's face. "Imagine how I felt coming here. Learning about Earth was as fascinating for me as it is for you to learn about Elustria. Did you have a chance to practice any spells?"

"Yes, the first book I devoured was a spell book you recommended. It did a good job of explaining everything, but I didn't learn anything there that's going to help me protect myself." I remembered the voicemail I'd received yesterday. "Is Casper back yet?"

"No. Why? Do you need something?" Mikael appeared eager to help.

"The assassin left me another voicemail. I wanted Casper to listen to it."

"I'll let him know if I see him before you do." Mikael leaned forward, his eyes taking on a more earnest intensity. "You're safe here. I know it may not feel like it after Bolivia, but there's really not much cause for you to worry about defending yourself. There's a reason you've only encountered the assassin outside the Armory."

Mikael's words were reassuring. I still needed Casper to have all the latest information, but there was no need to be scared. "You're right, but I want to continue in my mother's footsteps. I'm not saying I'll ever be as good as she was," I hastily corrected, "but I want to continue her legacy. That's why reading about Elustria and our history didn't seem like a chore."

Mikael leaned back in his chair. "I'm glad to hear that. We can always use another good mage. Have you tried getting the talisman off again?"

I looked at my fidgeting hands and forced them still. "No. To be honest, I don't really see much point anymore. When I first came here, I wanted it off because it scared me; I couldn't understand it. Now it's becoming a part of me, of who I am. I can understand the bond you and Sadie were talking about with your wands."

"That's understandable." Mikael nodded to my desk. "I see you have your wand with you now. Do you prefer using it over the talisman?"

"In some ways it's easier, but it feels more foreign, if that makes sense. It's a nice learning tool, but I feel more ownership of the magic when I use my talisman, even if it's more difficult to control."

"That's fair. We do need to figure out how to take the talisman off, though, so you might want to try. Once you've mastered the stone, it will obey you in all things. If you tell it to release around your neck, it will."

That didn't collate with my experience. While I couldn't exercise fine control of the magic of my talisman, it had so far done what I'd wanted it to with this one glaring exception. "Dorran said I can't remove what's part of me."

"Ah. Dorran is wise. I'm still a little jealous that you got to meet him and I haven't. You just need to remember that taking off the necklace isn't removing it. Your talisman will always be a part of you and no one is trying to take that away."

"Why is it so important? I want it on now." Maybe that was the problem, the talisman knew I wanted it. I'd already accepted it as part of my life. As long as I could control it, I didn't see any reason to take it off.

"That's why Casper tried to take it off of you before you started working with magic. The more you want it on, the harder it's going to be to take it off. That's problematic, because the ultimate goal is to get you to Elustria. As soon as we can be sure of your safety, we fully intend to take you there. Once there, however, your talisman will need to be registered with the Magesterial Council. That can't happen if it can't be removed." Mikael shifted in his seat, as if there were more he wanted to say but couldn't.

"Wouldn't the Magesterial Council have a way of taking it off?" There had been a chapter on registering magical items with the Council in *Common Magical Objects and Their Uses*, but I'd only glanced over it.

"They're not going to let you keep a talisman you can't control. That's why we're hoping to remove it here." Mikael paused, as if figuring out how much to say. "The other reason we want to get it off is because your mother may have left a message in it, and we would like to examine it closer without triggering the defensive charms she placed on it. We think the charms will break as soon as the talisman releases itself from you."

"What kind of message?" My heart leapt at the possibility of discovering something more from my mother.

"We're not sure, but she would have wanted you to carry on her legacy, or if you weren't up to it, someone else. The problem is that Meglana often worked alone, so we're left without a lot of information. It's important that we not let all of her work be in vain."

Given all the progress I had made, I might be able to remove the necklace now. I cleared my mind, took a deep breath, and visualized the chain of the necklace breaking as I pulled on it. Nothing happened. Maybe breaking was the wrong visualization. I didn't want to damage the talisman. The chain may not hold the magic, but it was crucial in keeping the talisman safe with me. I tried again, this time picturing a clasp unhooking. Still no luck.

Frustration welled up inside me, but it wouldn't help anything. I pushed it aside and tried to believe that the knowledge would come with study and practice.

"Don't worry," Mikael said. "Try to take it off whenever you think about it, otherwise leave it to Casper and the rest of us to worry about. You're one of us now."

One of them—a mage. I'd found my place among my mother's people. I wasn't Serafina, Dark Sorceress anymore or Kat Thomas, scholarship loser. I was Kat, Mage-In-Training, daughter of Meglana. This was only the start of my quest to avenge my mother and uphold her legacy. I wasn't playing solo, though; this was a group quest, and I had a pretty good group.

Except for Analise. Every group had a pain-in-the-ass person no one wanted to play with but did anyway because they were family. She filled that role nicely.

CHAPTER 35

"*A*m I interrupting anything?"

I turned in my seat to see Casper standing in the doorway. Mikael and I had been working for hours. He'd proved a great resource to answer questions about my reading the previous night. His enthusiasm for the subject matter carried us on a natural course from my questions to the next level of learning. It had been such an engaging discussion that I didn't even notice the time passing until Casper interrupted us.

"No, not at all. Please, join us," Mikael said.

"How was your trip?" I asked.

"It went well." Casper sat in a chair next to Mikael, facing me. "How are the lessons coming?"

"I'm starting to get a handle on things. There's so much to learn, but I think I'll get there." My time with Mikael and Sadie had given me the confidence that I was capable of learning all of this. They didn't make me feel inadequate or slow, so I took that as a good sign.

"You've made good progress in a short amount of time. Sadie and Mikael have had nothing but good things to say. I bet you're laughing at the girl who came here scared of her talisman and wanting it off."

Casper's easygoing smile transported me back to the first time I met him. So much had changed since then. I now had casual conversations with a man who I had idolized as the creator of my favorite game. At the time, I had been terrified of the amber stone that seemed to act with a mind of its own. The bond I'd forged with the talisman over time made it mine. "I'm starting to feel more control over it, but that hasn't helped me remove it. I wish I didn't need to take it off to get it registered with the Council. I really just want to focus on developing the skills I need to defend myself and avenge my mother."

"It's just a matter of finding the right solution." Casper covered my hand with his own. "Your mother's genius far outstripped ours. I'm not surprised your talisman, which was once hers, is more difficult to control than most. We'll get there. Would you like to try now?"

"Sure. What do you want me to do?" What I really wanted was to learn how to fight, to use magic for more than just convenience and amusing tricks. But if I couldn't exercise even this most basic control over my talisman, I doubted Casper or anyone else would feel comfortable trying to teach me how to fight.

"I have another spell we can try in Cadaran," Casper said. "I thought you could try it by yourself first. Then, if it doesn't work, I can add my magic to yours."

"Just tell me what to say. It might help if you tell me the English translation so I can visualize it better."

"Very good." Casper sounded proud of my new knowledge. "Currend te degrilo. It roughly means to surrender and come undone."

Just like I had every other time, I closed my eyes and recited the spell, visualizing the necklace coming off. I reminded myself that I needed this to happen in order to register with the Magesterial Council. If I couldn't get the talisman off, becoming a real mage wouldn't even be an option. Despite my earnest effort, the chain didn't budge.

"Ugh." I slammed my fist on the desk in frustration, which did nothing to help get the necklace off, but it did hurt my hand a little.

"No, no, don't get frustrated," Casper said. "That won't help anything. We'll get there. Do you want to try it with me now?"

I shook the frustration out of my hands and took a deep breath. "Sure."

Casper stood behind me and placed his hands over mine where they touched the chain. "Ready?"

I nodded and closed my eyes as I recited the spell with him. The sound of desks crashing into each other startled me, and I opened my eyes in time to see Mikael rush from his seat. When I turned to see what had happened, Casper lay motionless against the far wall, his eyes closed.

Fear gripped me. Had I just killed one of the few people in this world capable of helping me? When I reached him, the sight of his chest rising and falling sent relief pouring through me. Not dead, just unconscious. Not good, but not calamitous.

"I'm so sorry. I don't know what happened."

"It's not your fault." Mikael didn't look at me as he pulled a communication orb from his pocket and said, "Sadie." The orb expanded in size and floated in front of his face as Sadie appeared before him. "Casper's been injured. He's unconscious. I'm going to need your help. Meet me in the infirmary."

"I'm on my way," Sadie said. Before the orb stopped transmitting, I could hear Analise's voice in the background.

"It's that girl. She's going to be nothing but trouble. Clearly she doesn't want—"

The connection ended.

Mikael looked guiltily at me before turning his attention back to Casper. "Don't pay Analise any mind. I've got to take care of this. Go back to your room or the library or wherever. I'll call you when there's news."

Tears welled up in my eyes, and I knew if I tried to speak, I wouldn't be able to control myself. I strode quickly from the room to the teleportation ring, not even taking a second to marvel at how easily I was able to teleport to the living area. The tears stayed in place until I shut my bedroom door behind me and fell on the bed, feeling more alone than I ever had.

CHAPTER 36

$\mathcal{I}$ndulging in self-pity wasn't attractive. Loneliness overwhelmed me, but crying about it wouldn't solve anything. I grabbed my phone to call Nicole, but could I really talk to her about this? What would I say? She couldn't know the truth, and I couldn't bring myself to lie again. I had to tough this one out on my own.

I looked at my phone and saw my voicemail notifications. With all the focus on removing the necklace, I'd forgotten to tell Casper about Marcus's message. He needed to know, so I put the phone in my pocket to remind myself to tell him.

Regardless of what happened with Casper, I still had work to do. Before I'd fallen asleep the previous night, I'd found the instructions for working the cloaker. I needed to practice using it and performing the spells I'd learned so far.

I held the triangular stone in the middle of my palm in front of me and thought, "Conceal magic." Nothing happened. Last night, after finding the instructions, I'd moved quickly on to other reading, too excited to learn all I could to bother with practicing. According to the book, the stone should light up in some way to indicate it had been activated.

"Conceal magic," I said with my most authoritative tone. This time the stone flickered, then died. "Conceal magic." It flickered more strongly but still, ultimately, died.

"Voclevar." An intricate black design illuminated the face of the stone. The old language had done the trick. Certain Cadaran words had more nuanced meanings than their English counterparts could relay. This appeared to be one such instance.

"Endara." The black design disappeared. I put the stone in the same jeans pocket that held the communication orb. I hadn't yet had an opportunity to try out the orb, and given the tense situation, I didn't think now was the best time.

I'd had a chance to run through my entire repertoire of spells once before I heard anything from Mikael.

"Casper's going to be fine. Don't worry. You didn't do anything wrong." The benefit of communicating through orbs was seeing the other person's face, and Mikael's expression assured me he was sincere.

"Is there anything I can do?"

"Just keep practicing your magic. Casper really is fine. I'm sending some lunch up for you. Eat and practice, and we'll all get together in an hour or two. Sound good?"

"Yeah, just let Casper know I'm sorry."

"He knows. Have a good lunch."

After the call with Mikael ended, hot soup and a sandwich appeared. I wondered who had prepared the meal. Other than the helicopter pilot, I hadn't seen anyone except for the triplets and the new recruits. I doubted any of them spent time preparing food. From my research, there were magical devices to assist in cooking, but someone still had to put together the ingredients.

The soup made me feel a little better, and after I finished eating, it was easy to pick up the spell book and continue practicing my control. I decided to leave the wand untouched, figuring that the more I used the magic in my talisman, the more likely it would be to obey me in other matters. If I could learn to control the magic in the amber stone the same way I could the wand, I couldn't even imagine the possibilities.

CHAPTER 37

My hands manipulated the ice in front of me into a likeness of Casper as I'd last seen him against the wall. Emotion charged the memory and focused my efforts to wrangle the talisman's magic. Not to brag, but I could definitely see a future for myself as an ice sculptor. It baffled me that in only a few hours I had developed this level of control, yet I couldn't do something as simple as remove the necklace.

"The resemblance is uncanny."

I jumped at Mikael's voice and quickly dismissed the ice sculpture of Casper. I turned around to see one of the orbs in my room displaying Mikael's face.

"Thanks. How is Casper?" It'd been hours since Mikael had last communicated with me. The time had flown as I honed my control of the ice spell. If I hadn't been so worried about Casper, I'd be celebrating my victory.

"As I told you, he's fine. I'm afraid there have been some developments. You need to go to the map room. Do you think you can get there by yourself?"

"Of course. Is everything all right?" I asked. Mikael's uneasy tone put me on alert.

"No, but Casper will explain when you get there."

Mikael's face disappeared and nerves assaulted my stomach. He had said Casper was fine and that Casper would be the one talking to me, so at least I knew I hadn't killed him. There must be a development with Marcus.

It took two tries with the teleportation ring to get to the map room. I'd only been there once, and my anxiety over what awaited me blurred my concentration.

When I entered, Analise and Casper stared at me. A quick survey of the room showed no sign of Mikael or Sadie. The atmosphere was eerily still. Unable to bear the intense stares, I broke the silence. "Mikael said something was wrong."

"That's an understatement," Analise mumbled under her breath just loud enough for me to hear.

Casper reproached her with a look then focused on me. "Marcus, a known assassin for hire, came to Magical Games headquarters today asking questions about you. I guess we know who killed Meglana now. The question is, how would he know to go there?" Casper stood perfectly still, as if sheer willpower kept his anger in check. The tight control he exercised over his voice made me fearful of the rage that would require such restraint to conceal. "I understand him tracking your talisman. That's to be expected, but it's been days since you were there. He found us in Bolivia before he found my business. He shouldn't have any idea who I am, at least not my human identity."

Shit, after all he had done for me, my stupid forgetfulness had brought trouble to his door. If only I had remembered sooner, he could have prepared for this. "I forgot to tell you. I meant to, but then you were traveling, and when you got back we were trying to get the talisman off, and it slipped my mind."

"Tell me what?" Casper's eyes narrowed to dark slits. Storm clouds seemed to roll across his face, waiting for the lightning to strike.

Cold fear crept around my rib cage and up to my heart. To an outsider, Casper might appear calm. But knowing the context surrounding the situation, I had a very different take on his demeanor. "I got a voicemail from him yesterday. He said to tell you that he says hi. After he saw us in Bolivia, he figured out who you were because of my computer. Turns out it wasn't destroyed by the lightning from my talisman."

"You knew this last night, and you neglected to tell anyone?" Analise stepped toward me, and I genuinely thought she'd hit me.

"I tried to call Casper, but he was gone. I told Mikael this morning about the voicemail. He said not to worry and that he'd let me know as soon as Casper was back."

"That doesn't excuse this deceit. There are two other people in this facility you could've told, but you chose not to." I don't know what kept Analise from physically assaulting me. She clearly wanted to.

"I'm sorry. I don't know why I should have thought to tell you or Sadie after telling Mikael." I didn't say more even though I wanted to point out that she was illustrating why I hadn't felt comfortable telling her.

"Yeah, well sorry isn't enough. You've exposed this entire operation, endangered the work we're trying to do here," Analise said. "Some of us have spent our entire lives fighting for something. This isn't pretend for us; it's not a nice little vacation from our real lives."

Defensiveness propelled me a step toward her. "I don't think that at all. I'm sorry, I didn't mean to endanger anything or anyone."

"And how do we know you're not a mole of some sort? It's all just so convenient how you suddenly appear with a talisman more powerful than any we've seen, and yet no one can get it off to examine it. You almost killed Casper here with it. How do we know you're not using it as some kind of cover to attack him? An innocent little girl who can't control anything. It's all the fault of that stone. I'm not buying it anymore." Analise crossed her arms around her chest, which at least meant she couldn't hit me.

"That's not true. I never meant to hurt Casper. I want to be a part of this work like my mother."

"A likely story."

I turned to Casper to see if he believed any of what Analise was saying. "You found me. You know the truth."

"What I know is that you've led Marcus, an assassin, to my company. No one in Elustria knew of my identity here. This entire operation is now in danger. I can't allow that. I can't allow him to find out that we're using *Wizards and Fae* to recruit new mages, to restore the birthright of our brothers and sisters on Earth. This cause is too great. It's bigger than all of us. You've brought trouble to my door and given us nothing to justify the risk."

"She's been playing us this whole time." Analise moved next to Casper just in case I didn't feel ganged up on enough already.

"No, I haven't. I swear." My heart raced, and I gulped in air. Was this what a panic attack felt like? I'd never had one before. This couldn't be happening.

"I have to agree with Analise. All of the evidence points to it. I know you're Meglana's daughter, and maybe that's blinded me to your true nature, but you've done nothing but lie to us since you got here. If you didn't want that talisman around your neck, it would come off at your command. Your mother spent her entire life searching for more power. After she passed it all to you, you came here hoping that your talisman would give you cover to kill us and claim some of our power for your own."

"That doesn't even make sense. I can barely do magic." This had to be a nightmare. I must have fallen asleep after going to my room.

"I don't know what makes sense anymore," Casper said. "I don't know what the truth is. All I do know is that Marcus is getting closer, and he's not going to stop until he finds you. I cannot justify endangering our entire operation for one person. I'm sorry. I really am. Enzaro!"

The world went dark.

CHAPTER 38

*T*he freezing asphalt scratched my cheek and hands as I moved to stand. Thick clouds filled the sky, making it impossible to judge the time. Little bits of snow swirled around my face before making their way gently to the ground. I pulled my phone from my pocket, but it had no signal. Without a signal, the battery would die quickly, and I didn't have a charger with me. I turned it off and put it in my pocket opposite the cloaker and communication orb. My ID and credit card were still between my phone and its case. That was all I had with me.

It only took one try to get the cloaker operational. Out here on my own, I was vulnerable to more than just the elements. Marcus had proven that he wouldn't stop looking for me. Supposedly, the cloaker would continue to work until deactivated, but I made a mental note to check on it periodically.

Protected as much as I could be from Marcus, I took stock of my surroundings. I had no idea where I was. The Armory had been north of the Magical Games headquarters, but I'd slept during some of the helicopter ride. Even if I had been awake, I doubted I would've gathered any information that would prove useful now.

The asphalt beneath my feet was crumbling and in disrepair.

Potholes dotted the one lane road. To my right, all I saw was an endless stretch of blacktop surrounded by trees so thick they concealed any light that might have indicated a building. No turnoffs appeared on either side of the road. To my left, the horizon appeared slightly lighter, as if there might be something if I continued down the road that disappeared around a bend. Assuming I hadn't been out of it all night, the air would be getting colder. I chose to go left, hoping I was correct. If I wasn't, there wouldn't be time to rectify my decision before I froze to death.

As I walked, I remembered my family vacations to Lake Powell and sang the country songs we'd listen to on the drive. The hot Arizona sun warmed me now, and the songs helped me push forward despite the fact that I shivered so much it was a miracle I could walk at all.

One foot in front of the other. I lost myself in a mental playlist of songs I associated with happier, warmer times. I focused so strongly on moving forward that the sight of a gas station on my left surprised me. The artificial yellow light inside called to me, and I ran to it. Warmth hit me as soon as I opened the door, and for a few minutes all I could do was luxuriate in it. My skin itched as the blood started flowing again.

"Can I help you find something?" A man who appeared too young for his balding head stood behind the counter.

"My car broke down, and I had to hike here." With the imminent danger of freezing to death taken care of, I needed to come up with a plan. "I actually need to get back across the U.S. border. How far of a drive is it from here?"

"You're looking at three hours."

"You know anyone headed that way?"

"Nope, but plenty of truckers stop in here. Might find one that'd welcome the conversation. On these long hauls, the radio can get pretty boring."

"Do you mind if I hang out here while I consider my options?"

Hitchhiking was the only viable plan, but I wasn't completely comfortable with it.

"Not at all, especially if you buy something."

Using my credit card wouldn't be wise with Marcus having access to my computer. I would need to change the password to my online credit card account first. This qualified as a good reason to use some of my precious battery life. After I updated my password, I powered my phone down and grabbed a coffee and donut.

"If anyone comes in who is headed south, will you send them my way?"

"Sure. You won't have to wait long."

The donut took the edge off my hunger, and I paced around the convenience store, sipping my coffee and thinking about what I could do. I needed to get to my car, but that would require crossing the border, and I had the same ID problem now that I did earlier. If I could get a ride, I could stop before the border and then cross by foot. The battery on my phone should be able to last long enough to navigate me to my car if I kept it off until then.

The risk of freezing to death wandering in the wilderness was high, but I didn't see any other option. At this point, calling anyone for help would only endanger them. No human could protect me. They would only end up as collateral damage. Once I had my car, I could develop a plan.

"Nick says you're looking for someone headed south."

I turned to see a middle-aged man wearing jeans and a flannel shirt. A trucker hat covered long brown hair pulled back in a pony-tail. Whiskers surrounding a mustache completed the stereotypical picture. He may have looked messy, but he smelled fine, which was the first criteria for someone I'd potentially be spending hours with in close quarters.

"Yeah, I am. I don't have any cash on me, but I have a credit card. I can buy snacks or diesel for payment."

"Don't worry about it. I'll appreciate the company."

The thought of voluntarily getting into a truck with a stranger seemed unwise. I tried to convince myself otherwise. If he meant me harm, surely he'd let me buy him some diesel first, get the most out of the experience. Or maybe this was a nice-guy act to lure me in.

Nick spoke up from behind the register. "John here's a good guy. Known him since he was a kid. I go to church with his mama. He'll get you where you're going safe."

Plenty of criminals had mamas who went to church, but I'd already established that hitchhiking was the only option, so I might as well go with a guy who had a recommendation. The likelihood that this was an elaborate operation, waiting for vulnerable young women to come stumbling out of the woods to kidnap them, seemed far-fetched. "All right. Thanks for the offer."

John led the way to his truck. I'd never been in a semi before, and the amount of space in the red cab surprised me.

"Have you been driving truck long?" I asked.

"Since I was old enough to. I inherited the business from my daddy. What do you do?"

My first instinct was to lie, but there wasn't much harm in telling the truth, especially since I didn't have plans to return to that life. "I'm a college senior majoring in political science."

"So are you going all the way across the border with me, or am I dropping you off somewhere along the way?"

"If you'd drop me off at a rest stop or gas station at the last exit before the border crossing, that'd be great."

"That doesn't sound very specific."

Lying on the spot when I needed to was not a strong suit of mine. "I don't have the right ID to get across the border. After I'm close enough, I can call my roommate to bring my ID."

"If you want, you can hide in the back of the cab. They're not going to look. This is the Canadian border we're talking about, and I know the officers pretty well. This late at night, they might not even be checking."

I didn't want to risk being caught, especially since I had magical objects in my pockets that couldn't be easily explained. But this way the risk of death due to exposure was significantly reduced. Staying alive outweighed the possibility of getting caught. "I don't want to get you into any trouble."

"You won't." He seemed pretty sure.

Three hours later, John stopped and lifted the mattress behind the seats to reveal a storage compartment underneath. "Just sit in there and don't make a sound."

I assumed the fetal position in the cramped space. After we got moving again, it only took a few minutes to reach the border. When the truck slowed to a stop, I strained my ears to hear what was being said, but the beating of my heart was too loud in my ears to hear much of anything.

We were only stopped for a few minutes, and then we were cruising back down the road. I drew a deep breath, willing it to calm my nerves and slow my heart. It wouldn't be long now. Before we'd stopped, I'd used my phone to find the closest gas station to my car, and it was there that John let me out of the compartment.

"Thanks for the lift and the help at the border. I really appreciate it. Are you sure you don't want me to buy you something for the road?" It really didn't seem fair to leave him with nothing.

"No, I'm fine. Glad to help. Good luck to you."

"You too." Just like that he was pulling back onto the freeway.

According to my phone, it was a ten-minute walk to my car. Excitement filled me at the prospect of seeing my baby again. It was like coming home. I didn't have much juice left in the phone, but I turned on the flashlight app. Even with the phone lighting my way, it was still slow going to make sure I didn't sprain my ankle on a rock or pothole.

Three minutes out from the car, I swore I heard something and saw movement out of the corner of my right eye. I swung around, casting the light of my phone in front of me but seeing nothing more than trees. It had probably been a rabbit or some other small animal. Just in case, I pulled the cloaker from my pocket to confirm it still worked. The black design glowed back at me. Marcus wouldn't be able to track me as long as it was on. Hopefully it didn't require any kind of charging.

A few steps later, I saw movement again and whirled. This time, there was someone there.

"Ahhh!" I screamed.

"Shh! It's all right. It's just me." Alex took me in his arms and held me close until I calmed down.

It couldn't be him, but I felt his firm muscles under my hands, smelled his earthy scent. "How?"

"How do you think? I've never seen anyone as attached to something as you are to this car of yours. I knew you'd come back for it."

That still didn't make sense. "How?"

Alex laughed at my confusion. "We'll talk later. Let's get you to your baby and get the heater blowing."

With Alex guiding me, I didn't need the phone. He grabbed the keys from where I'd left them in the wheel well and helped me inside. I was still in shock and stared at him in amazement as he got into the passenger seat.

"What?" he asked when I couldn't stop looking at him.

"You're here. I just can't believe it. Why? You left to get away from me."

He reached over and put the key in the ignition then turned on the heater. "It didn't take me long after I left to regret it. Regardless of any attraction I may feel on my own or through magic, I should've been there for you. I definitely shouldn't have kissed you. I can control myself better than that."

"Don't worry about it." I really didn't want him to regret that kiss.

He brushed right past my comment as if I hadn't spoken. "Once I told Casper I was leaving, it was impossible for me to find the Armory again. I searched, but once I realized he'd hidden it by magic, I knew there'd be no way for me to find it. I figured you'd come back for this car eventually, no matter how things went at the Armory, so I came here and waited for you."

"But I may have never come."

Alex shrugged. "It's not like I had anything better to do."

The relief at seeing him, at having him so close, made me happy enough to cry. Instead, I leaned forward and took his mouth in a kiss. It was every bit as good as I remembered.

"Thanks for waiting for me," I whispered.

"Sure. Any time." He pulled away. "We need to get you somewhere warm with a bed."

I could go for that.

"A bed for you to sleep on," Alex clarified. "I didn't mean it any other way."

"Uh-huh." I started the car and headed to the freeway.

CHAPTER 39

*I*t would've been easy to find a hotel nearby, but something didn't feel right about staying so close to where I'd left my car. Marcus knew I had gone to Magical Games headquarters from my apartment, and this area was on the way. So instead, I got on the freeway headed west, and told Alex all that had happened after he left.

"As soon as it became apparent that you needed protection more than ever, he kicked you out? Classy." Great, I'd given Alex more ammunition for his dislike of Casper.

"I can understand that he wants to protect his operation. The other mages I met there, they lost their parents too. I can't be the cause for other people dying."

"That's total bullshit. You are much too nice. You're the vulnerable one. He's the mage with protection, facilities, money, and not to mention other mages who, given what I know of Casper, probably aren't too shabby either. He doesn't strike me as the type to associate with people much below him."

While I didn't want to cast aspersions on Casper, having Alex's support meant a lot to me. After an hour of driving, I pulled into the parking lot of a hotel, one that included a hot breakfast and appeared busy from the packed lot. There was a feeling of safety in numbers.

Once we got checked in, the first thing I did was take a shower. The hot water warmed me down to my bones, something my car's heater had been unable to accomplish no matter how long I kept it at full blast. The front desk clerk had given us a tube of toothpaste and two toothbrushes. Add to that the hairbrush I kept in my glove compartment, and I had everything I needed to freshen up.

When I stepped out of the bathroom, I found Alex lying on the bed looking at the room-service menu.

"They have twenty-four-hour room service here," he said. "We could order something, if you want."

My frugal instincts immediately said no, but my credit card had plenty of room on it, and given the path my life was taking, keeping a good credit score wasn't high on my list of priorities.

"Sure. Order whatever you want," I said. He handed me the menu, and we both ended up ordering the biggest steak on it.

"How long do you think we can keep running?" Alex asked. "At some point, your money is going to run out."

"I'm not planning on running forever." I'd had plenty of time to think on the drive, and I decided I wasn't cut out for this kind of life, constantly looking over my shoulder. If there was a way to go to the Magesterial Council, I could get help from them. Dorran had warned me against trusting the Council, but he had also told me to trust my gut. And I was pretty sure he'd been full of shit and just wanted to threaten me so I wouldn't harm the world with my talisman. Casper had planned to take me to the Council eventually, and Alex had wanted me to go from the beginning. It was the only option left.

"But with the cloaker, you could theoretically hide forever," Alex said.

"Do you really believe that? Because I don't. Marcus will find me. I want to continue improving my skills and go to Elustria to learn more about my birth mother. The cloaker can buy me some time, but that's it. If there are some shifters you trust, we can see if I can use the same portal they do and go to the Council. I don't think Marcus is going to be monitoring shifter portals. He's focused on finding me through my talisman and the information he has on me."

"I used to know some shifters who lived in an enclave on the Oregon coast. I trust them. They won't betray us. I think you're right. Marcus is more likely to focus on tracking your talisman and hunting you than on monitoring portals. And at this point, we really don't have much choice if you think he'll find you no matter what."

"We can travel together in the direction you think we need to go to find someone who has a portal. While we're doing that, I can be studying."

A knock on the door interrupted us. I moved to answer it, but Alex waved me back onto the bed while he went to the door. The arrival of food put a hold on our conversation. The steak wasn't great, cooked far longer than a medium rare should be, but after the gas station donut I'd had earlier, I didn't mind. Between the steak and the garlic mashed potatoes, I was more than satisfied after devouring it all.

"You should probably get some sleep," Alex said once I'd finished.

"We need to settle on a plan."

"I'm open to what you said earlier, but how exactly do you want to go about it? How are you going to continue to learn magic with no one to teach you?"

During the drive with John, I'd considered that very question. The solution was both obvious and crude.

"The same way I did magic the first time: the game."

"You can't be that foolish. Marcus has access to your game account on your computer. He might be able to track you through that. And I don't trust Casper. I'd rather you not give him a trail to follow either."

"I've already thought of that. I agree I shouldn't log in to the game or really into any of my accounts. Once the stores open, I want to go buy a cheap, little laptop. I should probably get a new phone as well. The quests in *Wizards and Fae* are full of spells. There's dozens of fan sites on the Internet that have compiled databases of all the quest lines in the game. I'm betting the 'made-up' language in the game is Cadaran or at least based on it. All I need to do is access them and learn what I can from the spells. Between the theory I learned at the Armory and the spells Casper put in the game in order to find latent mages, I'm confident I can make progress."

"Do you really think you'll find spells there that are of use to you? Wouldn't that present something of a dangerous situation for latent mages to have access to that?"

"No, because they don't have a talisman. In the case of the game activating the magic of latent mages, the game code itself is the magical object the mage is interacting with. My mother enchanted it but only with a low level of magic, just enough to create a blip for Casper to find. It worked differently for me because I had a talisman. If my mother hadn't stripped my spark when I was little, the magic would've activated for me the first time I played the game, but not big enough to actually cause ice to come out of my hands."

"If you think it'll work, I'll support you and protect you while you do it." Alex's sincerity and commitment to helping me were overwhelming. Since my parents had died, I'd only had that kind of support from Nicole, and she couldn't be part of this.

"Thanks. You can also help in another way. I want to know everything about Elustria. I know you haven't been there in a long time, but I heard different things while at the Armory. Casper seems to think that Marcus is a sorcerer assassin. I was so consumed with learning magic that I didn't delve into the details of the situation with anyone, but I think I need to know more about whatever politics or conflict is going on, seeing as I'm now part of it."

"The animosity between mages and sorcerers is both simple and long enough to fill several volumes. I'll tell you everything I know, but we both need to get some sleep if we're going to do this tomorrow."

We stacked our dishes back on the delivery tray, and Alex left it outside the door. I set the alarm with just enough time for us to catch the last few minutes of breakfast and climbed into bed.

All throughout dinner, I'd wanted to reach out to Alex, to kiss him again, but there were more important matters at hand. With a little twinge of disappointment, I watched as he climbed into the other bed, turned off the light, and rolled over.

CHAPTER 40

The pizza at the food court of the mall tasted like cardboard that had accidentally been dropped into some sauce and cheese and then shaken off and served up on a plate. Bland, inoffensive music played, annoying precisely for its plainness. Across from me, Alex surveyed the scene, his eyes darting from face to face as people passed. He'd chosen this table in the corner because it gave him a clear view of the rest of the food court without the possibility of anyone coming up behind him.

This wouldn't have been my first choice·for a late lunch, but the mall had everything we needed: an electronics store for the new laptop I had out in front of me and the phone I'd already put in my pocket and plenty of clothing stores for me to grab a few outfits. My old phone was smashed in a trash can outside. The one saving grace of the food court was the free Wi-Fi.

The new laptop was the most basic model the store had. Practicing magic indoors was too great a risk, so Alex and I had decided that we would go to a remote area outdoors where I could practice while he patrolled the perimeter, alert to threats. That meant that I needed to download the spells I would be practicing.

Nerves caused my mind to go blank. The game was full of interesting spells, many of which I knew would come in handy, but I couldn't recall any of them. My mind remained keenly aware of each passing minute that Marcus could be drawing closer. My thoughts wandered to the smashed phone in the trash can. Was there a way for him to track it there? I'd feel a little better once we were moving again.

There were dozens of fan sites to choose from, but I'd have to explore them all later. I chose The Codex, one of the sites I frequented with Nicole. I created an account with a new email address and looked up my character profile. Players could publicly display information about their characters, and the site pulled in information from the game to display stats and quest history.

Seeing Serafina in her familiar armor was like seeing an old friend. The title "Hades Killer" floated above her head. A mixture of pride and remorse filled me. I had been so proud of my accomplishment, but I knew now that it hadn't been real. At the same time, even though I was in a bad situation, that quest had also opened up my destiny to me. I didn't know how to feel about it, and instead of dwelling on it, I clicked on my quest history.

Page one of eighty-seven loaded: years of quest history, chronicling my time in-game. As I scanned the list, I couldn't help the memories flooding in of sitting in front of my computer, chatting with Nicole as I worked on progressing in the game. It was odd how with each quest I could remember what we'd talked about. During *Feeding the Troll King's Champion*, Nicole had been telling me about the loser she was dating at the time. And while I ground through *Infiltrating the Troll King's Guard*, she'd regaled me with the story of how she'd dumped him—the loser, not the Troll King. In fact, the long Troll King quest line could be a good source of material for me. I clicked on the quests and copy and pasted the text to a word processor. I didn't have time to reminisce.

"Remember, we can stop somewhere else if you need to get more. Just grab enough material to study until then," Alex said, his eyes never wavering from their scan of the area.

"All right, let's go."

I finished copying over the quest line as well as the standard spells Serafina used and put the laptop away in the carrying case I'd bought for it. Alex grabbed the shopping bag with my new clothes in it, and we went to the car.

As I drove farther west, Alex read the quests to me from my laptop, and I had him flag the ones I'd want to take a look at when we stopped. Driving through Idaho, it wasn't difficult to find places out in the middle of nowhere. Most of the state was either desert or ski resorts with little towns sprinkled about here and there. The trick was to find a place that would be hard for us to be seen, and that meant getting far away from the freeway.

The flat landscape resulted in a good line of sight, which was bad for us. We also had to avoid grazing land, of which there was plenty. The last thing we needed was a run-in with an upset rancher, even if the chances of being caught were slim. And while I enjoyed beef, I didn't want to inadvertently kill a cow.

An hour after leaving the mall, I parked off to the side of an old dirt road that looked like it hadn't been used in ages. "All right, hand me the laptop. I want you to give me plenty of space. I don't want to accidentally hurt you."

Alex handed over the laptop and got out of the car. "I'll be patrolling. If you hear me growl, I want you to stop what you're doing and come back to the car. I really don't think Marcus will find us here, but if he does, I don't know how much of a match I'll be for him, so you might want to practice that spell that makes fire rain from the sky. Just an idea."

I smiled. "Noted. I'll practice for four hours, then we'll meet back here."

"Sounds good." Before my eyes, Alex shifted into his panther form. I'd never get tired of seeing it. He ran north to start creating a perimeter, and I headed about a hundred meters east to give me some room to work with. Not only would it break my heart to damage my car, but it would make this whole plan a lot more difficult logistically.

Alex's suggestion had been a good one, but I didn't like the idea of playing with fire in such a dry climate. Starting a brush fire was a very real risk. Instead, I pulled up a similar spell that was part of Serafina's regular rotation. In-game, it rained down deadly purple droplets. I had no idea what they were or what they would do, but they had proven effective at killing most things in-game. I looked at the spell in the word processor and committed it to memory.

"Acidic downpour," I shouted while casting my hand in front of me and feeling like an idiot.

The English translation proved ineffective. My guess was the purple substance didn't have an English equivalent.

"Acruvio regnian." While saying the spell, I pictured what it looked like in-game. A few purple sprinkles appeared and burned the ground like acid. Not the impressive display I'd hoped for, probably because I didn't know exactly what I was doing. It might be better to move along to the elements I was familiar with.

Next.

CHAPTER 41

At the end of four hours I'd created a cyclone I could control, summoned lightning strikes, refined my skill at using ice as a weapon, and made the discovery that I could use my power to accurately throw rocks at a target. I'd also learned a neat defensive trick.

"How did it go?" Alex asked when I met him back at the car.

"You tell me." I cast a concealment spell I'd been working on. Since it could keep me concealed without alerting someone to my presence, I prioritized learning how to execute the spell nonverbally.

Alex's eyes widened and he started forward. "Kat?"

"I'm here." I raised my hand and waved at him. This particular spell transformed my skin and clothing to blend in with my surroundings. I reappeared before Alex. "What do you think?"

"That was amazing. If you hadn't moved, I wouldn't have been able to see you at all. And if I hadn't seen you disappear, it would've been nearly impossible for me to pick up that little bit of movement without knowing exactly what I was looking for."

"Yeah, I'm a long ways off from offensively being a match for anyone, so I thought I should have some good defensive and avoidance skills. The offensive spells are a little harder, but I've got some

243

up my sleeve." I hadn't been able to successfully execute any spells that didn't use elements I knew. While playing the game, I'd never noticed how many spells used poisonous green fog, purple acid, or sprays of deadly gold light.

We headed to dinner, and I tried my best not to reveal the most important lesson I'd learned: that there was no way I could possibly survive an encounter with Marcus.

CHAPTER 42

"Can you order dinner for us? I'm going to do some more research." We'd just settled in to our new hotel room, and I wanted to check out The Codex and troll for new spells. The forums were awash with people debating the virtues of this spell over that.

As I'd found out earlier, not every spell translated into the real world, and there were also considerations in-game that I didn't have in real life that would skew my results, things such as health and magic meters that needed to be replenished. Seeing as I had an assassin actively searching for me, my general plan was to seek out spells people thought were overpowered.

"Sure," Alex said. "I assume you want some kind of steak?"

"Yeah, that'd be great." While practicing magic was not physically taxing, it did drain me. From the reading I'd done back at the Armory, magical ability was thought by some to be like a muscle that grew stronger with use. Not many people had ever been in my position before, and I could attest that this theory about magic was true. Most people learned magic gradually; I was cramming it all in to save my life—literally.

The Wi-Fi in the hotel was slow, especially when I was anxious for content. As expected for this time of night, the forums were a hive of activity. I scanned the list of topics on the main forum page.

elemental wizards nerfed...again!
    Magma Lake way OPed

That was a good thread to click on. My character didn't have that spell, so I'd have to look it up in the database.

help plz n00b confused
    Anyone else offended by the hunting lions quest line?
    new buff added to dark magic tree is dark sorcerer best class?
    Latest Hades Killer is Serafina, Dark Sorceress!

That caught my eye, not just because of my name but because of the correct grammar. The author of the thread was GreyMist. Count on her to brag for me. I clicked on the thread and read her post.

The newest Hades Killer is Serafina, Dark Sorceress!

This was linked to my profile page so people could check out my stats and see proof of my new title.

Anyone seen her around? She hasn't been online in a while, and I want to congratulate her.

Nicole had been there the night I got my title. Something must have happened. This was her way of reaching out to me, of trying to make contact since I no longer had my phone.

A knock sounded on the door, and Alex answered it, making way for the server bringing our dinner.

"It's time to eat," Alex said as he unloaded the tray of food on the table and placed my plate next to my laptop.

"I can't right now. This is important. My best friend's trying to get a hold of me."

"Whatever it is can wait. You need to eat, and it'll be better hot."

"It's serious, Alex. I don't have my phone for her to call me. The only reason she'd be this cryptic is if something bad happened."

"Yes, that's important. It's also important that you eat. She'll still be there when you're done. If I'm going to protect you, you have to do your part, and that means taking care of yourself."

Alex's yellow eyes bored into me as he looked down from where he stood next to my chair. And of course, it was at that moment that my stomach decided to release a growl that could rival any of Alex's.

"Fine, but I'm doing it because my stomach says so, not because you do."

"That's totally fair," Alex said while unsuccessfully suppressing a laugh.

As I ate, I couldn't keep my mind from wandering to what Nicole could possibly want. It wouldn't be anything good. A post like that was practically code, and she wouldn't do that just to chat. Marcus must have done something.

The food helped not only relieve my hunger but also calm my anxiety. Good decisions are rarely made on an empty stomach, and when I finally pushed the plate away, I had a much more level head on my shoulders to deal with the issue.

"Don't worry, I'll clear." Alex put our dishes outside the door while I opened my laptop.

The message had been a cry for me to get in touch with her in a way that didn't make use of my normal accounts. Underneath her avatar, a green circle showed she was currently online. I clicked on her name and chose the option to send a private message.

I momentarily worried this might be a trap, but it was unlikely Marcus had found a way to hack her. The only reason he had access to my information was because he had my computer. This wasn't a CIA assassin; he didn't have technical knowledge.

User4276: It's Kat. What's wrong?

I didn't want her to think I was someone trolling her. She was the only person in-game who knew my real name. I hit "send" and hoped that she'd get it before logging off.

My sense of time was warped as I waited for her to reply. After hitting the refresh button a ridiculous number of times, a new message appeared.

GreyMist: This Marcus guy is looking for you, and he means business. He showed up at my house. He's called me, emailed me, contacted me in-game. He has access to your computer, which is why I haven't messaged any of your accounts. He says all he wants is to talk to you, and he gave me his phone number to pass on to you. I tried calling you, but your number isn't working.

My worst nightmare had come true.

User4276: Give me the phone number.

GreyMist: I don't think it's a good idea for you to call him.

User4276: Just give me the number. I'll give it to the police.

I had absolutely no problem lying to my best friend when her safety was at risk.

GreyMist: 555-210-4798. But seriously, don't call him. This guy is creepy.

User4276: Don't worry about me. I'm safe. If you have someone out of town you can visit right now, do it. I don't want to freak you out, but this guy is bad news. He shouldn't be there long. He's after me. So just get away for a little while, and I'll let you know when it's safe.

GreyMist: You're really freaking me out. I don't like this AT ALL. What's going on?

User4276: I've picked up a stalker. I can't tell you more right now, but I'll message you as soon as I can, probably with this account. I had to ditch my phone because of this guy.

GreyMist: I'll check in regularly. My cousin lives a couple hours away. I'll go visit her.

User4276: Good. Leave tonight. If something happens or you need anything, message me here.

GreyMist: Will do. Keep yourself safe.

User4276: You too.

The little green light below her avatar went gray when she logged off.

I sat back in my chair, my mind whirling and my stomach churning at the danger I'd placed my best friend in. There wasn't even a question in my mind as to what I should do. I pulled my phone from my pocket and began to dial.

"What are you doing?" Alex asked. He snatched the phone from my hands before I even realized he was standing behind me.

"Marcus is harassing my best friend. He showed up at her house. He says all he wants to do is talk, and he gave her his number for me to call. I'm calling it." I made a grab for the phone, but Alex had cat reflexes even in human form.

"Oh no, you're not. He wants to do more than talk."

"You don't know that." Sure, I assumed he wanted to do more than that too, but we didn't know. "I'm not going to let him hurt my best friend. This is my mess, and I may not have asked for it but neither did she, and I'm not going to let her pay the price. She's the only friend I had after my parents' death, the only person I could talk to. I'm not going to let something happen to her for being my friend."

"I understand how you feel, and I admire you for it, but Marcus will not hesitate to kill you. I know you're getting better with your magic, but this is a man who's been practicing his entire life, the man who killed your mother, the woman many people say was the most powerful mage they'd ever met."

"Well then this only has one ending, and we both know it. He's going to kill me no matter what. I'd rather he not kill my best friend too. And even if I can escape him somehow, even if we get a safe portal to Elustria, I'm still not going to let him hurt her. I might not know what I'm doing with my life, but I do know that I'm not the type of person who'd let someone else get hurt because of me. If I can't even say that about myself, then what's the point of living?"

Alex's eyes showed his weakening resolve. I knew I wouldn't be able to get my phone from him unless he voluntarily gave it to me. The only weapons I had against him were words, and I saved my sharpest for last.

"Your father understood what it meant to die protecting someone. You came back to protect me. Let me protect my person. You wouldn't let an innocent person die, would you?" I searched his eyes for an answer, and made sure he knew from the way I leaned toward him that I wasn't going to let him get away without answering.

A tense moment passed before Alex visibly deflated. "No, I wouldn't. You're right about that. I'll give you back your phone but only if you talk to me first. We need a plan. You're not going to call an assassin who wants to kill you and invite him here without some kind of plan. You don't have to die. The only way you're going to get out of this alive is if we work together. So let me help you."

"Deal." I admired that he gave me the phone as soon as I agreed instead of waiting for me to follow through.

"He's going to want to meet you," Alex said as he sat opposite me.

"I know."

"Where were you thinking? A public place would make it harder for him to do anything."

"It also endangers the general public. He might not be willing to reveal magic, but if I'm threatened by him, my talisman might take over. Besides, if he's a sorcerer, he'll be able to teleport me away. A public place doesn't provide much safety. I also won't feel comfortable defending myself in public."

"We'll go somewhere remote then, where you can use your magic."

"When? I want to get it over with, but I should probably sleep tonight." Sleeping was a pipe dream. Adrenaline must have been rushing through my veins, because I didn't feel much fear at the prospect of death. No other outcome seemed likely, but the reality that I would soon be dead didn't penetrate. No matter how much my mind knew it was true, my emotions didn't react.

"Do you think there's any way he can track where you are if you call him?" Alex asked.

"If he were a human with advanced tech skills, yes. But even for a human he'd have to be pretty smart to figure out how to do that since this is a new phone. I don't think it's a realistic possibility."

"Let's meet him tomorrow. That'll give us tonight to rest and prepare."

I dialed the number Nicole had given me. The ringing was over-shadowed by the pounding of my heart.

"Hello. This is Kat, I presume."

"You're right. Stay away from my friends." I sounded much more badass than I felt.

"I have no desire to hurt your friends. I have no desire to hurt you. I want to talk; that is all. You are in possession of something that I don't think you quite understand, something that I need."

"If all you want to do is talk, then talk. No one's stopping you."

"The kind of conversation I want to have needs to happen in person." He obviously thought the word "conversation" meant some-thing different than most people.

"If I agree to meet you, do you promise to stop harassing my friends?"

"Of course."

Asking the question was stupid. What kind of response did I expect? The word of an assassin meant nothing. "I'll meet you tomorrow. I'll text you the location in the morning, and we can meet at eleven."

"Can you tell me what state you're in?" Marcus asked.

"Not until morning."

A brief silence said he didn't like my answer. "Very well. I'll see you then. And I hope it goes without saying that notifying the authorities or speaking to anyone else about this meeting would be ill-advised."

"I understand."

The line went dead, and I would soon join it.

CHAPTER 43

*T*he next morning, nerves made eating difficult, but I needed my strength. After I choked down breakfast, Alex and I went to the meeting place we had chosen. It was in the middle of nowhere.

"Remember, you have to maintain your element of surprise," I told Alex when we were at the location waiting for Marcus. "Don't stay too close. I'm pretty sure I can hold him off or at least distract him."

"I know. I'll let you handle yourself. At the same time you're attacking him, I'll leap on him from behind. He may be a sorcerer, but I'm pretty sure even sorcerers need their heads attached to their bodies."

My stomach churned at the mention of what Alex would have to do, what I would have to see. In trying times, though, it was amazing what I was willing to stomach. "It's five 'til eleven. You should get in position."

Alex nodded and shifted. He ran to a spot we'd found where he could crouch unseen behind some bushes. We didn't have any realistic hope of winning a fight, and the element of surprise gave us the only edge we would have. Perhaps talking was really all Marcus wanted to do. Perhaps this was a giant misunderstanding. Perhaps pigs could fly. I had to hold on to any sliver of hope I could.

At exactly eleven o'clock, a man appeared on the horizon, walking toward me. My skin crawled when I saw him, and I knew this was the man who had killed my mother. Long black hair was pulled up into a sloppy bun. Blue eyes focused on me with alarming intensity. He wore jeans and a green polo that looked brand new. In my mind, I'd expected something closer to the clothing Casper wore.

"Kat, how nice to finally meet you," he said when he stopped five feet in front of me.

"I can't say I feel the same."

"Put your mind at ease. I am a wand-wielder, and as you can see, my wand is tucked safely away. I only wish to talk."

The absence of a wand didn't ease my mind. As far as I knew, Marcus was a sorcerer, so he didn't need a wand. I wouldn't let him trick me into a false sense of security. "You'll forgive me if I don't take the word of a murderer."

"Yes, that is the most sensible place to start, isn't it?" Marcus's calm, measured tone irritated me. "The unfortunate truth is that things did not have to go that way with your mother. Regrettably, we could not come to an agreement. I'm hoping you will be more reasonable. All I need is that necklace, and I'll be on my way."

"I may not know much, but I know this talisman is mine. It holds my magic and was bequeathed to me by my mother. You have no right to ask for it."

"I see Casper has been educating you. Did he give you the cloaker you're using as well?"

I wanted to keep Casper out of this as much as possible. He wasn't helping me anymore, and I didn't want to give Marcus any reason to target him. "No, I stole it from him. I have nothing to do with Casper."

"Ah, so it's just you and the panther who's hiding behind me?"

Alex sprang from his spot, but it was too late. In one swift motion, Marcus drew a wand and made short work of Alex, placing him under a binding spell. Then he held his arms out as if in surrender. "I don't wish to hurt you, Kat. I merely wish to talk."

I shot a torrent of ice arrows from my hands, but they didn't even faze Marcus. With a flick of his wand, a protective shield appeared in front of him. I'd been counting on his distraction to hide the moment I disappeared. Too committed to the plan to change course now, I performed the concealment spell and ran to my left. Unless he had keen eyes, he wouldn't be able to see me.

"Come now, Kat. That's not going to solve anything. All I want is the talisman. Just give it to me, and I'll leave you alone. I'll even unbind this shifter boy for you. You've already proven quite willing to be agreeable when your friends are in jeopardy."

I hadn't anticipated Alex being a weakness, but it might have been better if he'd left me to do this on my own. I cast more ice arrows, my mind unable to recall another spell. Even coming at him from a completely different angle, Marcus easily blocked them.

"That's all right, Kat, I can do this all day. I'm not so sure your friend will enjoy it." A twist of his wrist and Alex let out a scream, a horrifying sound in his cat form.

"Stop!" I disengaged the concealment spell and revealed myself to him. "Leave him alone."

"All I need is to remove that talisman from you. This doesn't have to end the same way it did with your mother. Just let me—" He reached out his hand and the talisman reacted. A force of white light catapulted Marcus six feet into the air. He landed on the ground with a thud. The spell binding Alex broke, and he pounced on top of Marcus. Alex swiped with one of his great claws, carving deep grooves into Marcus's face.

Marcus screamed, and then Alex was flying in the air. Marcus held him suspended a few feet off the ground.

"Don't you worry, Kat. You'll see me again soon. You've given me the information I need. I won't fail next time." He disappeared, using the same concealment spell I had. I saw his movement and tried to catch him as he ran away, but he had to be using some sort of enchantment to increase his speed. I threw everything I had at him: a whirlwind, a hailstorm, an energy burst whose damage I hadn't been able to accurately measure yet. None of my spells hit their mark. When I lost sight of Marcus, Alex fell to the ground, the spell broken. He shifted into his human form and came to my side.

"What do you think he meant when he said I gave him what he needed?" I asked.

"I don't know. Maybe nothing. But I believe him when he says he'll return. We need to get out of here."

I nodded and let Alex lead me to the car. "How long until he returns, do you think?"

"I'm guessing not long. He won't want to risk us getting too far away or losing us through a portal to Elustria."

I floored it on the way back to the freeway, a giant cloud of dust trailing the car down the dirt road. Every few seconds I glanced in the rearview mirror, convinced I could see Marcus in pursuit. I'd survived my first encounter with an assassin. I didn't know how long my beginner's luck would last.

CHAPTER 44

*B*ack at the hotel, my laptop took forever to load The Codex, or maybe it was just nerves making it feel that way.

"What are you doing? Pack it up. We're leaving." Alex already had the shopping bag packed with my clothes and toiletries.

I'd had time to think on the drive back, and nothing had changed. I couldn't run now for the same reason I couldn't run before: other people's lives were at risk. All I could do was come up with a better plan for the next time I met Marcus. "I'm not running. I'm coming up with a game plan."

"Are you crazy? He could've killed you."

"You're right, but he didn't. He had a wand, so he's not a sorcerer. He says he wants the talisman, and I believe him. Why would he want me dead? The only reason is so he can remove the talisman from me."

"Do you think you can figure out how to get it off before he comes back?" Alex's skepticism made his question sound patronizing.

In some ways that would make things easier, but I wasn't sure it would ultimately be better. If I'd learned anything during all this time, it was that the magic in my talisman was extraordinarily powerful. It didn't belong in the hands of a murderer.

"No. I'd give it to him if I thought it would stop the violence, but he wants it for its power. Maybe that's why my mother gave it to me, to protect it, to keep it from falling into the wrong hands. I couldn't abuse its power if I wanted to, but a man like that? One who terrorizes my friends? There's no telling what he'd do with it."

"So what exactly is your plan?"

"There has to be a way to beat him. There's always a way. I just haven't figured it out yet. You can either help me or you can stand there staring at me."

Alex put the bag down and pulled the other chair around the table to sit next to me. He looked over my shoulder at the computer screen. "Tell me how I can help."

The attraction I felt for Alex in that moment was the strongest it had ever been. It wasn't the raw attraction that had been between us at the Armory or in Buenos Aires. This was the overwhelming bond that could only be forged under the immense pressure we found ourselves under. We were partners in that moment, in every sense of the word. While I knew it would be better for me to die than Nicole, who was innocent in all of this, I had an overwhelming urge to live. A sense filled me that things were getting better, that if I could just crest this mountain peak, I'd have the entire world at my feet and someone standing next to me to enjoy it all.

CHAPTER 45

*A*fter hours of deliberation, we settled on a rotation of spells and a general strategy then headed to the desert to practice. This time we would use Alex's senses to alert me to Marcus's presence when he eventually found us. Until then, I'd be practicing.

"Are you sure you want to do this?" Alex asked when we got out of the car. "I can find us a portal to Elustria."

"Yes, I'm sure. He knows where Nicole lives. I'm not going to leave her in danger."

"Then we can bring her."

"I can't ask her to give up her life to be a second-class citizen in a foreign world. It's not fair." Nicole would probably jump at the chance to go to a magical, alternate dimension, but the reality wouldn't live up to the dream. A human didn't belong in a world of magic. And I wouldn't put my best friend in the position of deciding her future under duress.

"Please, I don't want anything to happen to you." Alex placed a hand on my shoulder, and his gaze pleaded with me to reconsider.

"Then let me practice. We don't know how much time we have until he finds us."

Alex sighed and dropped his hand. "Fine. When he gets here, I'll growl. That's your signal to stop practicing and get ready. Don't worry about me. He won't kill me, not when he can use me as leverage."

Before I could say anything, he shifted and ran off to start his patrol. I tried not to think about the fact that I may have just seen him for the last time. A sentimental goodbye would have only cut into my practice time.

CHAPTER 46

*S*pell after spell flowed through me. The talisman responded to my commands as if we'd worked together my entire life. The amber stone probably felt the threat, and it performed well under pressure.

Earlier, I'd been unwilling to use fire because of all the dry brush around, but Alex and I had decided that a brush fire, even one that got out of control, would be better than Marcus getting his hands on my talisman. Anyone who was willing to kill for power shouldn't be entrusted with any.

During practice, I successfully created a magma lake, threw fire-balls from my hands, and made fire rain from the sky. My control of water was more than adequate to douse the flames as long as I acted quickly. In the real fight, I wouldn't bother. Even if the fire didn't directly hit its target, it would produce enough heat to present a problem for Marcus. I practiced the sequence again, casting the magma lake, using a cyclone to carry the flames upward to obscure my target's view, and then casting a fireball.

A roar sounded somewhere to my right. I swung around and crouched low, my eyes and ears on high alert for any threat. My instincts urged me to run to Alex, but the smart thing was to stay put. Marcus didn't want Alex; he wanted me. If he was attacking Alex, it was to draw me to him. I wouldn't be foolish enough to fall for such a trap.

The stillness following the roar was more unsettling than the roar itself. I scanned the horizon, but I couldn't see any sign of movement. Even the wind had ceased to blow. All I could hear was the sound of my breath and the ring of silence. My eyes darted from side to side, looking for Marcus. My thighs screamed from my crouched position, but I didn't dare move.

A blinding pain cracked through my head. White light flooded my vision.

And then there was nothing.

CHAPTER 47

*D*ust tickled my nostrils where I lay prone on the ground. My nose crinkled in preparation to sneeze, but I held it in. The last thing I remembered was Alex's roar and then a bright flash of white light. Until I knew where I was, sneezing did not seem wise.

The light penetrating my eyelids was too dim to be outside in the middle of the day. Beneath my hands, I felt hardwood. I had no idea how much time had passed or where Marcus and Alex were. A quick mental check of my body revealed no serious injuries other than a massive headache. None of my limbs bent in unnatural positions, so shock wasn't hiding a broken bone. If I'd been bleeding enough to cause concern, I doubted I would have woken up. Only after I determined I was in no immediate, physical danger did I notice what was missing: an ache where the amber stone should be pressing into my chest.

Marcus had succeeded. I had lost my talisman.

A chair scratched across the floor. I wasn't alone. As much as I wanted to maintain the charade that I was still passed out, I had to risk cracking open one of my eyelids to see where I was. The sound of the chair had come from in front of me. I could get away with a peek.

Light poured in through a single small window, illuminating motes of dust floating in the sunbeam. Outside the window, I could make out a tall pine tree. I wasn't anywhere near where I'd been with Alex. The sparse furnishing and bare wood walls had a utilitarian feel, like a hunting cabin. A desk and chair stood a few feet in front of me. On the desk were marks where Marcus's hands had wiped away the dust, and there sat my talisman. Beyond the desk, Marcus stood with his back toward me. A communication orb floated in front of him, and a woman's face appeared.

I had to come up with a plan—not that my plans had worked out well so far, but it seemed the smart thing to do. I could play dead, and he might leave me alone. After all, he wanted the necklace, and he had it. But that meant letting him steal a part of me, the only part of my mother I had. I felt bereft without my talisman. I'd grown used to its weight lying on my chest. When I called out for magic, it had responded like an old friend. Now when I called out, nothing but silence echoed back at me. Playing dead may save my life, but what kind of life was I returning to?

If I fought now, there was every chance I'd die. It was likely. But I was likely to die either way. If he realized I was alive and conscious, he wouldn't let me live. I'd seen too much. I couldn't bear the thought of just lying there for him to kill me. If I died, I wanted to die fighting.

"I have the talisman, just like you asked for," Marcus said.

"Excellent." The woman in the orb spoke with a dignified air. "As soon as you deliver it, you will receive your payment. And what about Meglana?"

"Meglana proved difficult, but she ultimately succumbed."

Flames of fury roared through my body and licked at my fingertips, my hand itching to hold my talisman in its palm. My only hope was to summon it to me, but without anything to direct the magic, I didn't know if the talisman would respond.

The necklace sat directly in the line of sight of the woman Marcus spoke with, so I'd have to wait until they were done. When they were, I would only have a few seconds. The spell would have to be performed silently. With every fiber of my being, I needed to command my talisman to come to me. I was the stone's true owner. Surely it would recognize that.

"Very well," the woman said. "We thank you for your service."

"I don't care about your thanks; I care about my payment."

"Yes, Marcus, I figured. When you get back to Elustria, you will be paid, but don't take any side trips with the talisman. We'll expect you here tonight."

"Trust me, I don't plan to stay in this wretched world any longer than I have to."

"I'll have your payment waiting. Our business is done." Her face disappeared, and I had my chance.

Come! The talisman flew into my outstretched hand so fast that I was already performing the first spell in my sequence by the time Marcus turned around.

Magma lake, cyclone, fireball.

Without thinking, I went from spell to spell, performing them perfectly. The practice had paid off. Marcus's stunned face could barely comprehend what was happening as he struggled to counter.

I wanted to place the talisman around my neck, where it belonged, but I didn't dare stop the barrage of spells. I feared I'd drop the talisman or he'd somehow find a way to take it from my hand, but all of his attention was directed at blocking my attacks. His clothes were already falling victim to the flames. He'd have to first repel my spells before he could even think of casting any toward me.

"We can talk. You don't need to do this. I didn't kill you." Marcus had the unique ability to snarl while pleading.

"I've heard all the talking I need to from you. I don't believe for an instant you were going to let me live. Even if you were, you killed my mother."

"She deserved to die."

He picked a horrible time to speak. The rage coursing through me fueled the fireball I conjured to an intensity beyond my control. It flew from my hands and struck Marcus with lethal force. Not only did he fall over dead, the entire room went up in flames, trapping me in the corner.

Marcus's lifeless eyes held my attention amid the inferno raging around me. I watched them, looking for any sign of life. They didn't blink. The skin around them crinkled and puckered as it burned to a crisp.

Sweat drenched my clothes. My slick palm made holding onto the necklace difficult. Before my eyes, a clasp appeared on the broken chain. I secured it around my neck, and the stone took its rightful place on my chest.

I called down a torrent of water, but it was no match for the flames. The heat formed a wall almost as impenetrable as the fire. I had to get out, but there was no easy escape. The best option was to run through the fire to the next room.

I doused myself with water then summoned an ice shield, but I didn't have faith that it would hold. I dashed across the floor, leaping over Marcus's body, and slammed the door behind me. My heart raced with adrenaline, and I leaned my forehead against the door for a second, allowing the relief of my escape to wash over me.

When I turned around, Casper stood staring back at me.

CHAPTER 48

"What are you doing here?" The last person I had expected to see was Casper. He stood in the middle of a teleportation ring in the corner of what appeared to be a living room.

Casper ignored my question and ran to the door I'd just closed. He threw it open and called down a rain of enchanted water. With a flick of his hand he washed it all away: flames, water, everything. The only thing that remained of the fight was Marcus's body.

"You killed him?" Casper's surprise would have offended me if I wasn't as shocked as he was.

"He tried to kill me first." I took the same defensive tone as a child who was found hitting her brother.

"Don't tell me Marcus couldn't get it off either." Casper eyed the amber stone resting on my chest.

Something about the way he said that, his tone, threw me. "No, he got it off. I took it back. How did you know I was here?"

"The cloaker you took from the Armory has a GPS locator in it. We like to keep track of our mages, for safety."

"I thought you could only teleport to places you've already been." Casper's presence didn't make sense.

"I've been here a few times. It's a Magesterial Council safe house."

"What?" My unease grew with each passing second. I took a step backward, putting distance between us.

"That's right. Marcus was sent by the Magesterial Council."

"I thought they were the good guys. You and Mikael told me that I needed to get the talisman off so I could register with the Council, that I wouldn't be able to go to Elustria until then."

"That's all true. It's also true that they sent Marcus after your talisman."

Alex had seemed sure the Magesterial Council was good. They were the authority over mages in Elustria. It didn't make sense that they would send an assassin to kill my mother.

"If you don't believe me, check his pockets. He'll have a council medallion to identify himself as being on official Council business. It's the equivalent of a badge."

I didn't want to go anywhere near Marcus's body; I certainly wasn't going to touch it. "Why would the Council send someone to kill me and my mother?"

"He didn't kill you. Didn't you think it was odd that he left you alive after taking off the talisman? Doesn't that suggest his plan was to keep you alive this entire time? We told you that the Council wouldn't allow anyone to have a talisman they can't control."

"But he killed my mother, and she had to have been able to control the talisman."

"The Council was always jealous of Meglana's power. Did Marcus contact anyone once he had the talisman?"

I couldn't say anything. I couldn't even think. I nodded absentmindedly, answering his question out of instinct and not conscious thought.

"There's not much time then." Casper reached out toward me and was violently thrown back. I immediately went on guard. Pieces of the puzzle fell into place.

"You were hoping Marcus would catch me, that he'd be able to get the talisman off, and then you were going to steal it for yourself."

"Clever girl." Casper lunged at me and cast a spell. I threw up a shield that absorbed the blow and then cast an energy bolt, which he easily parried. I cast another, and he parried again.

"And what exactly are you going to do, Kat? You have nowhere to run, nowhere to hide. Humans can't help you, and you don't even belong with them anymore. You've become greedy in your magic. You were so scared of it before. You couldn't wait to get the talisman off, and now you won't let it go even to save your life. You'll have no place in Elustria now that you've killed an agent of the Magesterial Council. If you give me the talisman, you can live with us at the Armory. We'll give you a wand. You can join our fight, take up your mother's legacy."

My mind couldn't process what he was saying. My only thought was to get out of there alive. I used all my power to throw him back and stepped inside the teleportation ring. Marcus had to have put a connected one near where he'd captured me. I closed my eyes and pictured the desert where I'd been, hoping that the magic would work even though I didn't have a precise location in mind. A vise squeezed around my body, and a second later, I was standing alone in the desert.

CHAPTER 49

"*A*lex!" I screamed as I turned around, desperately looking for any familiar landmark. I had no idea where I was, only that I had to be in the same general area where Marcus had kidnapped me.

"Alex!" He could be dead. At the very least, he was wounded. I pulled the cloaker out of my pocket and threw it as far as I could. Marcus had to have placed this teleportation ring earlier in the day, so there was no chance that Casper had been to it before. He couldn't instantly follow me, but it wouldn't take him long to find out where the cloaker was. When he did, I wanted to be as far away as possible.

I ran west, searching the ground for Alex's body and yelling his name, hoping I'd chosen the right direction.

"I'm here!"

I whirled to my left and saw Alex shift from human to panther and run toward me. A few feet before reaching me, he shifted back to human form in mid-stride. "You're alive. Praise the moons, you're alive."

He pulled me close, holding me so tight that I had difficulty breathing, but I didn't mind. When he broke away, he looked down

271

at me with his yellow eyes and brushed my hair back from my face. I thought he might say something, but instead, he leaned down and kissed me. All my tension melted away. My relief at seeing him alive poured through that kiss.

"I hate to put a stop to this," I said as I pulled back, "but we need to go."

"Of course." Alex was instantly all business. "The car's this way. It'll be fastest if I carry you."

After he shifted, I let myself relax on his velvety back. I found myself wishing I could always travel this way. It only took a few minutes to get to the car, and in no time I was pulling back onto the road.

"What happened? Where's Marcus?" Alex asked once we were on the freeway.

"He's dead."

"You killed him?"

I wished people would stop sounding so surprised. "Yes. He got my talisman off, but I took it back and killed him with it." I still didn't understand how I was able to summon the talisman to me when I didn't have an object to channel my magic.

"Then why are we running?"

"Because it turns out he was working for the Magesterial Council. After Marcus removed the necklace, Casper showed up to take it for himself. The magic cloaker had a GPS locator in it, so I chucked it as soon as I teleported back."

"Whoa, back up and tell me everything that happened."

I related the entire story, leaving out nothing.

"You're sure Marcus was sent by the Council?" Alex asked when I was done.

Now that I thought about it, I wasn't completely sure. I hadn't searched Marcus's body for the medallion. "I don't know what to believe anymore. Casper knew who Marcus was, yet he still let me believe he was a sorcerer. Everyone at the Armory seemed to know my mother, so either they were all lying or they did work together. Do you think Marcus was sent by the Council?"

Alex thought a moment. "Given everything I know, yes. What everyone says about your mother is true: she was very powerful. The fact that she was even on Earth would put her afoul of the Council unless they specifically sanctioned it. If she really did work with Casper, then I believe it's entirely possible she was operating without the Council's approval. Whoever sent Marcus, whether it was the Council or not, isn't going to stop."

I didn't need Alex to tell me that. "And if he was sent by the Council, then killing him probably wasn't the best idea. He might not have intended to ever kill me. I might have killed an innocent person. He left you alive."

Alex placed his hand on my knee. "Don't think that. Even if he didn't intend to kill you, even if he didn't threaten the people you care about, he did take your talisman. In Elustria, that's the most serious violation a person can make against a mage. You did what you had to do. As soon as Marcus realized you were awake, he probably would've killed you. You had no choice. The moment you woke up, one of you was going to die. Don't let what Casper said get to you. He was messing with your mind."

Justified or not, I'd taken someone's life. I didn't quite know how to deal with that.

After a few awkward moments of silence, I changed the subject to something lighthearted. "Praise the moons? What was that?"

A bashful smile crept up Alex's face. "It's a stupid saying from my childhood. In the shifter world, it's the moons of Elustria that light our path at night, give us direction. They're even worshipped by some. I suppose it's a habit that's hard to break."

"No, I like it." Alex's obvious discomfort made me smile.

"So what are we going to do?" he asked.

"I'm not sure, but I'm a mage now. I want to keep learning and practicing. Casper won't be able to track me anymore, but it's only a matter of time before he or someone else finds me. I want to be better prepared. I know this is more than you signed up for."

"Don't even say that. I'm staying with you." Alex's tone left no room for doubt.

"Yeah, but I bet you're wishing you had never agreed to deliver that necklace."

Alex laughed. "And I bet you're regretting opening the door that night."

I glanced at the man sitting next to me and felt the weight of the amber stone on my chest where it belonged. I could honestly say that I didn't regret it one bit.

CHAPTER 50

$\mathcal{T}$hat night, after we checked into a new hotel, I opened my laptop while Alex slept. I'd made a promise to Nicole, and The Codex showed that she was online.

> *User4276: It's safe. You won't see Marcus again.*
>   *GreyMist: Good. I've been worried about you. What's going on?*
>   *User4276: Marcus was stalking me. He broke into my apartment and stole my computer. It's fine now. He's been taken care of.*

I'd eventually have to tell her more, but for right now, that would suffice.

> *GreyMist: Where are you?*

The answer to that question was too complicated and dangerous to tell Nicole, and I didn't want to keep lying to her. I fidgeted with my talisman as I thought of a reply. The amber stone warmed in my hand, the magic inside it ready to obey, and Alex lay beside me. I knew one thing.

User 4276: I'm right where I want to be.

Thank you for reading *Magic Born*! Is Alex really sleeping? Since this is Kat's story, Alex's point of view didn't really fit, but you can find out what he's thinking in an optional extra scene by going to https://CaethesFaron.com/mbscene.

THE MAGIC BORN SERIES

Magic Born

Magic Unknown

Magic Betrayed

Magic Hunted

Get sneak peeks and stay up to date on new releases by signing up for the author's Insider Newsletter. You'll also get a free copy of the Insider exclusive story *Magic Tracked*, a prequel to *Magic Born*:

http://CaethesFaron.com/magic-tracked

ABOUT THE AUTHOR

Caethes's writing is influenced by her observations of this imperfect world and the flawed characters who inhabit it. She enjoys playing RPGs and making up complex backstories for her avatar and the characters she encounters. Caethes has lived in seven states and is always looking for the next place to call home with her husband and dogs. She currently resides in Florida where she's often found at theme parks when she's not writing.

Join her Facebook reader group:
CaethesFaron.com/fbgroup
Contact her:
CaethesFaron.com/contact
Visit her site:
CaethesFaron.com

Printed in Great Britain
by Amazon